FELI... ...REEN

COOKING UP
A WITCH

A SCOTTISH WITCHES MYSTERY

PROLOGUE

FIONNA

"My mom says I'm a woman now." Tara sounded very grown-up Then she stifled a giggle with her hand. "Have any of you started your period yet?"

Andrea, whom everyone just called Andie, just shook her head. She was the same age as Tara but didn't seem concerned about lagging behind.

Fionna felt the heat rise to her cheeks and wished she could hide her face behind her hair. But her mother had insisted on taming Fionna's wild red mane into a French braid. Fionna found it didn't flatter her round face, but she knew better than to argue about things like that.

She put the end of her braid in her mouth and chewed on it, then mumbled something that might be taken for a "Yes, of course."

Tara didn't even pay Fionna any attention. She was already busy recounting all the details of her seminal experience, blithely ignorant of how uncomfortable it made Fionna.

It was a sore subject with her that she still hadn't started menstruating at age seventeen. Tara was five years younger than her, but starting your period at twelve was totally normal these days. Fionna had read all about it.

She didn't even fall into the late bloomer category, as she was exhibiting all the other signs of puberty, like her plump figure, acne on her back, and sweat patches under her arms on a hot summer day like this one.

It felt incongruent that she hadn't gotten her period yet. Ordinarily, she'd have gone to the doctor about it. But that would have meant talking to her mother first.

Her mother already had a long list of things that were wrong with Fionna, so adding an embarrassing disease would make everything even worse.

Oh, her mother wouldn't say anything outright. But she had a way of showing her disappointment in her daughter that was more hurtful than a scolding.

In a way, Fionna welcomed the rare passive-aggressive comments that were directed at her. At least they suggested her mother hadn't totally given up on her.

Fionna looked around to check whether her mother's reprimanding eyes were on her.

Small groups of women and girls were seated at tables spread out across the manicured lawn behind the house. The garden was walled in by hedges, and the Argyll Forest bordered the back, so this Midsummer celebration was well hidden from view of strangers.

The women were passing the time before the sunset ceremony with talking, eating, and drinking.

Fionna's mother, Rosa Simmonds, was seated at the center table. To her left, as always, sat coven leader Mary MacDonald.

With her unkempt black hair, her warty, lined face, and her old-fashioned, dirty-looking frock, Mrs. MacDonald fit the cliché of a witch to a T.

Rosa was the exact opposite. She looked distinctly average. Her gray hair was neatly tied up in a bun, her cheeks shone apple red under the wire rims of her old-fashioned glasses, and her lips were drawn into a perpetually benevolent smile. She matched the stereotype of a kindly Scottish grandmother.

The impression was deceiving.

Yes, Rosa was older than other mothers of girls Fionna's age, but she was far from retired. The Helensburgh police station would be lost without their capable receptionist. Rosa had no intention of stepping down, not from her job, nor from all the volunteering she did in the community.

As for the kind, warm-hearted façade... Well, maybe it wasn't exactly a façade. She just had no warmth left over for her daughter.

Rosa met Fionna's gaze, frowned, and made a gesture to indicate that her daughter should quit chewing on her hair. Fionna spit out the braid, and drool stuck to her chin. She quickly wiped it away.

But her mother had seen it. The creases on Rosa's forehead deepened, and she leaned over to Mrs. MacDonald to whisper something in her ear.

Fionna jumped up and fled into the house.

What had she been thinking, even contemplating telling her mother about her problem? Rosa would go to Mrs. MacDonald instead of making an appointment with a doctor. The coven leader would invite her over to her house, which gave Fionna the creeps, and would perform some magical mumbo jumbo.

No, she'd rather wait. Surely she'd get her period soon, and once she turned eighteen, she wouldn't have to tell her mother about anything anymore. Then she could move out, start an exciting life away from all of this, show everyone what she was really made of.

It was refreshingly cool inside the house. Nevertheless, Fionna felt drawn to the freezer compartment of the refrigerator. She had a hankering for a cold treat. She'd just eaten two pieces of raspberry cream pie, but there still was a hole in her stomach.

Unfortunately, there were none of her favorite popsicles left. Fionna closed the door and decided to check the large freezer in the basement.

As she descended the stairs and entered the dark, cavernous cellar, she immediately felt more at ease.

It might have seemed strange to outsiders that this should be her favorite place in the house, but she had loved it since childhood. It had been beyond her why playmates hadn't enjoyed coming down here. Maybe it was the old-fashioned fireplace with the cauldron suspended above it that had turned them off, Fionna thought now. Or the single light source that didn't reach into all the dark corners.

Fionna shrugged. She didn't have to worry about what other people thought because she rarely had anyone over anymore. That was just fine with her. She didn't have to justify her apparently weird preferences.

"Fionna?" A raspy voice drifted over from the shadows to her left.

Fionna was already bent over the large freezer in the section of the basement that served as a pantry. She turned around.

"Hi, Grandma," she said, as the old woman appeared from behind one of the tall bookshelves dividing the room on the other side. "What are you doing down here?"

"What do you think?" Matilda Simmonds held up a book. It was bound in old Moroccan leather and must have been part of her rare book collection.

"I mean, why aren't you upstairs with the others?"

"There isn't anything to celebrate yet. I'd rather prepare for the ceremony here than stuff my face and make small talk."

6

Fionna nodded as she turned around, opened the lid of the freezer, and rummaged around inside. When she turned with a popsicle in her hand, she realized her grandmother had been eyeing her critically the whole time. Embarrassed, she lowered her gaze and fiddled with the plastic wrapper.

"And what are you doing in the basement, lassie?"

Without looking up, Fionna stammered, "I was...Tara said something, and…" Finally, she sighed and faced her grandmother. "I want to tell you something, but please don't share it with Mom."

"Spit it out."

Fionna put the popsicle down on the lid of the freezer. She went over to her grandmother, who had taken a seat in her old and worn armchair. Fionna pulled the footstool close and sat down.

Picking at her fingernails, she confessed. "Tara got her period. She asked everyone else if they had gotten theirs yet. I didn't say anything, but Grandma... I'm already seventeen, and I haven't had my period yet. Isn't that weird?"

She looked up at Matilda, who was eyeing her with an impenetrable stare. "Remember when you used to come to me to ask about your father?"

Surprised, Fionna nodded. She had no clue how this was related, but it had been a similar situation.

As a small child, Fionna had noticed that all the other kids seemed to have fathers. A man had never been part of the Simmonds household. As far as Fionna knew, her mother and grandmother had never even dated.

Fionna had always known she was different. It hadn't been so bad, because she belonged to a community where everyone was a little out of the ordinary. Still, even the girls in her coven had fathers. Or grandfathers. And periods, apparently.

Even back then, Fionna hadn't dared to ask Rosa about it. But she'd needed to talk to someone—so she'd turned to her grandma.

Afterward, she'd wished she'd never asked, and neither Matilda nor Fionna had breathed a word about it since.

Until now.

"Of course. Of course, I remember." A cold shiver ran down Fionna's spine.

"Well, this has to do with your father. You'll probably never get your period."

"Why?" Fionna didn't understand what one thing could possibly have to do with the other.

Matilda was silent for a moment, turning the book in her hand. "How well do you know your Bible, lass? Are you familiar with the fall of man?"

"Umm..." Fionna cleared her throat. "Eve persuaded Adam to eat the forbidden fruit from the Tree of Knowledge, and God expelled them from the Garden of Eden. They were punished with—among other things—severe pain in childbirth...which links this to menstruation? Eve was cursed with her period?"

"Well. It says nowhere in the Bible outright that God cursed Eve with menstruation." Matilda sounded sarcastic. She narrowed her eyes until they seemed like dark slits in the dim light. "But Adam and Eve were the first humans. After Eve, every woman had to endure it. Cycles, menstruation, painful childbirth. God commanded his children to be fruitful and multiply. So every ordinary woman since Genesis has had to go through it. But you, my child, are different."

Matilda now smiled so the gaps in her teeth showed. The old woman refused to get dentures.

Fionna swallowed. "I'm not a normal woman, not a child of God, and that's why...that's why I don't get my period?"

8

Matilda nodded.

Fionna didn't know how to react to that. She was used to being an outsider, but she had never felt so left out.

"Do you believe that? Creation, the fall of man…the way it's explained in the Bible? Do you think we're all sinners? Women especially? I mean, you, who descended from Eve…" Fionna stammered.

Matilda gave a hoarse laugh. "Not literally. It's a story, that's all. It's a good story, don't you think? Women have cycles, and they menstruate because it's natural. We're mammals. Part of nature. But it comes down to the same thing where you're concerned, lassie. You aren't natural. You're different."

Fionna swallowed, then nodded. Her question had been answered.

She got up, picked up her now melted popsicle, and went back up the stairs.

In the garden, nothing had changed.

The sisters of the Tarbet coven were sitting at the tables, eating, drinking, and chatting.

Tara and Andie had their heads together and were giggling.

Fionna sat down next to them.

But she didn't join in their conversation.

She was too preoccupied with the terrible things Matilda had told her.

I'm not natural. I'm too different. I'm a freak.

CHAPTER ONE

ABBEY

"Where is My Mind" by the Pixies interrupted the silence in the breakfast room of Dessie's B&B.

Without looking at the display, Abbey declined the call. She had chosen the ringtone for her boss, Ken Sly, for good reason. He'd already tried to reach her several times this morning, and Abbey thought about switching her phone off.

Sly wasn't just disturbing her own breakfast of porridge and fruit, but that of several other guests as well.

Suddenly, loud construction noise filled the room. Abbey shrugged and pushed her phone away. She wouldn't need to worry about disturbing anyone if this went on.

"Everything all right? Can I get you…?"

Abbey looked up at the owner of the B&B, Dessie McKendrick.

Dessie was English, so Abbey usually had no problem understanding her—unlike the locals with their thick Highland accent. But the noise from outside had drowned out the tail end of the B&B owner's question.

"Pardon?"

"Can I get you another coffee?" Dessie gave a contrite smile. "I'm terribly sorry about the noise. I'd hoped the crew wouldn't get started before breakfast was over. My partner and I are building a house next door. I'm still living here, in a room in the B&B, and Declan has an apartment in Helensburgh. We had to remedy that situation, considering there's going to be three of us soon." She patted her round stomach.

"Oh, when is your baby due?" Abbey asked out of politeness.

"In three months. I just hope our new home will be ready by then, or else we'll have a problem." Dessie laughed nervously.

"I don't mind the noise," Abbey reassured her. She wasn't here on vacation—she had a job to do. Only she wouldn't tell Dessie that.

"I'm so glad. Let me get you a refill."

Dessie took the empty cup and went back to the kitchen counter.

Black Francis sang about feet on the air again.

Abbey sighed, swallowed the last bite of porridge, and picked up her phone to answer the call.

"Hello, boss."

"Fine, I've been trying to reach you all morning," Sly growled. "Had a nice lie-in, did ya? You're not in Scotland to skive off."

"Sorry. It's hard to get a signal up here," Abbey lied.

Her boss couldn't argue with that. From his perspective, in his big corner office in London, the sleepy Highland village of Tarbet had to appear like the worst kind of backwater.

The sort of place you'd send your least valuable employee to.

"Give me an update already!"

"Umm, I would, but there really isn't anything to

12

report. I got here late last night. I haven't gotten very far with my investigation yet."

"You'd better not screw this up, Fine," Sly ranted. "You know how important this client is…"

Abbey, having heard his speech numerous times already, rolled her eyes and tuned out.

"Of course, I understand, boss," she said, when Sly seemed finished.

She put on a smile for Dessie, who set down a fresh cup of coffee in front of her.

"I've already done the hard work for you," Sly continued talking.

Yes, her boss had done some research and the initial investigation. Because he didn't trust Abbey with anything.

It hadn't been too hard, though. The client had suspected his clerk of stealing the valuable rare book that was missing from his collection.

All it had taken was questioning the employee, who had quickly broken down. After admitting to having sold the book online to a rare books dealer, the clerk had been forthcoming with the address.

The recipient of the stolen book was an F. Simmonds of Tarbet, Scotland.

Abbey had been deemed just about capable of going to Scotland to retrieve the book. Even so, Sly clearly didn't trust her to complete the task.

"Don't be so uptight when you talk to that Simmonds guy." More unwanted advice. "Flirt a little. Use what you've got."

Abbey had gotten quite used to suppressing her emotions when her employer talked to her. She had known from the beginning that it wouldn't be easy to break into her chosen profession, which was still dominated by men—and a certain type of men, like Sly, at that.

She had applied for the position at Sly Investigations

with her eyes wide open, knowing that the large detective agency was known for its ruthless work culture. She'd been aware she'd have to prove herself to her male colleagues.

But enough was enough. Sly just wouldn't give her a chance. All he used her for was a honey trap when jealous wives hired the agency to prove their husbands' infidelity. And that was if she was lucky. Otherwise, he only found her useful as an assistant who took phone messages and picked up the dry cleaning.

Sly's suggestion to use her feminine assets in this case still rubbed her the wrong way, and she had a hard time not letting anger creep into her voice.

The only reason Sly had sent her to Scotland was that he assumed F. Simmonds was a man. She had been prepared to prove herself with this job, even if it seemed menial, but it just came down to the same old thing. All Sly thought she was good for had to do with her looks.

It was already a sore point for her.

"I'll do my best," Abbey got out through clenched teeth. After some more "good advice," Sly finally let her go.

Abbey tossed the phone into her purse on the chair next to her. She took a few deep breaths and had a sip of coffee.

"Bad news?" Without waiting for an answer, Dessie placed a chocolate muffin in front of her. "Here, we baked these for the guests, to make up for the noise. You're welcome to take it with you if you're full up right now."

"Thank you." Abbey drank more of her coffee, lost in thought. Sly wanted her to act quickly. He envisioned her ringing Simmond's doorbell and seducing him so he'd readily hand the book back.

Abbey didn't think that was wise. She'd rather find out as much as possible about this Simmonds character before she contacted him.

She was determined to solve this case and prove her worth to Sly. But she would do it her way.

"Dessie?" she called over to the B&B owner. "Could you help me with something?"

"Sure, what do you need?"

"I collect old cookbooks, and I heard there's a rare books dealer in Tarbet who specializes in that kind of thing."

"A used bookstore?" Dessie frowned. "No, we have nothing like that here."

"I don't think it's a store. Just a dealer who conducts their business at fairs and online, something like that?"

"Hmm. I do know someone who collects old books, but I thought it was more of a hobby—"

"That must be the person I'm looking for. There can't be that many antiquarian book collectors in Tarbet, right?"

"Umm…maybe." The screeching sound of a saw penetrated the walls of the breakfast room. Abbey cast a glance toward the construction site.

She didn't want to take advantage of the nice B&B owner, but a little guilt-tripping might play to her advantage.

Dessie pressed her lips together. "Well, if you're interested in buying a book from Fionna, I guess there wouldn't be any harm in giving you her address."

Fionna…F. Jackpot! "I would be so grateful, thanks!" Abbey pulled a pen and notepad out of her purse to jot down the address. "I can just go by and pay her a visit, right?"

"I don't know." Dessie sounded skeptical. "Maybe you should call first. Hang on. Andie, my employee, will know Fionna's phone number."

Dessie went to the kitchen counter where a petite young brunette was busy tidying up.

Abbey couldn't hear what Dessie said, but the younger

woman's reaction was pretty easy to read. Andie widened her eyes and shook her head in dismay.

Dessie screwed up her nose, smiled sheepishly, and pointed toward the construction noise.

Andie put the dish towel down and came over to Abbey's table, closely followed by Dessie.

Abbey tried to look as guileless as possible.

The young woman introduced herself as Andie MacLeod and then said, "Fionna won't receive customers at the door. You can't just stop by. You'd better contact her first."

"Okay. Well, I was hoping to pay her a visit. I collect old cookbooks, and I've heard of a rare book dealer in Tarbet. From what Dessie told me, that can only be this… er…Fionna Simmonds. I thought I'd look her up while I'm here."

Andie frowned. "Cookbooks? That's the first I've heard of that." Now she looked uncertain. "It's possible, I guess. Until a year ago, Fionna couldn't make toast or boil eggs, but she recently discovered a passion for cooking. She even started working in a restaurant. So it's possible that she's now buying and selling cookbooks, too…"

"Great!" Abbey exclaimed. "Then we share that passion. Please, would you give me her phone number? I'll call and ask her if I can come by. I'd love to see her collection, and I'm looking to buy, too, so it would certainly be to her advantage."

"You know what?" Andie seemed to come to a decision. "I'll call her. Fionna can be a little…antisocial. I'm her friend, so I know when to catch her in the right mood. I'll set up an appointment with her, all right?"

"That would be just wonderful, thank you!"

And that, Sly, Abbey thought to herself, is how it's done!

CHAPTER TWO

FIONNA

Fionna held her breath while she concentrated on squeezing the piping bag so the whipped cream icing came out perfectly.

She was in charge of desserts today, and she certainly didn't want to disappoint Drew.

She'd only been working at Drew's restaurant, a converted old church called The Kirk, for four months. At first, she'd been so insecure that she'd gladly stuck to fixing side salads and washing the dishes. But now, she was ready for greater challenges.

Drew had hired her on a whim, despite her lack of experience, and it amazed Fionna how much he trusted her. Today, he was even letting her try out her own dessert recipes. She'd hate nothing more than to let him down.

Drew was the most wonderful man she'd ever encountered in real life. He was romance-novel material, for sure.

Fionna loved those little creases around his chocolate-brown eyes when he smiled. And how his unruly dark curls always escaped from his chef's hat.

But Fionna also had the utmost respect for him. And not only because he had worked in a trendy restaurant in

Glasgow before opening The Kirk and was regarded as a celebrity chef by the locals. He would have every right to be arrogant, but he was warm, supportive, and so nice to her.

He was just a dream.

Fionna would have sighed if she hadn't remembered the cake she was decorating. One last cream rosette, and she'd be done.

"Fionna!"

She winced as she squeezed the piping bag with a little too much force. The delicate spiral of cream turned into a bulging worm. Great!

Annoyed, Fionna turned around.

"Thanks a lot, Sally! Now my cake is ruined."

The waitress, a plain woman in her mid-forties with mousy hair, shrugged. "Sorry."

Fionna wiped her forehead with the back of her left hand.

Maybe she could carefully remove the offending cream worm with a teaspoon…

"Um…Fionna…"

She pursed her lips and slowly turned her head in Sally's direction. "Yes? How can I help you?"

"There's someone asking for you. In the restaurant."

Fionna looked at her cake. She really should fix it. And she liked being on this side of the swinging door, where she didn't have to talk to guests.

On the other hand, could it be that the guest wanted to compliment her on a dessert? That really would be something.

Earlier, a couple of guests had ordered Fruitful Pockets, her very own recipe. Well, almost her own. Anyway, it was something that Drew had let her try out. Delicate short-bread pastry with a sweet but slightly tart rhubarb-apple-blackberry filling.

Fionna didn't enjoy talking to strangers, but she was also extremely proud about pulling this off. So why not?

"I'll finish the cake and then I'll come out, okay?" Fionna said.

She managed to remove the worm and pipe a perfect last rosette. After washing her hands, she went into the restaurant.

Sally was busy with drink orders at the bar, but she saw Fionna and pointed toward the old nave.

The entrance, bar, a few small tables, entry to the kitchen, and an old church organ were all in the transept of the old church.

Three steps led up to the longer nave, where most of the tables were set up. Columns and a balustrade partially blocked Fionna's view, so she couldn't see who was up there.

But once she had ascended the steps, she immediately knew who had asked for her.

The gorgeous blond woman waved at her.

Fionna rolled her eyes, but she was secretly pleased to see Penny Reid.

The woman had become a friend, and Fionna didn't have many of those.

Actually, aside from Penny, there was only Andie, who was a few years younger than her. They had always just gotten along as if by default. Andie was calm and level-headed, if a bit serious.

Penny was the exact opposite. Too much so for Fionna's liking. Also, she was intimidating, drowning out everyone else in the room with her confidence, beauty, and strong personality. No wonder she'd always had a reputation of being a witch with a "b."

But last summer, Fionna had gotten to know her better. A young pregnant girl had turned up in Penny's rose garden, and the herb witch had needed Fionna's help.

It turned out Penny had her insecurities too, and she wasn't nearly as selfish as everyone made her out to be.

In fact, it was Penny who Fionna had to thank for her new career. The herb witch had sort of coerced her into learning how to cook. If it wasn't for Penny, Fionna wouldn't have found her new passion—or met Drew! To say nothing of the ten pounds Fionna had lost since learning how to cook healthy meals for herself.

So now Fionna greeted her new friend with a smile.

Penny and her partner, Chris, were seated at a small rustic table for two.

"Hey! We've been wanting to come and get a taste of your cooking for a while," Penny said. "We finally made it. This is so great! Who would have ever thought!"

Fionna didn't blame Penny for being so blunt.

After all, at twenty-five years old, she'd never had a proper job. She didn't even have a degree. She'd just never bothered after finishing high school early. Staying home with her mother had been the easier option.

Fionna's love for old books had turned into an income stream without her even trying very hard. She'd always adored her grandmother's special collection, and over the years she'd added to it. In learning where to find these treasures, she had also begun to dig up books others were searching for and sold them at a profit. She had a website for bibliophiles, and customers contacted her through that, but she was also active in forums.

She liked to work online and under an avatar. Fionna didn't really view it as a business—she certainly had never done any bookkeeping and had never filled out a tax form in her life. But it earned her a pretty penny.

Her mother had never commented on it, as usual. Rosa had not once encouraged Fionna to find a job, and she hadn't asked her to move out, either.

Fionna didn't like living with her mother, but at some point it had become somewhat of a personal challenge. How far could she push before she finally provoked a reaction in Rosa?

Slowly, Fionna was reaching a point where she was giving up. She had made significant changes in her life, and getting this job was one of them. She would move out as soon as she found an apartment that suited her.

"So, what can you recommend?" Penny asked. "I really want to try one of your dishes."

Fionna blushed. "Umm…I don't really cook, you know. That's Drew's job."

"Why not?"

"Um…I'm still new at this, learning the ropes."

Penny looked at her with big green eyes. "But you could fix it if something goes wrong. You know…you could make the dishes taste good just like that." She snapped her fingers.

"What do you mean?" Fionna asked with indignation, knowing full well what Penny was getting at.

"You could season the food with a special ingredient." Penny winked.

"I don't—"

Chris cleared his throat. "Penny is just teasing you. There's no need for the vague hints either, Penny. There's only one other table occupied this early in the evening, and I don't think they can hear us all the way on the other side of the room."

"Killjoy." Penny pouted, but her eyes sparkled. "Not to beat around the bush, Fionna, but why don't you just put a spell on a salt shaker or something, so the seasoning makes all your dishes taste delicious? You could easily pull that off, right? Enchanting objects is your specialty."

Penny was right. Every sister of the Tarbet coven had a particular magical talent, passed down from a mother or grandmother. Penny was an herb witch, and Fionna's gift was enchanting objects—as far as the coven knew.

"I would never do that," Fionna said.

"Nobody cares if you spice things up with a little magic." Penny waved off Fionna's moral objection. "Everybody just wants their food to taste good."

"I care." Fionna's voice trembled. "This job...it has nothing to do with magic. Here, in the restaurant, I'm just a normal person. I want to come by my success honestly... without the help of magic." Fionna noticed the heat rising to her face. She was probably bright red.

Chris nodded. "Good for you."

Penny now looked serious, too. "Yes, good for you. I mean that." Then she laughed. "So, what should we order?" She looked at the open menu. "Is there anything you had your non-magical hand in?"

"Actually," Fionna couldn't help but sound a little proud. "I'm making the desserts today. Drew even let me try my own recipe. It's called Fruitful Pockets, and it's traditionally Scottish. I hope it's good. So far, only the guests over there have ordered it, so I haven't had any feedback yet."

Fionna looked over toward the table at the far end of the main aisle where an elderly couple had just finished their desserts.

Sally was with them, and she seemed distressed.

Fionna frowned and strained to listen to the conversation. There seemed to be a problem with the bill.

Nobody had a problem hearing Sally when she raised her voice. "No, you don't understand. Forty-nine pounds. Four. Nine. Not ninety-four."

She pushed the wad of cash on the little plate back across the table.

"*You* don't understand," the man replied resolutely. "The rest is for the chef."

Sally stared at him. "You're supposed to tip twenty percent, not a hundred percent. That's…I can't—"

"Wait, I think I have some more change…" The elderly customer dumped all the coins from his pockets onto the table.

The waitress looked at him incredulously. "Is that supposed to be a joke?"

"Come, dear," the man said to his wife. She stood up, and he helped her into her jacket.

"Oh look, I have this." The woman pulled a few bills out of her jacket pocket. "For the chef. The dessert really was delicious."

Sally was speechless. She stared at the couple as they left the restaurant, then shook her head and gathered the money strewn on the table.

"Wow!" Penny said. "Your Fruitful Pockets must be superb if they felt compelled to tip all the money they had on them. I definitely want what they had!"

"Your dessert really was delicious." Penny complimented Fionna as she and Chris said goodbye after their meal.

"Thanks! Did you try it, too?" Fionna asked Chris.

He raised his hands. "Sorry, no. I don't have a sweet tooth. I ordered the cheese selection."

"Well, it seemed to be a big hit with most of the guests," Fionna said excitedly. "Sally said customers who ordered the Fruitful Pockets tipped insane amounts today."

"I guess you can perform magic in the kitchen without a spell," Penny said happily, waving goodbye.

Fionna beamed. Her friend couldn't have given her a nicer compliment. She practically skipped back into the kitchen.

She thought her first foray into restaurant cooking couldn't have gone any better—until Drew approached her later.

The restaurant had just closed, and Fionna was tidying up the kitchen.

"Fionna, your Fruitful Pockets were a tremendous success," Drew congratulated her. "Sally said we received record tips."

Fionna blushed. "I'm sure that was also because of your great dishes and Sally's excellent service."

"I don't know. Are there any left? I would love to try one, since all the guests have been raving about them. Sally, too."

Fionna almost jumped up and down with excitement. "Sure! I'll heat some up and bring them out to you."

Drew and Sally ate their desserts in the dining room as they finished the closing tasks, and Fionna got nervous again.

The guests seemed to have enjoyed the Fruitful Pockets, but they weren't professional chefs. A compliment from Drew would mean more to her than anything else in the world.

Her heart was racing as she scrubbed the perfectly clean stainless steel counter for the third time.

Finally, Drew came back into the kitchen.

Fionna turned around, squeezing the sponge so tightly, foamy liquid dripped out. "What did you think?"

Drew's puppy-dog brown eyes lit up. "Fionna, they were sensational."

"R...really?"

Her boss nodded. "I had a feeling during the interview, when you did a few sample dishes, that you had a hidden talent." Drew took off his chef's jacket. "That's why I hired you, even though you had no experience. I thought to myself, that girl has something. Good thing I listened to my instincts."

Drew disappeared into the storage room, which also functioned as an employee coat room and office.

Fionna stood stock still and stared after him. She couldn't believe it. It was the first time in her life that someone had told her she had done something sensationally. And not just someone, but Drew!

When Drew came out of the storage room wearing his black leather jacket, Fionna couldn't help but beam at him.

She'd always tried to hide her feelings for her boss. But today was different.

"Wait, I want to give you something." Drew took out his wallet and thrust a wad of bills into her hand.

Fionna's smile got wonky.

"You're doing such a great job here. Let's call it a bonus. A Christmas bonus."

"But…" Fionna looked at the money. It had to be well over three hundred pounds. "There's no need for that, and…it's March."

"You earned it." Drew put a hand on her shoulder. Instead of enjoying the touch, Fionna was only more rattled. Something didn't seem right about this.

"Okay, I'm off. Can you lock up, please? It's Sally's day off tomorrow, by the way."

Fionna nodded, her gaze still on the bills in her hand.

A bad feeling rose inside her, like bile in her throat.

She put the money on the counter and went into the dining room.

"Did you enjoy my dessert?" she asked Sally nervously.

Sally, who was sitting in the little nook next to the bar counting the day's earnings, nodded vigorously. "It was so delicious."

Fionna held her breath and waited tensely.

"I'm done here," Sally said, writing her numbers in the

cashier's book. Then she shoved the stacks of money across the table in Fionna's direction. "I want you to have this."

Fionna swallowed. "All of today's earnings?"

"Yes. And my tips, too. You earned it." Sally seemed completely serious.

Fionna didn't say anything, but Sally looked at her expectantly, so in the end, she just nodded.

"Um, Drew asked me to lock up." Fionna got out.

She was still standing at the table, trying to breathe calmly, when Sally returned with her coat and bag.

After a cheerful goodbye, the waitress left the restaurant through the front entrance.

Fionna sat down at the table and counted out the change as well as the tips for the day. After returning the change to the till behind the bar, she found an envelope for the tips and wrote Sally's name on it. Next, she filled out a deposit slip and put it in a bank pouch, together with the earnings of the day. After a moment's consideration, she put both the pouch and the envelope in the safe in the storage room.

With all that taken care of, Fionna went to the little corner of the kitchen that was reserved for paperwork. On the wall, there was a clipboard with the menu for that evening. Stuck next to it was the recipe for Fruitful Pockets that Fionna had copied from an old cookbook.

Collecting antiquarian books was a bit like a treasure hunt. Fionna loved the tingle in her belly when she saw a book listed for sale somewhere that she knew she had to have. It had started as a hobby, but her good instincts had led her to turn that passion into a profitable business.

But where this book was concerned, it had been more than a tingle. As soon as she had read the author's name, Fionna had known the book was meant for her.

She was so naive. She should have known.

Fionna read the recipe again, even though she had already read it so many times she knew it by heart.

The ingredients weren't unusual, but the wording was.

She'd thought it was just the author's quirk—it would have suited her.

For example, instead of simply listing rhubarb, the recipe called for "the very first rhubarb."

That's what had caught Fionna's attention, because the previous week she had seen "the first rhubarb of the season" advertised at the market.

She'd also had "free blackberries from many moons ago" on hand. Last September, she had picked wild blackberries and put them in the freezer.

It had been fun to follow the recipe to the letter. Fionna had bought elderberry syrup at a local farm for "sweetening drops of the region's finest elderberries." She'd even thrown salt over her shoulder, as described in the recipe, before adding some to her shortcrust pastry mix.

Yes, it was all too obvious, and Fionna should have known. But she wouldn't have thought that you could do so much damage with an unusually worded recipe.

There had been no coven circle, no summoning of the elements' energy, no actual spell...

Penny's words were still ringing in her ears. "You can perform magic in the kitchen without a spell."

"Apparently not," Fionna murmured to herself. She ripped the piece of paper from the wall, crumpled it, and threw it in the trash.

CHAPTER THREE

ABBEY

Abbey had trouble keeping the surprise from registering on her face when Fionna Simmonds opened the door and invited her in.

She hadn't known what to expect, but certainly not a grumpy-looking, chubby red-head who could hardly be older than herself. She certainly didn't fit the stereotype of a rare books dealer, and the fact that she lived in a neat cottage in a remote village in the Scottish Highlands seemed even more incongruous.

Then Fionna led Abbey down the basement stairs, not bothering with an introduction or small talk.

Abbey's sense of surrealism turned to unease. And when she stood in the cavernous basement, the bad feeling in her stomach was no longer something she could ignore. If she hadn't had to prove something to her boss, she would have run back up the stairs.

She dragged her feet as she followed Fionna beyond the first row of bookshelves.

The shelves were modern-looking, solid metal constructions that contrasted with the old fireplace and cauldron closer to the door.

Abbey swallowed. It occurred to her that the air was quite dry down here, not at all like you would expect in a damp old basement. The ceiling was barely visible in the dim light of a single bulb, but Abbey noticed the walls were made of crumbly old bricks. Hardly the environment best suited for preserving valuable old books. There had to be an expensive dehumidification system installed, even though Abbey saw no evidence of it.

But who knew what was hidden in the shadowy corners?

An icy shiver ran down Abbey's spine at the thought.

Get a grip, Fine, she scolded herself.

She had a job to do and couldn't afford to act like the cliché of a weak and helpless female Ken Sly had cast her as.

Determined, she caught up with Fionna. The young woman had hardly said a word since she'd opened the door. It was obviously up to Abbey to get the conversation going. "I'm particularly interested in old cookbooks," she said, her tone a touch too cheerful. Abbey cleared her throat. "Do you have any of those?"

"Yes. A few." Fionna disappeared behind a shelf. A light turned on. "Come over here."

Abbey followed Fionna with a queasy feeling. But the source of the light was a desk lamp. It illuminated a large table covered with books.

Relieved that the mystery of one of those dark corners was solved, Abbey came closer.

The wooden surface of the desk bowed under the weight of stacks of books, and Fionna added two more volumes she'd pulled from nearby shelves. "Why don't you take a look at these? I'll get more."

Abbey pretended to thumb through a cookbook of Scottish recipes from the 1950s as she looked around. On the desk were a wide variety of books, from how-to manuals to romance novels. Nothing struck her as particularly valuable.

But then, she didn't have a clue about antiquarian books. She could only hope that Fionna would bring her the recipe book that had been stolen from Sly's client.

"Do you have anything in particular in mind?" Fionna asked when she returned with another book under her arm. "A certain time period? A region or country?"

She blew a strand of red hair out of her face as she dropped the heavy tome onto the desk and the stacks threatened to topple. "Sorry, but I have little practice with walk-ins. I'm used to handling things online."

Abbey smiled. "Not a problem. The young woman in the B&B...Andie?...She already mentioned that. I guess I'm looking for a cookbook with Scottish recipes." She looked at the leather-bound volume titled *Renaissance French Cuisine* that Fionna had dropped onto the desk. "I should have specified."

"I should have asked." Fionna picked the heavy book up, and Abbey pretended to help her, pushing over a pile of other books. Some of them fell to the floor.

"Oh no, I'm so sorry."

"No, my bad. I really should keep things tidier down here, but like I said..." Fionna grumbled, and the rest of her words were lost as she bent down to gather the volumes up from the floor.

Abbey took the opportunity to survey the rest of the books on the desk. She was now pretty certain that the client's stolen copy wasn't among them.

"Here, let me help you." She grabbed the books Fionna was picking up from the floor—and almost yelped when she read the title of one of them.

Magical Highland Cooking.

It was the book she was looking for!

Abbey tried to keep cool.

"Oh, this looks interesting," she said with an even voice. Abbey sat down at the desk chair and flipped through the book. Her heart was racing.

"What?" Fionna got up from the floor and bumped her head on the edge of the desk. "Ouch."

Rubbing her head, the red-haired young woman straightened. "Oh, no, that...um, give it back." She reached out to take the book, but Abbey pulled it quickly out of reach.

"No, it's exactly what I'm interested in. What do you want for it?"

Fionna got very flustered. "No, it isn't for sale. That's mine. P-p-please..."

Abbey shut the book before Fionna could grab it, hugged it to her chest, and stood up quickly.

Fionna stared at her for a moment. Then she crossed her arms in front of her chest, trying to make herself as tall as Abbey—an endeavor that was doomed to fail—and said in an ice-cold voice. "Give me my book back. And then leave."

Even though Abbey could have easily taken on the distinctly unathletic-looking young woman, something in Fionna's tone made her sound very scary.

Abbey swallowed. She mustered up all her confidence. Then she said, "This book was stolen, and you acquired it illegally. The rightful owner hired the detective agency I work for to retrieve it. So you will let me do my job—unless you want me to involve the police."

"The rightful owner?" Fionna snorted. "Don't make me laugh."

Abbey hadn't expected that reaction. She tried not to let it rattle her.

"Yes," she said. "The person it was stolen from."

"If that person really is the rightful owner, why aren't the police here?"

"Because...the police..." Abbey faltered. Then she took a deep breath and continued. "He most likely reported it. But the police aren't going to investigate as extensively as my agency to find a stolen book—"

"Rubbish," Fionna interrupted her. "I can tell you why the client didn't report the theft. For the same reason he won't want the police involved. Your threats are empty. Give me my book and go away."

Fionna reached out to grab it from Abbey, but the private detective took a step back. Her back hit the cold brick wall. She raised her chin defiantly to cover up the fact that she was shivering. "Oh yeah? What would that reason be?"

Fionna looked at her for a moment, then sighed in exasperation. "Your client stole the book in the first place. It's not his."

Abbey had to admit there could be something to Fionna's claim.

Threatening to call the police was just a bluff. Her boss had specifically told her not to involve the authorities, under any circumstances.

Nevertheless, she said, "You can't know that. Do you want to take the chance? I understand you deal...let's say under the table. This could end badly for you."

"Yes, I know it with absolute certainty." Fionna didn't let herself be intimidated. "I am the rightful owner of the book."

"You aren't the owner just because you paid the thief. It was stolen, so—"

Fionna snatched the book from Abbey. "The book is mine. The proof is written in black and white. Look."

Fionna put the book on the desk and opened it.

Taken aback, Abbey needed a moment. Curiosity won her over, so she stepped closer.

Studying Fionna for a moment, she eventually took her

eyes off the young woman and looked where Fionna pointed.

It was the name of the author.

"Matilda Fionna Simmonds," Abbey read aloud.

"My grandmother wrote the book," Fionna explained.

Abbey got goose bumps, but she tried to keep her tone light. "Well, that doesn't make the book yours. Imagine if JK Rowling's granddaughter would claim all the Harry Potter copies ever printed as hers. That's ridiculous."

Fionna waved her hand impatiently. "This isn't a commercially distributed book. My grandmother made it with a printing press. Only five copies were produced—and none of them were ever for sale. This is the kind of book that was meant to stay…in the family. I'm absolutely certain of that."

"Look. I'm just doing my job here. I don't know how the client got hold of the book—I only know that it was stolen from him. He hired my firm to find it. If you aren't willing to hand it over, I'm just going to have to tell him where it is. If he calls the police, it's your—"

"He won't."

Abbey pressed her lips together. She considered her options for a moment.

Fionna would not budge.

Abbey would have to wrestle her to get the book, and while she was fairly confident she would win, wrestling matches weren't something she wanted to add to her job description. Also, secretly, she thought Fionna was right. If the client had come by the book honestly, there wouldn't be any reason he couldn't call the police. Abbey's assignment was to find the book—and she had succeeded.

So Abbey nodded and then retreated, weaving her way through the tall shelves until she reached the staircase. Fionna followed her.

Once Abbey had reached the top of the stairs, it was as if a heavy load had been lifted off her chest.

An older woman with her gray hair in a bun came through the front door just as Fionna was about to open it for Abbey. The woman looked at Abbey with raised eyebrows, then turned her skeptical gaze on Fionna.

"She wanted to buy a book," the red-haired young woman said with a squeaky voice. She no longer bore any resemblance to the confident person who had just stood up to Abbey.

"I wouldn't let strangers into the house if I were you," the woman said.

"We just went to the basement for a minute." Fionna bowed her head. "It was pretty clear the sale wouldn't happen, so—"

"The basement?" the woman said sharply. "Fionna, you should know better!"

"Um, I'd better go." Abbey waved goodbye to Fionna and ducked through the door.

She got no response, so she hurried down the cobbled walkway toward the street. Breathing in the clear Highland air, she felt relieved to leave the oppressive atmosphere of the Simmonds house behind.

CHAPTER FOUR

FIONNA

Fionna quickly disappeared back into the basement so she could escape her mother's scolding words.

She picked up her grandmother's book from the desk and flipped through it.

When Fionna had seen it offered on a rare books site, she had been so excited. Her grandmother had authored a book!

She should have known, though, that it was more than a cookbook. And now it turned out it had been stolen.

After her discovery of the book's existence, Fionna had rummaged through her grandmother's personal documents until she found a reference to *Magical Highland Cooking*. That's how she'd found out only five copies of the book existed.

They must have been intended for members of the coven. Fionna was a hundred percent certain they had never been meant to leave Tarbet.

Abbey Fine's detective agency was located in London. Their client had to be from thereabouts, too. Instead of reporting the book theft to the police, he had hired an agency that wasn't afraid to get their hands dirty. It was clear to Fionna that this dubious client had acquired her grandmother's cookbook illegally.

Fionna opened to the page with the recipe for Fruitful Pockets again and examined it carefully. There really were no instructions for a magical ritual or any other indication that the recipe really was a spell—other than the oddly specific ingredients and the strange wording. Fionna studied all the recipes again and again throughout the night. She got little sleep, and she wasn't much wiser come morning.

The titles were the only sign of what the spells were for. Fruitful Pockets had literally made her pockets bountiful. Everyone who had eaten her dish had been eager to fill Fionna's pockets with money.

Fionna was inclined to try another recipe, just to make sure it hadn't been a fluke.

Her gaze lingered on the recipe for Loose Tongue Terrine. Her assumption was that people who ate it would have a loose tongue and reveal things they ordinarily would keep to themselves.

That didn't sound as if it could cause too much harm.

Fionna scanned the ingredients and then looked at her watch. If she hurried, she could get everything from a store in Helensburgh and prepare the terrine in the restaurant before her shift started.

Having decided, Fionna flew up the stairs to her attic room. While packing an overnight bag, she called her friend Andie to ask if she could stay with her.

She needed to take herself and the cookbook to a safe place. Abbey knew where Fionna lived—and she would report that back to her client. Who knew how far the original thief was willing to go to get the magical recipe book back?

〜

"Fionna, you really have outdone yourself," Drew complimented her after he sampled some of the tongue terrine.

"Really?" Fionna asked, not because she was fishing for compliments or because she was thrilled that her crush had such a high opinion of her. She just needed to find out if the magical recipe had worked.

Fionna was very nervous. Dying to know if Drew reciprocated her feelings, she had wanted him to try the dish first.

She knew the truth could be brutal, but she needed to know if he was just being nice to her because he was a friendly guy. It was better not to have any false hopes. What was the likelihood that such a confident, attractive, talented man would fall in love with a naive, socially awkward, and slightly overweight woman like her?

Fionna desperately wanted to know how Drew felt about her, but now, as push came to shove, she couldn't bring herself to ask him directly.

"So…Drew," she stammered. "Is there anything else on your mind? Something you want to confide…um, tell me?" Fionna twisted the button on her chef jacket.

Drew sighed. "There is something. It's bad."

Fionna's heart sank. She prepared herself to be let down gently.

"The restaurant is so very close to my heart. I gave up a well-paid, prestigious job at Jus d'Ox in Glasgow for this passion project."

"Oh. Yes. I know." The conversation seemed to be going in a direction Fionna hadn't anticipated.

"I invested every penny I had." Drew pushed his dark curls back. "And now it looks like I'm going to lose everything. My dream is about to go bust." He hung his head.

Fionna looked at him, aghast. Drew had never let on about any of this. He always seemed positive and in good spirits. The restaurant was doing well, wasn't it? They certainly seemed to be fully booked most nights. And everyone only had good things to say about The Kirk.

Drew looked the picture of misery.

Fionna really wanted to give him a hug. Instead, she wiped an imaginary stain off the kitchen counter with a dish towel.

"Why do you think that?" she asked in a small voice.

"A building inspection showed that we need to do renovations to comply with safety guidelines. They're minor, but they have to be done, or else we'll be shut down. I don't have the reserves to close the restaurant temporarily and hire contractors."

"Oh my god, I'm so sorry," Fionna said. "I wish there was something I could do."

Drew managed to smile at her. "Thanks, that's sweet of you to say. Unfortunately, the only way to help me would be to let me know the winning lottery numbers. So unless you're clairvoyant…"

"Let me think…" Fionna wasn't clairvoyant, but she knew a couple of people who were. They couldn't just predict lottery numbers, of course, but maybe there was another way…

"Fionna, I was only kidding!" Drew laughed.

"Oh, right, of course." Fionna did her best to return a smile.

She should have known that it would be a mistake to let people eat this terrine. She didn't want to know things that weren't her business. Drew had never intended for his employees to know his situation.

How ridiculous that she had been worried about his reciprocation of her silly romantic feelings. Drew had real problems.

"Anyway, I don't know why I just told you that. Forget about it, it's not your concern. I'll think of something. The terrine really is delicious. I'm sure our guests will love it. The first couple of orders have been served already."

"Really?" Fionna had an uneasy feeling in the pit of her stomach. The recipe worked a little too well. What had she been thinking?

"Um, I'm just going to ask Sally if she's had any feedback yet," she said to Drew, who was busy at the stove again.

Fionna's worst fears were confirmed when she heard the loud voices in the dining room.

This early in the evening, there were only three tables occupied.

A middle-aged couple was arguing.

"I don't have to sit here and listen to this," the woman said, incensed. "Especially not on our anniversary!"

Fionna craned her neck to see what was on their plates, but the pillars blocked her view.

"What's going on?" she whispered to Sally, who was standing behind the bar.

"The husband told his wife not to eat such rich food because she needed to watch her weight."

"Oh, my!"

Sally seemed nonplussed. "I think it's great. I love it when people argue in public. It's like a soap opera. I adore soap operas. I spend my mornings watching the episodes I taped the evening before, while I'm working."

"Okay." Fionna chewed on her nails, still craning her neck to see what was going on in the section of the restaurant where the customers were seated. "Um…what starters did they have?"

"She had the trout mousse; he had your tongue terrine."

"Shoot."

"Why do you say that? Don't worry, it's yummy!"

Fionna stared at Sally. "Did you try some?"

"Yes, Drew brought some out for me to sample." Sally leaned closer and said in a conspiratorial voice, "He's cute, isn't he?"

"Who?"

"Drew! He is an absolute dish, don't you think?"

"Um…sure. Drew is very attractive."

"I think so. Although he isn't really my type." She paused for dramatic effect. "I have sexual fantasies about Prince Andrew."

Fionna coughed. "The disgraced Prince Andrew, Duke of York?"

"Yes." Sally sighed. "I know. *I'm* the disgrace. I mean, I'm Scottish, born and bred. I just can't help myself. Go ahead, call me a traitor to my people. I feel terrible about it."

Fionna suppressed a chuckle. "Don't feel bad. Not about that."

"Oh, but I *am* bad." Sally leaned very close again. "Sometimes I'm a *very* bad girl."

"O…kay." Fionna took a step back.

"I even dream about a threesome with Andrew and his brother, King Charles. It's the ears that do it for me. I fantasize I'm holding on to them and just riding—"

"Stop, stop!" Fionna raised her hands and hightailed it back into the kitchen.

Inside, she leaned against the door frame and tried to shake off the mental image.

"Are you all right?" Drew asked her. "You look like you saw…something very unpleasant."

"I heard something unpleasant. Listen, I want to take the tongue terrine off the menu."

"What? Why? It's delicious."

"Um, I remembered I left the tongue too long in my car. I went shopping and totally lost track of time. I'm worried it has gone off. I know it's so stupid. Maybe it'll be fine, but if someone gets food poisoning, that would be really bad, right? Better safe than sorry. If you and Sally are okay tomorrow, we can still serve the terrine tomorrow. It'll keep, and nothing is wasted. I'd just feel so much better if we leave it off today. I'm sorry," Fionna babbled on.

"If you feel that's best." Drew interrupted her. He eyed her quizzically. "It doesn't seem like you to forget. I'm sure everything is fine. It tasted good. But yes, better safe than sorry. We'll serve it tomorrow."

"Thank you," Fionna said, relieved. She quickly went back into the dining room to wipe the terrine off the chalkboard and tell Sally.

She just hoped she wouldn't hear any more unsavory details about the waitress's sex life!

Andie's shift at the B&B started very early—much earlier than Fionna usually got up. But when Andie's alarm clock went off, Fionna didn't follow her inclination to pull the duvet over her head.

Yawning, she rose, too.

Fionna had stashed the Loose Tongue Terrine in Andie's fridge. Once her shift had ended last night, she had packed up the dish and taken it with her. Fortunately, there had been no more embarrassing incidents, and Fionna wanted to keep it that way.

Now, she was worried that Andie's parents would see it and sample it. She would have to take care of it.

Andie had been asleep when Fionna had let herself in with her spare key the previous evening, so she hadn't had the chance to explain anything.

She remedied that at the breakfast table over a strong cup of coffee.

Fionna quickly summarized for her friend how she had gotten hold of the cookbook, what its recipes really could do, and that Abbey Fine had been hired to take the book from her.

Andie had to leave for work, so Fionna decided to accompany her to the B&B. She wanted to make copies of the recipes in the book. They had also come up with a plan about how they could use the Loose Tongue Terrine to their advantage, so they took it with them.

"It's not that I don't believe you," Andie said, pulling up the collar of her coat. There was an icy wind that morning. "I just would like to see it with my own eyes."

"It works like a charm. I don't know how, though; it seems far too simple. That's why it didn't occur to me the recipes could be magical."

"I agree. No ritual, no need for the coven—or at least the energy of other witches—none of the usual magical tools or ingredients?"

"No. And I didn't even have the book with me when I was cooking," Fionna said. "I mean, I could understand if the book was enchanted and somehow responsible for enchanting the dishes, too. It looks like I'm doing it just by cooking the copied recipes. That's weirding me out a little."

"But that's your magical gift—to enchant objects, right? Like, when you enchanted the book you gave to Pari to read her thoughts. That's similar. Maybe your grandmother did something like that with the book, too. It stands to reason that you inherited that skill from her."

"Yes." Fionna turned red. She didn't want to be reminded of giving Penny Reid a tool to spy on someone's innermost thoughts. It hadn't been one of her proudest moments. "But you know, it's one thing to enchant a book and another to transfer the enchantment onto a recipe. The magic has to work independently, if you know what I mean. I've never come across anything like it."

"Seems like strong magic. Your grandmother must have been one hell of a witch. Is that why you always say her magic passed down to you? Your mom must have the same talent."

"Technically, but Mom's magic is so much weaker, it can hardly be compared. She can also do elemental magic, but just the basics. Like…she can turn water into ice cubes, but she wouldn't be able to populate the water with fish. She can make a scratchy sweater soft, but she can't turn the sweater into a flying kite. You know what I mean?"

Andie nodded. "I think so. Your magical skills can do more complex stuff."

"And I can transfer magic to an object, so that someone else can make use of it. Sticking with the example of the enchanted sweater, I can make a piece of cloth have the qualities of protective armor. That's what I do when we waulk the tartan every year. And that's what I did with the tartan shawl for Dessie, when it acted as a protective shield for her. Like I said, I'd understand if the book was directly responsible for the spells. If my grandmother transferred the magic of the recipes into the book. But it isn't—I left it at home. It's the recipes themselves. So the source of magic is once more removed. Powerful stuff."

Andie unlocked the door to the B&B, and Fionna was glad to get into the warm house.

"Maybe it's just you," Andie said, as they hung their coats on the rack. "Because you have the same magic as your grandmother. Maybe everyone else would need the book. That mysterious client of Abbey's wouldn't go to such lengths to get it back otherwise. He could have just copied the recipes."

Fionna followed Andie down the hall to the kitchen and breakfast room. "True. The book itself must have value. I'll take another look at it. I have a feeling it has to do with the last section under the heading of Specialties. Those recipes sound even weirder than anything else in the book."

In the kitchen, Fionna got the terrine out of the insulated bag, placed it on the counter, and unwrapped the aluminum foil.

Andie eyed the dish skeptically. "Do you think Abbey will eat this?"

"Why not?"

"Beef tongue? Gross."

"Hey, it's delicious," Fionna replied indignantly.

"If you say so. Well, I don't have to eat it."

"Yes, and you'd better make sure nobody else gets a bite, either. It should work out okay, since you said Dessie won't be here." Fionna got out the cookbook. "I'd better get to the office and make my copies. I don't want Abbey to see me here before she eats the enchanted dish, and I especially don't want her to see the book."

"I'll bring you a cup of coffee once I get everything set up."

"I'd appreciate that, thanks!"

Fionna went into Dessie's little office, turned on the copier, and began making copies. Her coffee arrived soon, and she drank it while flipping through the book again.

Soon after, Andie returned. "Abbey is in the breakfast room—and she ate the tongue!"

They rushed back. Fionna scanned the room for the private investigator. When she locked eyes with Abbey, Fionna hesitantly raised an arm to wave at her.

Abbey waved back.

Fionna took heart and walked over. "Hi. I'm glad to see you here. I wanted to…apologize," she improvised. "I know I came across as rude the other day. It's just…my grandmother's book means a lot to me, and I feel I have the right to keep it."

She anxiously shifted from one foot onto the other, waiting for Abbey's answer.

"To be honest, I totally understand, Miss…can I call

you Fionna?"

"Sure."

"Please call me Abbey. I always feel self-conscious when I talk to someone my age and they call me Miss Fine."

"I know what you mean."

"Have a seat, Fionna."

Fionna sat down, her body stiff with tension. After what she had experienced last night at the restaurant, she didn't know what she could expect from Abbey.

"I mean, a formal address helps create a professional distance, and it implies a sense of respect. It makes me feel like an impostor, though. In reality, I'm just a shy girl like you, trying to prove myself in my profession. I mean, I have more going for me than just a pretty face, and I want to show that."

Fionna glanced at the remains of the tongue terrine on Abbey's plate. The spell seemed to be working. The tough private eye Fionna had met yesterday would never have shown her vulnerable side like that.

"Anyway, I understand you, Fionna. I called my boss yesterday, and he confirmed our client hasn't reported the theft. He doesn't want the police involved. Your assumption that our client stole the book in the first place is probably correct."

"Oh, okay…so you won't call the police on me?"

Abbey shook her head. "That was an empty threat." She took a bite of the cheese scone on her plate. "God, this is delicious," she raved, still chewing. "My mom would have a fit if she saw me eat this. I always have her voice in my head when I indulge in something that wouldn't be in her diet plan. My mom used to be a model, and she would have loved to see me follow in her footsteps. Thanks to her, my subconscious has me on a permanent diet."

Fionna looked Abbey up and down. She really had a great figure. Tall, slender, and athletic. It was nice to hear from one of those beanpoles that they couldn't eat anything they wanted and just never gain weight. That sort of false modesty really grated on her.

"I get that. My mom is also very dominant. She used to give me a hard time when I was a child. She was always on about me having to watch my weight. But she doesn't do that anymore. She's kind of given up on me, I guess. Sometimes I wish she would still give me that hard time. I used to try to provoke her…"

Stop! Fionna told herself. She had to remember that Abbey was only so open and vulnerable because she had ingested the tongue terrine. It wasn't like they were friends now.

"Um, what do you think the client's next move is going to be?" Fionna got back to the more important topic.

"I don't know. I'm supposed to pressure you. Or come up with some other way to get the book. Be creative, my boss said." Abbey snorted.

Fionna's eyes widened. "You mean he wants you to steal it?"

"Pretty much. I'm not prepared to do that, though. There's proving myself, and then there's crossing the line. The only thing is, my boss implied I mustn't return to London without the book, or else I won't have a job to come back to."

"Oh no. What are you going to do?"

"I don't know." Abbey put the scone back on her plate. "I've already put up with so much for my career. My boss isn't really interested in helping me develop my skills. He isn't giving me opportunities to show what I can do. So I'm not really sure what the point is in working for him. And now this…I'm not a thief."

"Why don't you talk to your boss again?" Fionna suggested. "Maybe he can convince his client that it isn't worth pursuing the stolen book."

Abbey gave a bitter laugh. "You don't know my boss. He has no scruples. He doesn't care about the circumstances. A paying client is a paying client, no matter what." She picked up her cup of coffee.

"I assume he's paying Sly a lot for him to be putting so much pressure on me. That makes me wonder. How valuable can this book possibly be? I'm not familiar with the rare book trade, although I know some collectors pay insane amounts. You did say there were only five hand-printed copies, so I get that the book is rare. But…it was made by an old woman in a remote Highland village. What's so special about it?"

"I don't know. It's valuable in my eyes, of course, because it's personal. For someone else? Who knows? Um, I really have to go now. Why don't you call me or come by before you do anything? Maybe we can find a solution together."

Abbey nodded. "All right."

"Okay, see you soon." Fionna said goodbye.

She waved at Andie and quickly went to the office to grab her book. She sent Andie a text.

I'll update you later. She started asking awkward questions, and I needed to get out. Thanks for your help!

When she left the B&B, Fionna thought about what to do with the book. She couldn't keep lugging it around. That wouldn't be safe, either. Abbey wouldn't steal it from her, but what if her boss sent someone else to do the heavy work?

Fionna decided she would return the book to her basement. It might be the best place to hide it, among the many other books on her shelves.

Maybe she could come up with a protection spell…or a glamour that would make it look different.

Lost in thought about how she could create something like that, Fionna hurried home.

CHAPTER FIVE

ABBEY

Abbey set off for a walk to clear her head. Her mind felt foggy, almost like she couldn't remember clearly what she had done and talked about in the last half hour. She'd had breakfast and talked to Andie and Fionna. Hadn't she been far too chatty, considering how she had left things with Fionna yesterday?

No matter how much Abbey disagreed with her boss, her reservations about her job weren't any of Fionna's business.

Just a couple of steps into the Argyll National Forest and Abbey felt much better. Maybe it was the clear air or the serene woodland scenery. The walk turned into a long hike.

When the sun came out from behind the clouds at noon, flowers opened their buds and insects woke up. Birds were singing, and Abbey even spotted a black grouse.

Spring was undeniably in the air.

It felt like a sign. Should she follow nature's example and make a fresh start?

By the time she reached Arrochar, her stomach was growling. She stopped at the local pub and ordered hunter's chicken. Succulent with bacon, cheese, and barbecue sauce, it tasted nothing like the dry chicken fillets her mother usually served with a plain salad.

It was a revelation. Abbey devoured the entire large portion. And because the cozy atmosphere next to the open fire invited her to stay a little longer, Abbey ordered a coffee and rhubarb crumble for dessert.

Afterward, she looped back through the forest, taking the long way to Tarbet. At a bench on the edge of the village, she watched the sun set over Loch Lomond.

She was feeling slightly guilty about taking the entire day off work and dodging her boss's calls, but the day had been so rejuvenating that she pushed the feeling aside.

At the B&B, Abbey pulled her keys out of her pocket. She studied the set, trying to figure out which one was the front door key, when a male voice startled her.

"Abbey Fine?"

Abbey spun around. A man walked out of the shadows of the front garden and took an easy step across the low bushes that framed the walk to the door. It was too dusky already for Abbey to make out his face. The light above the entrance didn't reach very far.

Instinctively, Abbey backed up against the door. "What...what do you want?"

The man kept his distance and raised his hands defensively. "You are Abbey Fine, right? I've been waiting for you."

"And you are?"

Abbey half turned to put the key in the door—luckily, it was the right one—then quickly looked over her shoulder.

The stranger was now holding something in his hand.

"Stay where you are." Abbey tried to hide the panic in her voice.

She jerked at the key to get the damn door to open.

The man took a step in her direction. Now she could make out his face.

There wasn't anything particularly alarming about him at first glance. He was young and nearly crossed the line from ordinary to attractive. With his very pale skin and reddish-blond hair, he wasn't Abbey's type, though.

And then she noticed his eyes. His irises were pitch black and as small as pinheads.

A chill ran down Abbey's spine. Every instinct in her body told her that this was a person to be wary of.

"I also have a key, so please don't be alarmed when I follow you into the B&B," the man said, just as Abbey pushed the door open and rushed into the house.

"If you have one, use it," she said and slammed the door in his face.

She hurried to her room, but the man seemed incredibly fast. He was already catching up to her.

"Wait," he called.

Abbey's fear turned into annoyance. She stopped and turned to look at him. "What do you want from me?"

"My name is Magnus Magnusson, Jr. My father hired Sly Investigations to track down a stolen cookbook. I believe you were assigned to retrieve the book?" He said the last sentence without an accusatory tone, but Abbey knew what he was getting at.

"I haven't gotten hold of the book, and now you came here to take over?"

"Not exactly. I thought we could work together." Magnusson gave her a charming smile. It was so slick that Abbey knew he used it often—presumably to win over members of the opposite sex. He looked her up and down with those terrible eyes of his, and she supposed it was meant to be flattering. "Let me just say that it will be a pleasure to be your partner."

"Ugh." Abbey turned toward her room. "I'm exhausted. This will have to wait until tomorrow."

"Let's meet for breakfast at eight," Magnus called after her. "Can't wait."

Abbey locked her door from the inside and leaned against the frame. She took a deep breath, then got her phone out of her travel bag.

She'd left it in her room so she could think undisturbed, not expecting that she'd be gone all day.

Her heart beat faster when she looked at the display.

Nine missed calls from Ken Sly.

"Crap."

With a queasy feeling in her stomach, she called her mailbox.

"Fine, where the devil are you?" Sly's exasperated voice was loud. "I've been trying to reach you all day. Our client's son is on his way to Scotland. To finish what we started. Because you've failed miserably. Fucking embarrassing, Fine! For you and my agency. You'd better be nice to him, if you know what I mean. Be a good girl for a change, and don't screw this up any more than you already have. If you want to keep your job."

Abbey had had enough. She pressed the end call button.

Sly couldn't have been more clear. If she wanted to keep working for him, she'd have to respond to Magnusson's slimy advances. She'd have to do whatever he wanted.

That was the end of the line for her. She wasn't a thief, and she most certainly wasn't a prostitute.

She would have to bide her time, however, because she didn't want to let Magnusson loose on poor, unsuspecting Fionna. Abbey needed to warn her—and if she pretended to go along with Magnusson, maybe she could mediate between them.

Once that was done, she would tell Sly he could shove his job.

~

When Abbey came into the breakfast room the next morning, she looked around for Andie, but only Dessie was present.

"Is Andie here?" Abbey asked her.

She wanted the young woman to warn her friend about Magnusson.

"No, it's her day off," the B&B owner replied curtly. She seemed run off her feet.

Magnusson was already seated at one of the tables and waved her over.

"I took the liberty of ordering breakfast for you. You strike me as the kind of woman who likes it sweet, am I right?"

Abbey looked at his large Scottish fry-up with envy but remembered her plan and smiled. "Thanks."

Dessie brought over pancakes with syrup.

"Go ahead, dig in," Magnusson said. "I love watching women eat."

The comment spoiled any appetite Abbey had for the sweet breakfast, but she cut a piece of pancake anyway and shoved it into her mouth.

Magnus propped his chin on his hand and gazed at her. "Do you know who you remind me of?"

Abbey was busy chewing and just raised her eyebrows.

"There used to be this TV series called Rizzoli & Isles. Based on Tess Gerritson's novels. Do you know it? You look exactly like the actress who plays Rizzoli."

"Isn't she at least twice my age?"

"A young Rizzoli, then. The actress started her career on Baywatch. You'd look good in a red bathing suit, too."

Abbey had the urge to ask Magnusson if these sorts of ridiculous compliments usually worked with women. Instead, she focused on her pancakes.

The bites she'd already eaten lay like bricks in her stomach.

"So what's your plan?" she asked, eager to change the topic.

"To take you out for dinner, of course. Champagne, caviar, whatever your heart desires."

"I meant, what do you plan to do about the cookbook?"

"Well, we'll pick that up first, before we travel to Glasgow, where we can switch to a more suitable luxury accommodation."

"How do you plan to do that? Just go to the rare books dealer and…persuade her to hand it over?"

"Exactly."

"And how do think that will go?" Abbey took a sip of coffee. She suspected Magnusson planned to win Fionna over with his charming personality. He seemed to have a high opinion of himself. Fionna might not be the most worldly person, but Abbey couldn't believe the young woman would fall for that routine.

"Don't worry your pretty head about it. Leave it to me."

"All right, let's go, then." Abbey stood up. She just wanted to get this over with.

Magnusson grinned. "I can see you're as eager to get to that hotel room as I am."

On the way to the Simmondses' house, the creepy man wouldn't stop with his inappropriate innuendos. When they got there, Abbey had a headache from clenching her jaw. She didn't know how much longer she could take this before she told him exactly what she thought of him.

When Fionna opened the door to them, Abbey cut

Magnusson off. "Hi! So sorry to just turn up. This is Magnus Magnusson, Jr., the son of my client, the...owner of the cookbook you recently acquired. He has come to see to it that it is returned to his father."

Contrary to Abbey's expectations, Fionna didn't shout abuse at them or slam the door in their faces.

She just looked sad.

"Even if I wanted to give it to you," Fionna said, "I can't. The book is gone."

CHAPTER SIX

FIONNA

Fionna blinked. She felt dizzy.

Shaking off the feeling, she discovered she stood in the middle of her kitchen without knowing how she'd gotten there or how long she'd been standing there.

Confused, she shook her head to get rid of the last of the cobwebs that seemed to have wrapped themselves around her brain.

What had just happened?

Abbey Fine had come by, and she had brought a creepy man.

The man was...the client's son. The son of the man who must have stolen her grandmother's book at some point.

Why had she let him into her house?

But she had. That was one of the last things Fionna remembered. She had led Abbey and...Mr. Magnusson into the house.

He had asked her questions, and she had answered.

It deeply disturbed Fionna that she didn't remember

one word of the conversation. He must have asked her about the book, of course.

The only reassuring thing about it was that she couldn't have told him where the cookbook was.

It had disappeared during the night.

Fionna had a suspicion who was responsible for that, and she only hoped she hadn't told Magnusson. But why would she have?

Suddenly Fionna remembered the copies she had made of the recipes.

She ran upstairs.

Her room was such a mess that it wouldn't have been easy for anyone to find them, even if she had told them about them. Again, it didn't make sense that she would have disclosed this secret, but a lot about Abbey and Magnusson's visit made little sense.

In her room, Fionna swept clothes off the couch, then lifted the cushion. She exhaled in relief when she saw the stack of paper exactly where she'd left it.

She pulled it out and dropped down on the sofa.

Still not sure what to make of her memory loss, Fionna leafed absentmindedly through the recipes.

Were there witches in Magnusson's family? Maybe they could use the recipes, and that's why the cookbook was so valuable to Abbey's client?

Fionna had never met or heard of any witch outside the Tarbet coven, but she assumed they existed.

When she got to the title section that said "Specialties," she reread the line. "Those who are normally immune to the effects of the other recipes will not have a defense against the specialties."

The Fruitful Pockets had not affected Penny. Fionna believed she had been immune because she was a witch. If she understood the warning correctly, witches would not be immune to any of the specialty recipes.

Fionna wanted to test that theory, but she would start by giving the Loose Tongue Terrine to someone in the coven. She didn't really want to try any of the specialties. They were even more strange than the recipes in the rest of the book, and Fionna had a bad feeling about them.

What if Magnusson was interested in the book precisely because of these specialties? Fionna didn't want to think of them as dark magic, because that would have meant that her grandmother had practiced this forbidden art…but they did look an awful lot like it.

Fionna had a knack for not dealing with something that she suspected would turn out unpleasant.

This was different, though, and Fionna knew she had to get over herself.

She forced herself to take a closer look at the specialties.

There was one particular recipe that sent shivers down her spine. It was called the Devil's Children.

It was a kind of soup with disgusting and nausea-inducing ingredients like "veal in an early gestational stage" and "squab fresh from the nest."

Nausea turned into gagging when Fionna got a good notion of what the Devil's Children recipe might be intended for.

Hurriedly, she stuffed the stack of recipes back under the sofa cushion.

She knew who the perfect test subject would be to try her theory about the effect of the Loose Tongue Terrine on witches.

Her mother.

There were questions she had for her. Questions Fionna had been afraid to ask for years.

It was time to ask them, but Fionna secretly crossed her fingers that her immunity theory would prove true.

The answers she got might be too terrifying for her to cope with if her mother told her the truth.

CHAPTER SEVEN

ABBEY

The old woman watched Magnus like an eagle watches its prey.

Abbey wriggled restlessly on the wooden bench in Mrs. MacDonald's kitchen. She held the teacup in her hand, but there was no way she would drink out of it.

There was a rim on the inside of the cup, as if tea had been sitting in it too long and the cup hadn't been washed properly. To make matters worse, there was something floating in the tea that certainly didn't belong there.

Abbey was far too upset to be properly disgusted by the teacup—or the entire grubby kitchen. Something definitely told her to run, but she didn't know if it was Mrs. MacDonald's house or Magnus Magnusson, Jr.

The last half hour had been very disturbing.

Abbey had believed Fionna about the missing book, but Magnusson had expressed his doubts. He had questioned...no, downright interrogated her.

Even more disquieting was the fact that Fionna had answered so readily.

Abbey had thought it strange when Magnusson had

performed a dramatic gesture in front of Fionna and stared into her eyes. But she'd initially believed Magnusson was coming on to Fionna in his obnoxious, overbearing, and overly self-confident way.

When Fionna answered in a strange monotone voice and an almost robotic manner, Abbey knew something was wrong.

It seemed to her that the creepy man had hypnotized Fionna and that the young woman was in a trance.

Abbey was still working up the guts to interrupt the whole disturbing scene when Fionna told Magnusson that her mother and Mrs. MacDonald were the suspected book thieves.

Abbey just stood there with her mouth open when Magnusson asked about Mrs. MacDonald and Fionna answered, "She's the head of the coven."

Coven? Abbey was certain Fionna couldn't mean that literally.

"Why did Mrs. MacDonald take the book?" was Magnusson's next question.

Fionna shrugged. "To keep it safe, I suppose. She doesn't trust me to look after it?"

"So Mrs. MacDonald has hidden this book in a safe place?"

"That's what I assume."

Then, without a moment's hesitation, Fionna described the way to Mrs. MacDonald's house, apparently also known as the Thistle Inn B&B.

When Magnusson walked out of the Simmondses' house, Fionna had just stood there, in the middle of her kitchen, not moving.

Abbey was torn between wanting to look after Fionna and keeping up with Magnusson. After a few seconds of fretting, she had run after him. "Hey! Is she all right?"

"Of course." Magnusson was already on the street, and

Abbey hurried down the steps. He turned to her. "I won't need you for this. Thanks, Abbey. Why don't you go back to Dessie's B&B and pack your suitcase?"

Abbey had received the unequivocal order from her boss to comply with Magnusson, and so far, she had kind of obliged. But now, she couldn't stand back. This was her case. It might be the last one she worked for Sly Investigations, and she wanted to see it through to the end. She planned to be there when the cookbook was found.

This couldn't be an ordinary book. Abbey wanted to see it and understand what all the fuss was about.

So she didn't go back to Dessie's, just followed Magnusson instead.

He didn't appear to take notice, but when he reached the Thistle Inn, he faced her. "Abbey. I don't need you for this."

She just shook her head.

He put both hands on her shoulders, looked deep into her eyes, and had opened his mouth to say something when a raspy voice interrupted them.

"I've been expecting you, Magnus Magnusson, Jr. Leave the lass be."

Magnusson's dark pinhead irises widened with anger. The black seemed thick as ink, and Abbey had the sudden fear his eyes would swallow her up if she didn't free herself from him.

"I said, leave her be. You are within my sphere of influence. It won't work, anyway."

Magnus's jaw tightened, and he took his hands off Abbey's shoulders.

It felt as if a heavy weight lifted off her.

Magnus put on a broad smile and turned his head. "Mrs. MacDonald, I presume? May I come in for a moment?"

"I'd rather talk here."

Abbey was now able to get a good look at the woman. She looked as old as she sounded, but she didn't give off an air of fragility at all. In fact, the petite elderly woman reminded her of the solid trunk of an old oak tree. Maybe it had to do with her posture…or her sheer presence.

Magnusson bared his teeth. "You aren't afraid of me, are you?"

The woman laughed, and it sounded as clear as a bell. "I do love a challenge. All right, come in, then. But she's coming, too." She pointed at Abbey.

Magnus didn't seem happy. "Wouldn't it be unfortunate if she became collateral damage? I still have plans for her."

"She won't. She's a tough one. You shouldn't underestimate her."

Magnus hadn't argued with that, but simply followed Mrs. MacDonald into her kitchen. Abbey had rushed after them. She had sat down when she had been told to and had accepted the cup of tea.

Now she was trying to keep up with the conversation while her brain tried to make sense of everything that had happened and what had been said.

She furtively eyed Mrs. MacDonald, who sat on a chair opposite her. If witches existed, they would look exactly like this woman, she thought, still not really believing that the word coven referred to a sisterhood of witches.

It had to be something else.

At least, that's what Abbey's rational mind kept insisting. Her body told her otherwise. The hairs on her arms were standing up, and she had a lump in her throat that wouldn't go away.

She forced herself to be analytical about the situation, starting with Mrs. MacDonald's appearance. There was something unnerving about it, and it wasn't just that she looked old, witchy, and repulsive.

There was the tangled hair. It was black, and on closer inspection, Abbey didn't detect a single gray hair in it.

What made the woman appear old was the wrinkled face. The lines were very deep and somehow looked... dirty. As if she never washed her face, and dirt and grime had accumulated in the furrows.

She had several warts—even a small one on her nose. A large, hairy wart on her chin almost disappeared in the dirty flaps of hanging skin.

Mrs. MacDonald was dressed in a rather old-fashioned-looking black dress that looked as if she never even took it off to sleep. The tartan shawl around her shoulders appeared clean and cozy, though.

There were other contradictions that didn't quite fit with the image of an ugly old lady who didn't take care of personal hygiene.

For instance, Mrs. MacDonald had applied a generous amount of pink lipstick. So much, in fact, that a lot of it was smeared on her teeth. This sort of embarrassing faux pas made people look away quickly, but now that Abbey paid closer attention, she discovered it distracted from the old woman's good teeth.

Yes, she had an overbite, and the pink shade emphasized some yellow staining. Other than that, though, the teeth seemed in excellent condition.

She'd already noticed the aura of strength that surrounded the old woman, even though she was so small, hunched over, and walked with the help of a cane. Every once in a while, Abbey caught her in a movement that seemed too nimble for a woman who otherwise appeared close to ninety.

Then there was the voice. It was old and croaky. Sometimes, though, she laughed like a young girl.

Abbey had the strong sense that Mrs. MacDonald

wasn't all she appeared to be. Her appearance seemed constructed so that an observer would quickly look away.

Abbey shuddered. The movement seemed to catch Mrs. MacDonald's eye. The old lady had been preoccupied with Magnusson so far. Even though neither had spoken, there seemed to be some sort of staring match going on.

Now two pairs of dark eyes were fixed on her, and Abbey's heart raced. She brought the teacup to her lips and drank, just to hide her face and do something.

"Good girl." Mrs. MacDonald nodded. "Now you, Magnus."

Not a muscle moved in Magnusson's face when he held up the cup as if to say "cheers" and then drank his tea in one big gulp.

He smacked his lips. "Refreshing. What is it, an herbal mixture to numb my powers? You cannot be so naive as to think that I didn't ward against something like that." He laughed.

Mrs. MacDonald kept a deadpan expression. "Of course not. You expected me to bring in the big guns. No need for that. Anyone with a knowledge of herbs would know how to stop you." She waved a hand. "That's just a potent mixture of goldenrod, birch leaves, and nettles. Within a few minutes, you'll have such a powerful urge to urinate that you'll have to excuse yourself if you don't want to piss your pants. Once you've relieved yourself, you'll feel like your bladder is going to burst again."

Abbey looked at her cup in horror.

"Dinna fash, lass." Mrs. MacDonald turned to her. "You drank an ordinary cup of Darjeeling."

Magnus didn't seem fazed. "What sort of cheap trick is this? *We* are the ones accused of trickery, remember? Do you honestly think I would—" He stopped speaking abruptly and his whole body tensed.

"Well, you're welcome to try to get information out of

64

me, search my home, or whatever you planned on doing. Or you can use the restroom. It's down the hall, first door on the left."

Magnus jumped up and ran out of the kitchen.

Mrs. MacDonald grabbed Abbey's cup and studied its contents. "Let's see."

Abbey was still trying to wrap her head around the exchange between the old lady and Magnusson when Mrs. MacDonald spoke again.

"You've already decided to quit. Don't take your boss's call personally. Be happy about it. Trust in yourself to succeed on your own and on your own terms. You can be a private investigator and maintain your integrity. Oh, and don't listen to your mother."

Before Abbey could answer, Magnus stormed into the kitchen. "You nasty old hag," he hissed. "You will regret this."

"You'd better drink a glass of water," Mrs. MacDonald advised him. "There's one on the counter. You'll need to hydrate if you don't want to end up in the hospital."

Magnus seemed to struggle with himself, then downed the water.

"Of course, it's a vicious cycle," Mrs. MacDonald said in a conversational tone. "You drink, you have to pee, you drink, you have to pee…"

Magnus cursed and set down the glass with a little too much force.

"Now, wouldn't it be grand if there were an antidote?" The old lady smiled at Abbey. "The good news is that I left an antidote in the form of a soluble powder for you at the B&B. The bad news is that you probably won't get there before you have to go again."

Magnus ran off, and they heard the bathroom door slam. Mrs. MacDonald got up to walk into the hall, and Abbey followed.

Outside the closed bathroom door, Mrs. MacDonald shouted, "This was just a little game, Magnusson. Like a cat playing with a mouse before it catches and eats it. You can't seriously believe you have a chance against me? You will not find the book. Your amateur magic tricks cannot compete against real magic—no matter what Magnus Senior has tried to instill in you. I would give up if I were you. The book belongs to us. Return to the mouse hole you crawled out of."

The flush of the toilet sounded in the hall. A short time later, Magnus came back out of the bathroom. His face was bright red.

"We'll see about that," he ground out. Then he left the house with his head held high.

Abbey looked questioningly at Mrs. MacDonald.

"Go on, shoo, shoo," Mrs. MacDonald waved her on. "Off you go. You don't want to miss your boss's phone call."

CHAPTER EIGHT

FIONNA

"So, how does it taste?"

Fionna asked with trepidation, watching Rosa chew her forkful of tongue terrine.

Rosa just nodded and tried another bite.

Fionna nervously moved the sandwich around on her plate.

"Mom?"

"Yes?"

"Did you take Grandma's cookbook?" Fionna sounded like a little child. She didn't dare look up.

Rosa placed her fork on the blue napkin next to her plate.

In order to try her plan, Fionna had asked Rosa to have lunch with her. It was convenient because Rosa only worked a half day at the police station. Still, Fionna had made a big deal out of it, because it was one.

Usually, Fionna and her mother ate separately. It was a habit carried over from the time Fionna had preferred junk food to Rosa's cooking. Fionna had always kept different hours than her mother, anyway, staying up late and getting up much later than Rosa. With the hours she now worked at the restaurant, this hadn't changed. The only difference was that Fionna now cooked for herself.

Rosa must have known that something was up. She hadn't said anything, probably waiting for a question like that.

Now she let her daughter squirm. Fionna was painfully aware of every second ticking by before her mother finally spoke.

"Is that a recipe from the book? Let me see if I can remember…ah, Loose Tongue Terrine, is it?"

Fionna flinched, then nodded.

"The recipe's spell has no effect on me. It doesn't work on witches. We are immune."

"Oh." Fionna had already suspected that, but of course, she hadn't been prepared for the humiliation that came with finding out her suspicion was correct.

"I'll answer your question, anyway."

Now Fionna looked up at her mother.

Rosa's face, just like her voice, remained impassive. It didn't seem to upset her that her daughter had had to resort to such a method to have an honest conversation.

"Yes, I took the book. I gave it to Mary for safekeeping."

"But…Why?" Fionna wanted to shout, "It's mine!" but bit her tongue.

"It's too dangerous. You can't handle a book like that, child."

"I'm not a child anymore, Mother." Fionna's voice betrayed her.

"Well, in many ways, you still are very young and naive, Fionna. And you are my child, so I'm allowed to decide what's best for you. You've already tried some of the recipes, haven't you? Tried to work a little magic with this one?" She pointed at the rest of the tongue terrine. "Who else have you given it to?"

Fionna wanted to defend herself, but Rosa didn't give her time to answer.

"The point is that you're far too irresponsible. The spells in that book are immensely powerful. They're out of your league. You'd only do harm with them. A book like that belongs with the coven leader."

"Maybe I was irresponsible for a long time, but I've changed. You just didn't notice, like you didn't notice so many other things. And that's the reason it took me such a long time to grow up." Fionna stopped herself.

She never argued with her mother. That's why they avoided each other as a general rule. If it came close to a blow-up, Fionna preferred to flee. But it had gotten to the point where that avoidance strategy didn't work for her anymore.

She couldn't let her mother treat her like she was a five-year-old.

"There wasn't much I could do with you." Rosa poured herself a glass of water. "Believe me, I tried. You were too young to remember. But it soon became clear that it was pointless."

"Maybe you should have tried a little longer," Fionna said quietly. "Raising a child is a process. Some children take longer in their development. It wasn't really fair to assume right away that I was a lost cause." Fionna looked out the kitchen window, focusing on the single yellow crocus on the lawn.

"You want to talk about what's not fair? Going through what I went through to get the special child I was promised, and then to have my hopes dashed like that…" Rosa sighed. "Everyone had high hopes for you. But you didn't meet them by any stretch of the imagination. I did what I could…" Her voice trailed off. Then she shook her head. "Anyway, you just don't remember. You were too little when all of this became clear. Your perspective is skewed. It's always easy to blame someone else. But the truth is that all I could do was be lenient with you. I never pushed you, never forced you to finish school, get a proper education. I let you live here, let you do what you wanted, didn't tell you what to do. It was an act of mercy on my part, but how would you know? So what else do you want from me?"

Rosa's voice had gotten shriller. It was out of character, and Fionna's mother must have realized that herself. She stopped talking, got up, and cleared the plates, carrying them to the sink.

Fionna answered calmly. "I want to know the real reason you took Grandma's cookbook away from me. I want to know the history behind the book and what it can do. What makes it so special? Why was that Magnusson guy here, and—"

"What?" Rosa spun around.

Fionna watched with interest as her mother's eyes widened with panic.

"Yes, the son of the previous owner of the cookbook—or should I say the son of the thief who stole the cookbook in the first place—was here. He insisted I give it to him."

"The son of…What did you say to him?" Rosa looked deadly pale.

Fionna shrugged.

"Fionna! What—"

"I didn't have the book, and I didn't know where it was," Fionna said. "Since you took it away from me."

"Okay. Okay." Rosa left the kitchen. "I really need to talk to Mary," she said, more to herself than Fionna.

Fionna stayed seated, frozen, unsure what to make of the conversation. Her mother had poked at all her insecurities. She had said a couple of things that were more than unsettling. Fionna didn't quite know what to make of them.

But she couldn't really think about that right now because there was something else that nagged much more at her: Rosa's reaction to Magnusson's visit.

She had never seen her mother that unnerved.

It had almost seemed as if she knew Magnusson. But that couldn't be, could it?

CHAPTER NINE

ABBEY

Back at the B&B, Abbey flopped down on the bed. The morning's events had been mentally exhausting. Trying to think of a logical explanation for everything Magnusson and Mrs. MacDonald had done and said had Abbey's brain in a scramble.

Fatigue was slowly taking over her body, but Abbey couldn't fall asleep. She was a rational person, someone who solved puzzles for a living, but all of this was just too mystifying.

Suddenly, Black Francis's voice jolted her out of her thoughts. The line about losing his mind felt surreal because Abbey could very much relate. It only took her a second to remember that the Pixies song was the ring tone for Ken Sly.

With a sigh, she answered. "Hi, boss."

"What the fuck, Fine? I just got a call from Magnusson Junior instructing me to take you off the case. He plans to retrieve the cookbook himself, and you, and I quote, are just 'getting in the way.' Didn't I specifically ask you to be nice to him? Could I have made it any clearer for your tiny brain to understand?" Sly's voice was booming in Abbey's ear. "Do you know what it means when Magnusson takes over without any involvement from this agency? We won't get paid; that's what it means."

Abbey said nothing. A strange sense of calmness washed over her.

"You've failed, Fine. Again. You are good for nothing if you can't even flirt with a client and make nice. I've had it with you. You're fired, do you hear me? Fired with immediate effect. I don't want to see your face in this agency again."

"Wonderful," Abbey said. "That saves me from writing a resignation letter. Have a great day."

She hung up, threw the phone in the corner, and closed her eyes. Having Mrs. MacDonald's prediction come true should have disturbed her even more.

Strangely, it had the opposite effect. She was so relieved to be free of Sly and the job she hated that everything felt very aligned.

Abbey took a deep breath, closed her eyes, and was asleep within seconds.

WHEN ABBEY WOKE up from her nap at noon, she felt happy and energized.

But as she took a shower, a queasy feeling came over her. She was unemployed. How would she pay her rent?

She thought about finding a lawyer, insisting on the notice period stipulated in her contract—and the seven days' pay that went with it.

Abbey discarded that idea pretty quickly. It wouldn't be worth the trouble and might saddle her with a huge bill. Sly would make her life a living hell.

She would rather just be rid of him.

But there was someone Abbey could count on in situations like this: her mother. Abbey hated asking her for financial support, but she'd have to if she couldn't find a new job by the time her meager savings dwindled.

After she got dressed, Abbey's growling stomach made her leave the room. In the hallway, she ran into Dessie. "Hey, is there anywhere close where I can buy a quick sandwich?"

"That hungry?" Dessie smiled.

"Starving."

"I just took a platter of sandwiches to the construction workers, and there are a bunch left." She held up the covered tray she was holding. "I was about to eat in the breakfast room. Care to join me?"

"Only if there's enough—"

"No worries, there's plenty!"

"All right, then."

Abbey followed Dessie into the breakfast room, and they settled down at one of the tables.

Over lunch, Dessie told Abbey about her plans to have someone else take over the day-to-day business of running the B&B so she could focus on establishing an acting school for children.

"I used to be an actress. I gave up my career a long time ago, but I discovered my passion for acting never really went away. Recently, I had the opportunity to help out at a college in Helensburgh when the acting teacher suddenly fell ill. It was so much fun, I decided to start teaching acting. Of course, I'll have to see how everything works out once the baby is born, but…" She shrugged. "Sometimes old ambitions never really die, just turn into new ones. Circumstances made me give up on my dream, but now I'm determined to pursue this transformed one."

Abbey sighed and put down her half-eaten sandwich.

"Oh," Dessie said. "I hope I didn't say anything to upset you?"

"No, no. It's not your fault. It's just that I got fired today. I stuck with this job for three years, even though it was anything but easy. Now it turns out it was all for naught. I won't get a reference letter, that's for sure."

"Oh, I'm so sorry to hear that. You're a private investigator, aren't you? Andie said something like that…"

Abbey waved her hand. "It's fine, really. I'd already made up my mind to quit. But to suddenly find yourself jobless and without a paycheck makes you question everything again."

"Well, it's just a job. It sounds like you're dedicated to your career. You'll find something else."

Abbey shook her head. "This business is…full of testosterone. I applied for a job at the most ruthless detective agency in London because I knew it would be tough, but it would prepare me for making it in this line of work. Now it looks as if I'm not cut out for it. I can't hack it in this business if I have…let's say, morals and scruples."

Dessie laughed. "Integrity, you mean? There is nothing wrong with that. On the contrary. I'm sure there are detective agencies that value integrity. Don't give up yet."

Abbey shrugged. "I'm sure you're right."

"I know a private investigator who definitely fits that description. His name is Christopher Harris. He's my future sister-in-law's partner. I'd be happy to talk to him and ask if he could use another employee. I know he's away on business at the moment, but when he comes back, I'll put in a good word for you."

"That's so nice. Thank you!"

"From what I've gathered, you're in Tarbet because you were working on a case. Since you've been let go, does that mean you plan on leaving early?"

Abbey picked up her sandwich. "No," she decided. "I'm staying. My agency might have fired me, but the case isn't over. I'm not going to leave before it is."

CHAPTER TEN

FIONNA

When Fionna arrived at the restaurant late that afternoon, she was greeted by a distraught Drew.

He tried hard not to let his emotions show and kept telling Fionna that he was fine, but eventually, she wore him down.

"The health and safety inspector is coming tonight. He wants to take another look. Then he'll give me a list of everything I need to change." Drew ran his fingers through his thick black curls. "Everything depends on this visit, Fionna. If his list is long, and I don't have the money for the necessary renovations…"

Drew shrugged and let his sad gaze wander around the restaurant as if he was already saying goodbye.

Fionna wanted to take on his pain. "It'll be fine." She tried to give him hope. "Maybe the inspector is in a really good mood today." She forced a smile.

Her attempts to cheer Drew up seemed to work. His face lit up a little. "Let's hope so." He turned toward the kitchen. "Let's prepare tonight's menu and make sure it's the best the inspector has ever eaten. Maybe that'll butter him up. That's all we can do for now."

"I'll be right there. I have to…take care of something first."

"No worries. You're early, as usual, anyway."

Drew disappeared through the kitchen door, and Fionna dropped her oversize bag on the table in the nook next to the bar.

She pulled out the photocopies of the cookbook recipes —it had felt safer to bring them with her rather than leave them at home.

Fionna flipped through them. She hadn't copied every recipe, only the ones that had looked interesting. Because the recipes in the Specialties section had confounded her the most, almost all of them were included in her selection.

She remembered seeing something that might help Drew tonight.

There, she found it: Fool with Rose-Tinted Spectacles.

If the inspector saw the restaurant through rose-colored glasses tonight, he wouldn't give Drew a long list of things to change, would he?

Ordinarily, Fionna would have been wary of trying another recipe from the book. She'd have tried to come up with something else to turn this situation around for Drew, possibly with the help of the other witches.

But she didn't have time. And this recipe looked so promising.

The Fool was a version of the dessert by the same name. A fool would be something they could whip up in a hurry, since they always had cream, fruit, eggs, and sugar in the restaurant pantry. It made it suitable for this occasion. If it was as complicated or time-consuming as the tongue terrine, there'd be no chance Fionna could pull it off before the inspector's arrival.

When she had a closer look at the ingredients, however, Fionna realized it wouldn't be as simple as she'd thought.

Fionna fished her phone out of her purse and called Penny.

"Hi, I need your help," she blurted out when the herb witch picked up.

"What's wrong?"

Fionna quickly described the situation. "I have a magical recipe, and I think it would help." She finished with her explanation. "But I need some unusual ingredients. Dried rose petals. Heather honey."

"I have both."

Fionna exhaled in relief. "Okay, so the other thing is cream made from milk from Highland cows. We have that at the restaurant—our supplier is an organic farm nearby. That leaves me with one ingredient I don't think I can come by at this time of year. Wild strawberries. We have strawberries in the freezer, but I'm pretty certain they aren't wild—"

"I have some. I pick wild strawberries and freeze them when they're in season."

"Really?" Fionna couldn't hide the surprise in her voice.

"Yes. I sometimes need them…" Penny cleared her throat. "Well, needed them. For love spells."

"Love spells?" Fionna scanned the recipe again. "Oh no, what if this is a recipe for a love spell?"

"What's it called again?"

"Fool with Rose-Tinted Spectacles."

Penny chuckled. "A love spell sounds about right. My love potions also contain rose petals."

"Crap."

"Why? The health and safety inspector is supposed to fall in love with the restaurant, right?"

Fionna remained silent for a few seconds. She had

doubts about this. Then she thought about Drew and the sadness in his eyes when he'd thought he'd have to give up his dream.

"I can't think of any other recipe offhand that would fit, and we even have all the ingredients for this one, which might be a problem with one of the others. I don't have any other idea how to help Drew in a pinch, and we're running out of time."

"He matters a lot to you, doesn't he?" Penny sounded serious.

"Drew? Yes…I mean…the restaurant does…and Drew, too," Fionna stuttered, then took a deep breath. "He gave me a chance when nobody else would have."

"Then let's do this," Penny decided. "What good are our magical gifts if we can't use them to help other people who truly deserve it?"

A year ago, Fionna would not have expected to hear those words out of Penny's mouth. It had seemed that the pretty herb witch cared about nothing but herself. Then she had taken in two strays—a pregnant girl named Pari and a black cat—and things had changed.

"No risk, no fun," Penny added. That sounded more like her.

Fionna had to laugh. But her fingers tensed around the stack of photocopies. "Ahhh. I don't know!" Her gaze fell on her grandmother's name on the title page. This was her legacy. If anyone was meant to use the recipes, it would be her, right?

And Penny was right. If she could help someone with her magic, why not?

"Okay. Let's do it! Bring the ingredients. And hurry."

79

"I KNOW you have other things on your mind today," Fionna said to Drew in the kitchen. "But I'd like to talk to you about making one of my dessert recipes. It's a strawberry fool. I think it's really going to wow the inspector. My friend Penny is coming over with some special, high-quality ingredients for it."

Fionna held her breath. She wouldn't blame Drew if he decided not to trust her with this tonight. Maybe he wanted to make sure the inspector had one of his own best dishes for dessert.

But her boss didn't seem to have any such qualms. "That sounds great," he said, continuing to mash potatoes, salmon, and herbs for the fishcakes. "Oh, I forgot to mention Milton is coming in for a couple of hours to help out. Just so that I'm available for the health and safety inspector."

Milton was the chef who cooked at the restaurant on Drew's days off and helped out when it got really busy. Fionna wasn't too fond of him because he was in the habit of staring at her.

It sounded as if Milton wouldn't be there long—but she hoped he wouldn't get in the way.

An hour later, Fionna had to concede that she'd worried unnecessarily. Milton wasn't paying any attention at all to what she was doing.

The reason was Penny, who had stayed in the kitchen, even though, technically, that wasn't allowed. Drew had other things on his mind, since the health and safety inspector had arrived, and Fionna could really use her friend's support.

It didn't bother Fionna one bit that Milton only had eyes for Penny now. It meant she could focus on the magical recipe without interference. Plus, it was to be expected.

Penny was stunningly beautiful with her long blond curls, green eyes, and slim but curvy figure.

In the past, the herb witch had used beauty spells to make herself even more attractive, but the young chef's adoration proved yet again that Penny didn't need magical help in that department.

Penny did flirt with Milton a little, to make sure Fionna was left in peace. Fionna just hoped Milton wouldn't get distracted and put too much salt into the dishes.

The Fool was pretty straightforward. Making the rose-petal jam took the longest. When it was ready, Fionna stirred it into the strawberry compote.

Still, she paid close attention to the quirky instructions. The cream had to be whipped with a counterclockwise motion, for example.

By far the hardest part was smiling the entire time the different parts of the Fool were assembled. When Fionna finally sprinkled candied rose petals on the finished dessert, repeating "Fata Morgana, I'm calling you forth" three times, her cheeks were hurting.

She probably looked deranged with that frozen fake smile, so she was extra grateful to Penny for making sure nobody noticed.

"Phew," Fionna said, when the Fools were finally done. She wiggled her jaw to relax her facial muscles. "Now, he just has to eat it."

"Well, he seems to be enjoying the meal so far," Penny said, who had checked on Drew in the restaurant. "He insisted that Drew dine with him, but your boss is just picking at his food."

"I bet he's too nervous to eat," Fionna guessed.

Sally entered the kitchen, letting them know that Drew and the health and safety inspector were ready for dessert.

"I'll serve it to the inspector; then he won't be able to resist." Penny winked at Fionna.

"Let's go together." Fionna grabbed one of the dessert glasses. "Otherwise, Drew is going to wonder why you're suddenly waitressing. And we'll have to serve one of the dishes to Drew, too. I'm glad he won't be eating it, but it'll look funny otherwise."

With a queasy feeling in her stomach, Fionna followed Penny into the restaurant. Drew, who looked very nervous indeed, and a stiff gentleman sat at a table in the nave's front.

"I hope this stuff is strong," Penny whispered to her. "He doesn't look like the sort who gets swayed easily."

Fionna had to agree. She plastered a smile across her face again as she put the Fool in front of Drew. "Strawberry Fool with rose petals, freshly made," she said.

Penny served the inspector his dessert. "You look like you enjoy something sweet now and again."

The inspector looked up from his notes and noticed Penny. His features softened a bit. "Well, I have to admit…" He cleared his throat. "I do have a sweet tooth."

"Then this is just the right dessert for you," Penny said. "Enjoy!"

The inspector didn't hesitate to dip his spoon into the fruit-compote-and-cream mixture.

Fionna didn't dare leave, but anxiously waited for his reaction. Penny stayed rooted to the spot as well.

The inspector didn't seem bothered. The Fool commanded all of his attention. "Oh, this is excellent," he murmured.

Tension seemed to drain out of Drew. He picked up his spoon and also had a taste.

"This *is* good." He smiled gratefully at Fionna.

"Glad to hear it," Penny said, and took Fionna's arm. "We'll be in the kitchen if you need anything else. For instance, second helpings." She winked at the inspector.

As Fionna and Penny made their way back to the

kitchen, more guests were arriving. Sally was busy showing four women to a table when the door opened again and a familiar face came through. Abbey Fine.

"Excuse me a second," Fionna said to Penny. She rushed toward Abbey.

"What are you doing here?" Fionna hissed. "I don't know what you and that Magnusson guy did to me this morning, but I didn't like it. Don't ever pull anything like that again. I already told you I don't have the cookbook anymore. Coming to my house and ambushing me like that is one thing, but this is my place of work, and—"

"Wait, wait," Abbey interrupted her. "I'm not here to interrogate you. I'm not here in any professional capacity at all. I was forced to accompany Magnusson to your house, but I despise his methods as much as you do. Me coming here has nothing to do with that. I just wanted to have dinner at this place I've heard so much about." Abbey hesitated. "I'm not even a private investigator anymore. I got fired."

"Oh." Fionna didn't know what to say to that.

"I do admit that I hoped you'd be here tonight because I wanted to apologize. I had no choice but to go with Magnusson to visit you, and I felt as ambushed as you did. I don't know what he did, exactly, but I wasn't comfortable with it."

Fionna tucked a strand of hair behind her ear. "I think…could it be that Magnusson hypnotized me? What did it look like to you?"

"Yes, exactly! That's what it seemed like. But so quickly? It was weird, right?"

"Very weird." Fionna met Sally's eyes across the restaurant. She indicated to the waitress that she would show Abbey to a table. "Come on, let's get you seated."

Sally pointed at a small table in the nave's front, on the other side of the main aisle from where Drew and the inspector were sitting. Fionna nodded, and Sally turned her attention back to the four women, who were ready to place their drink orders.

When Abbey had taken a seat, Fionna lowered her voice. "What did Magnusson ask me? And what did I answer?"

"You can't remember?" Abbey looked up in surprise.

Fionna turned red and gave a barely perceptible shake of her head.

"That's creepy. He asked the same question in a few different ways. He wanted to know where the cookbook was. You kept saying you didn't have it but suspected Mrs. MacDonald did. Eventually, Magnusson seemed satisfied you had nothing else to say about the matter. Then we left and paid Mrs. MacDonald a visit."

"You did? You spoke to Mrs. MacDonald, asked her directly about this?" Fionna couldn't quite believe Abbey had survived to tell the tale.

"Yes. And Magnusson and Mrs. MacDonald said a couple of very strange things I'm still trying to make sense of. I'll tell you about it. But first, I have a few questions."

"Umm, sure." At the mention of questions, Fionna realized she'd better stay on guard. "Later. Right now, I have to return to the kitchen. Sally will take your order."

She gave Sally a sign.

"Okay, see you later."

When Fionna entered the kitchen, she caught Milton with a spoon in his hand, leaning over one of her desserts. He looked up with a guilty expression. There was a dollop of cream on his nose. He reminded Fionna of a kitten caught in the act of licking the cream out of a bowl.

"They looked so delicious, and I just wanted a taste," he admitted. "But I couldn't stop, and—"

He was interrupted by loud music. It was coming from the restaurant.

"What the…" Fionna had a very bad feeling as she turned around to investigate.

She quickly figured out where the music was coming from. The health and safety inspector was playing the old church organ, which stood at the back of what used to be the transept.

Penny came rushing toward her. "I think we got the recipe wrong!"

"Oh, you think, do you?" Fionna shook her head, still staring at the formerly prim and proper inspector as he sang what seemed to be a sentimental love song with a surprisingly high soprano voice.

"He dedicated the song to me," Penny shouted over the thundering organ music.

"Why?"

"He said I'm the loveliest women he's ever seen. I'm the love of his life."

Fionna turned her gaze on Penny. "Did you use a beauty spell?"

"No! I didn't do anything. It's the Fool. But now that you mention it, his reaction is similar to someone targeted with a strong beauty spell. Something similar has happened to me before. I made most of the spell ingredients. Maybe that has something to do with it? And I told you it felt like a love spell. Let's wait and see. It might blow over quickly."

The inspector had finished his song. He now turned around and looked at the blond herb witch with the eyes of a lovesick puppy.

There was only one person who clapped enthusiastically, someone in the nave. Fionna looked up and inhaled sharply.

It was Drew. He had eaten the Fool and was affected, too. Her stomach sank at the thought of her boss being in love with Penny.

She looked around. There was Sally, standing right next to Drew. She'd probably rushed over to him when the health inspector's inappropriate behavior had disturbed the rest of the customers.

Fortunately, the only current customers were Abbey and the four women in their mid-thirties at a table further back. They were all giggling. There were bottles of wine and cocktail glasses on the table. It looked like a girls' night out, and they'd probably had a lot to drink already.

Drew now came down the three steps to the transept, his phone in his hand. "Bravo!" he exclaimed. "That was wonderful. I'd like to sing a little something, too. I'm not a gifted musician like Mr. Dudley here, so I can't play an instrument, but…" He walked over to the bar and tinkered with the sound system.

Fionna watched him with trepidation. Then she heard a loud giggle. At first, she thought it came from the table with the four drunk women, but they seemed to have returned to their animated conversation.

Abbey wasn't someone who giggled like that—and in any case, Fionna could see the private investigator at the table in the nave's front, where she was observing everything that was going on with big eyes.

There was the giggling sound again, this time directly behind her. Fionna turned around. Nobody was there.

"Did you hear that?" she asked Penny.

"Yes, was someone laughing?"

Another soft giggle.

Penny suddenly turned pale. "Oh my god," she gasped.

"What?" Fionna was alarmed. It took a lot for Penny to look that rattled.

"I just remembered something. What was it I heard you say in the kitchen earlier when you were finishing the desserts? Something about Fata Morgana?"

"Fata Morgana, I'm calling you," Fionna replied impatiently. "That was an instruction from the recipe. Like an incantation I had to repeat three times."

Penny grabbed her arm. "The Fata Morgana mirage is named after Morgan le Fay from the Arthurian legend. She lived on the island of Avalon, which was inaccessible to mortals. The name comes from when sailors on the high sea would see a mirage, most often an island…and when they got there, it had disappeared."

Fionna frowned. "So…the Rose-Tinted Spectacles… they create some sort of mirage, like an optical illusion. Is that what you mean?"

Penny nodded, then shook her head. "Maybe, but I fear it's much worse." A loud giggle drowned out her voice. "…actually summoned fairies." Fionna caught the tail end of Penny's words.

Fionna stared at her in disbelief.

"Think about it. Fairies love nothing more than confusing mortals. They love to see us make complete fools of ourselves. Fools, get it?"

Before Fionna could say anything, loud music flooded the restaurant again.

This time, Fionna recognized the song immediately. It was "You Sexy Thing" by Hot Chocolate.

"This song is for you, Fionna," Drew shouted. "I want you to know that I've always been attracted to you. You're incredibly sexy, and I want to show you how sexy I can be, too."

Fionna's hand went to her mouth. "Oh my god, no!"

The women at the back of the restaurant were standing up, cheering and clapping their hands to the rhythm of the song.

Drew pulled his sweater over his head and began to make movements vaguely aligned with the music.

Penny burst out laughing. "He's doing a striptease."

Drew's jeans were suddenly hanging below his knees as he clumsily tried to kick off his shoes.

Fionna could only stare at him. He certainly had the body for it, but his dance skills left a lot to be desired.

Then Drew caught her looking and grinned like a maniac.

Mortified, Fionna averted her gaze.

The women had come to the front of the nave. Abbey was standing now, too. Sally was next to her. Their faces showed a mixture of bewilderment and hilarity.

Drew had now freed one leg, and he lifted the other to fling his jeans at Fionna.

Then he continued dancing in socks and boxers.

Fionna squinted and quietly prayed, "Please don't take off any more clothes." She had dreamed of seeing Drew in the buff, but this was a nightmare.

Her boss gyrated his way to the bar, managed to pull himself up on the second attempt, and then proceeded to dance in what remotely reminded her of Coyote Ugly style.

The inspector, whom Fionna had completely forgotten, appeared next to the bar, hooting loudly and cheering Drew on.

As the song came to a close, Fionna was ready to exhale in relief that the terrible performance was over. But Drew's questionable playlist switched to "Let's Get It On" by Marvin Gaye.

As if on cue, Milton came out of the kitchen and started dancing. He did a few standard dance steps and pirouetted toward them.

Mr. Dudley popped up from behind the bar, two bottles of champagne in his hands. Too late, Fionna noticed he was shaking them. She wanted to charge toward him and take the bottles away, but Milton bumped into her.

Umm, no. He grinded against her.

Not sure what to do, Fionna stood frozen in place and looked around the room for help. Abbey stared at the dancing men with her mouth open, Sally looked as if she had a fever, and the four women clapped and jeered. There weren't that many options for a wild night out near Tarbet, so they seemed pleased that their tame night at a restaurant had turned into this.

Fionna caught Penny's eyes. "We have to put a stop to this," she yelled.

Penny nodded and laughed, pointing at the bar. Mr. Dudley had taken off his shirt, climbed onto the bar next to Drew, and joined in the bar-dancing fun. His pale, hairless chest looked puny next to Drew's. The four women didn't seem to mind. This might have looked like a poor man's Chippendales performance, but since the Chippendales would never come to Tarbet, they took what they could get.

"I need to lock the door so nobody else gets in and sees this," Fionna said, more to herself than to Penny, since it was so loud in the restaurant.

She hurried to the door, locked it, and turned the sign to say "Closed. Private Event."

On her way back, she gave the bar a wide berth to avoid being showered with champagne. Drew and Mr. Dudley had opened the bottles and were spraying the expensive sticky liquid everywhere.

Fionna got around the bar without getting wet and turned off the stereo.

"Boo, boo!" the four women shouted, giving her thumbs downs.

"All right, all right," Drew said, laughing. "It's okay. I wanted to demonstrate to Fionna that I'm the man for her, that I can be sexy for her—"

"And I for you, blond goddess," Mr. Dudley interrupted, bowing in Penny's direction.

"But now it's time to get serious." Drew jumped off the bar, walked over to Fionna, who had come around the bar again, and kneeled down in front of her.

"Fionna Simmonds," he said with a solemn voice, but still grinning. "Ever since I first met you, I knew we had a special connection. My feelings for you grew, but I've held back, knowing how inappropriate it is, since I'm your boss..." He put his hand over his eyes. "Oh, I know how inappropriate all of this is, Fionna. But I can't help myself." He lowered his hand and looked at her earnestly with his puppy-dog brown eyes. "Today I'm so overwhelmed with my feelings for you, I just had to show you my heart. It's not enough. I have the strong urge to make a larger commitment to you, my one and only. Fionna Simmonds. Will you marry—"

"Noooooo!"

Fionna turned around to where the strong objection had come from. It was Milton, who was running toward Drew, a butter knife raised above his head.

"Watch out!" Fionna charged at Drew to push him out of the way, but she ended up on top of him, sliding across the wet tiles.

Drew grinned and held on tight, but Fionna, aware of his mostly naked body, quickly disentangled herself from him.

She was standing again, pushing the hair out of her face, when she heard Milton's declaration. "Fionna is mine. I'm the one she's supposed to be with. Nothing will stand in the way of our love. Not anyone, and especially not you, Andrew Ross."

Drew had gotten up and now found himself facing off with Milton.

Even though the young chef was still brandishing the butter knife, it looked more comical than menacing, especially since Drew towered over the weedy little man.

"This is ridiculous," Drew said, frowning. "You don't even like Fionna. I, on the other hand—"

"Stop, both of you," Fionna finally managed to speak. "All of this is ridiculous. None of you are in love with me. Let's just all calm down."

"Fionna, don't say that!" Drew looked hurt. "Of course I love you—"

"No!" Fionna said forcefully, tears welling up in her eyes.

Humiliated, she ran into the kitchen.

She wiped away her tears, pacing back and forth.

Fionna hoped Penny would be able to control the situation in the restaurant, because she couldn't deal with it right now.

She had secretly dreamed of Drew confessing his love for her for months…but not like this! Obviously, Drew's feelings weren't real. They had to do with the Fool recipe. It pained her immeasurably to see the love in his eyes, knowing it was all just because of a mirage.

The worst thing was that she had brought all of this on herself.

She had to fix it.

Fionna told herself to stop crying and think of a solution. It wasn't easy, but she finally got a grip. Then she had an idea.

She grabbed her purse from the storeroom, found her phone, and called Andie.

After a brief explanation, she asked her friend to fetch a few things from her room and come to the restaurant. "Hurry!"

Andie didn't ask any unnecessary questions. This wasn't the first time a coven sister had had to help another in a magical pinch. She arrived twenty minutes later—an eternity for Fionna.

During the wait, Fionna and Penny, with the help of

Abbey, had managed to pry the knife out of Milton's hands and prevent Mr. Dudley from tattooing Penny's name onto his arm with a corkscrew and a ballpoint pen.

There had been talks of a duel between Drew and Milton, but Penny had put a stop to that. Meanwhile, Sally had fainted. Abbey had made her comfortable on a bench at the back of the restaurant with a cold washcloth on her forehead.

Fionna had topped up the four women's glasses and done her best to convince them everything had merely been a fun dare.

When Fionna's phone rang and Andie told her she was at the entrance, the red-haired witch trembled with exhaustion. Relieved, she unlocked the door and pulled Andie inside.

"Thank you, thank you," she said. "Did you find everything?"

Andie nodded and looked around the restaurant curiously.

"Listen up, everyone," Fionna called out, taking the bag from Andie. "My friend brought a few things for a fun party game. Who's up for it?"

The four women were enthusiastic, but the men didn't seem so sure.

"Why would we play a game?" Drew asked. "All I want is to show you how much I love you, Fionna."

Fionna took a deep breath and did her best to sound flirty. "But that *would* show me. Come on, play a game for me."

Drew stared at her with adoration. Next to him, Milton also gawked, his mouth open, saliva running out.

"Yes, yes, of course," they both mumbled.

"And you'll play for me, won't you Dudley-fuds?" Penny purred.

Mr. Dudley nodded eagerly, like a dog with his tongue out.

"Okay, let's get started," Fionna said with relief. "I have a ball of yarn here, and I'm going to hand each of you a piece of the string. You'll stay right where you are and hold on to it. Don't move. Okay?"

Everyone nodded.

After everyone except Abbey, Penny, Andie, and Fionna were connected by the enchanted string, Fionna wound the yarn three more times on the floor around the entire group, creating a circle. Then she placed crystals at the cardinal points on top of it. She spoke a spell and knotted the two remaining ends of the string together.

All the people in the circle holding on to the yarn were now completely motionless, like living statues.

Abbey, who'd been watching the whole ritual in amazement, came over to Fionna. "I can't believe this," she said, bending forward to get a closer look at one woman, who had frozen while twirling a lock of hair around her finger. "It's like in *Sleeping Beauty*, when all the occupants of the castle freeze in time."

"Careful, don't get into the circle," Fionna warned her. "I don't know how well the binding spell will hold with that many people. But I hope it'll give us the time we need to undo the Fata Morgana spell."

Abbey whirled around to face her. "Binding spell? Fata Morgana spell?" She looked at Penny, then Andie. "That means you're…you're…"

"Witches," Fionna finished the sentence for her. "Yes. That's exactly what we are."

CHAPTER ELEVEN

ABBEY

Fionna, Penny, and Andie explained to Abbey what being a Tarbet witch meant—or at least, they tried to, in as few words as possible. Then they told her about the cookbook and what Fionna had done with the recipes.

Abbey just sank down into her seat and said nothing for a while. After her brain had assimilated the information, she repeated, "Okay. A community upholding ancient traditions. Special traits passed down the female line." She looked at Andie. "Visions of past and future, usually about a person who needs help." Her gaze traveled to Penny. "Herb witch. Got it. But you…" She pointed at Fionna. "You enchant objects? So they have…magical properties?"

Of all the abilities, Fionna's seemed the most fantastical to her. She just couldn't quite wrap her mind around it.

Abbey snorted when she became conscious of what she was thinking. What about her mind? There wasn't anything rational about it.

The three young women exchanged worried glances. They probably thought Abbey didn't believe them.

But how could she stay an unbeliever after everything she had witnessed that day? Unless this was an elaborate prank, magic seemed the only explanation that made sense, no matter how ridiculous it sounded.

"And Mrs. MacDonald is your leader? The leader of your…coven?" A cold shiver ran down her spine. Somehow, the old woman being a supernatural made more sense than anything else she'd heard so far.

"Yes," Andie answered. "She's a very powerful witch. She's been the head of our coven for a very long time."

Abbey looked at the frozen figures inside the web of yarn. "Then she'd be able to fix this? I mean, she knows about the recipes anyway, right? She has the cookbook. Are you going to call her?"

Abbey was thinking of leaving if the old woman really turned up. Watching Mrs. MacDonald in action would no doubt be a scary sight to behold. On the other hand, Abbey was far too curious to turn down an opportunity to learn more about the witches of Tarbet.

"Absolutely not," Fionna said. "There is no way I'm going to ask Mrs. MacDonald for help. She'll bring my mother and…" She swallowed and shook her head. "No, no, no. We have to fix this by ourselves."

"Fionna," Andie said, looking alarmed. "I know how you feel about your mother. You're embarrassed and don't want to give her any more ammunition to talk down to you. But…" She pointed at the frozen people. "This isn't going to hold forever. What if the Fata Morgana spell doesn't wear off by itself? And even if it does, everyone is going to remember and know something strange has happened. Mrs. MacDonald will know what to do. Or do you have a better idea?"

"I'll figure something out," Fionna said stubbornly, holding her head high. "I left Abbey out of the binding spell for a reason." She sat down opposite Abbey in the bar nook. "Abbey, you don't know it, but you've been enchanted by one of the recipes in this book."

Abbey's eyebrows rose.

"Remember the tongue terrine you had for breakfast yesterday? It was a magic dish. It made you tell us some things you probably wouldn't have told us otherwise."

Abbey blushed. "I had a feeling I said too much. Did I mention my mother and my professional insecurities?" She shook her head. "I'm not usually that open with someone I just met. In fact, I don't talk about those things at all."

"That means you remember what you said?" Fionna seemed excited. "I figured you would, because Drew also seemed to remember telling me about his financial worries."

"Yes, I remember, but it's vague." Abbey frowned. "It's a little like remembering something you did while you were very drunk. There's sort of a sense of unease and embarrassment."

As she was talking about it, more memories of the conversation with Fionna resurfaced. Abbey now felt like she shouldn't feel embarrassed at all. She should be angry.

"Why did you do that?" she said heatedly. "You had no right."

"I'm really sorry." Fionna looked contrite. "We just really needed to know about the danger your client posed. I had to find out what he was up to. Everything else you said was…collateral damage. It didn't matter to me. But I felt I had no other choice. You wouldn't have told me if I had just asked, would you?"

Abbey calmed down. "Probably not."

Still, she felt very uncomfortable being reminded of how she had not been in control of the situation and remembering what she had said. Why did Fionna have to bring this out into the open just now, if she'd already found out from Drew that people remembered the effects of the spell?

Andie must have had the same thought. "You could have double-checked with Sally, Fionna. Remember, she had the tongue terrine, too. And she's still in the back there, resting after her fainting episode."

"Considering what Sally told me, I don't think she would admit to it, even if she did remember. Plus, she's still not really responsive. There's another important reason I left Abbey out of the spell. She might be able to help. If we don't find a better way."

Everyone looked at Fionna expectantly. It seemed as if she was trying to work something out in her head.

Then the red-haired young woman turned to Penny. "Do you have a way to erase everyone's memory of tonight?"

The herb witch sputtered. "What do you mean? Do you want me to give them some sort of drug? We can't do that!"

"We have to!" Fionna shot a desperate look in Drew's direction. "Drew is never going to be able to face me again. He'll definitely fire me. There will be rumors. We can't expect those four drunk women to be quiet about what happened here tonight. Of course, they'll come up with some explanation that makes more sense to them, like there was something in the food. Drew's reputation will be ruined. He'll lose the restaurant—if the health and safety inspector doesn't take care of that beforehand."

"Okay, I can see how all of that would be bad. But let's just take a step back. Abbey and Drew remembered the effects of the tongue terrine spell. But those wore off pretty quickly. This seems to last much longer. Didn't you say this recipe was from the Specialties section? What if this is different? What if it won't wear off? Shouldn't that be our first concern? To make sure Drew, Milton, and Mr. Dudley return to normal? Before we give them some sort of memory-erasing potion that might just make everything worse?"

Fionna turned pale. "Oh, my god. You're right. This wasn't just a simple spell. We called something forth. You heard it earlier, too, didn't you?"

Abbey looked at the witches in confusion. What were they talking about?

"You mean the fairies," Andie whispered. "I can see them."

Abbey held up her hands. "Hold up! Fairies? This is too much."

Fionna didn't pay any attention to her. "You can see them, Andie? Penny and I only heard them giggle, right?" She looked at the herb witch, who nodded.

"I only see them out of the corner of my eyes. They're like shimmering images." Andie looked down. "It's not the first time I've seen them," she murmured. "That's how I know what they are."

Fionna stood up. She was shaking and gripping the edges of the table. "Don't ask me how I know this…but I have a very strong suspicion that the Specialties section in the cookbook…that it contains recipes designed to call forth dark powers. No, not necessarily dark, because fairies aren't evil, right? Supernatural powers, then."

Penny cursed.

Andie's eyes widened. "This is bad. This is really bad."

"Why? Abbey asked. She felt pretty silly asking the question, since the others were so freaked out. But wasn't witchcraft supernatural? What was the difference?

"This is black magic. The worst kind," Andie explained.

"I'm going out on a limb here, but I assume that the enchantment won't just go away on its own," Penny said. "With a spell like that, we're at the mercy of the powers we called forth. They need to release the people from the spell."

"I guess it could be worse," Fionna said in a somber voice. "In terms of the powers we called, I mean."

"Yes." Penny sounded confident. "I know a little about fairies. I never saw one myself, but my mother had an affinity for them. She told me about them. Fairies have a strange sense of humor. They like pranks. If they find something funny, they do it. They don't care if they throw the mortal world into chaos. But they're also pretty easy to placate, if you know how. So here's the plan: We'll give them something they like, and then we'll ask them nicely to break the spell."

Fionna exhaled in relief. Color returned to her cheeks. "We can do that? It's that easy?"

Penny nodded. "I think so. Let me mull it over, and I'll come up with a solution."

"In the meantime, we should really get Mrs. MacDonald," Andie implored. "I'm sure she knows about the fairies, too. And if you want to do damage control and make these people lose their memory of this night…I don't think we can get around calling Mrs. M."

"I think so, too," Penny agreed. "Even if I were willing to drug these people…I mean, I could. There are herbs that repress some memories like that. I know of some spells. I've done it before. Remember, I gave someone's memories a vague, dream-like quality? But to erase memories completely? I wouldn't know how high of a dose I could give. We could do actual damage with that. Besides, to research all that and get the ingredients together, it would take time. Time we probably don't have."

Fionna grimaced. "That's what I was afraid of. That's the other reason I kept Abbey out of the binding spell. I believe there's someone who could easily help us, quickly, and without doing damage. Someone Abbey could contact and bring here. This person has mastered the art of hypnosis."

"Who?" Penny asked, but Abbey already knew who Fionna meant.

"Magnus Magnusson, Jr."

~

"HAVE YOU LOST YOUR MIND?" Andie gasped.

She was basically taking the words out of Abbey's mouth, who was too stunned to be the first to object.

Then her concerns spilled out. "Fionna, this man would do anything—and I mean anything!—to get his hands on the cookbook. I've seen what can be done with the recipes. Magnus Magnusson is bad news. Very bad news. He probably has some evil plans, and the cookbook is going to help him execute them. Before tonight, I might have told myself off for being so irrational and silly...but if there are witches, then there could also be an evil, super-natural villain...and Magnusson absolutely is this villain. Think about this, Fionna. You are too proud to go to Mrs. MacDonald and your mom? Get over it! Don't give Magnusson any power because of this."

"This isn't about pride. This is about proving, mainly to myself, that I can get out of a critical situation I created by myself. You don't understand—if I ask Mom and Mrs. M. here now, I'll never get out from under their thumbs. I need to solve this by myself." Fionna's voice had risen. She clearly felt very passionate about this.

"Yes, but Fionna," Andie tried to soothe her. "If you drag Magnusson into this, you're going to get yourself into even more trouble. This is not the solution."

"Not necessarily." Fionna wouldn't let herself be dissuaded.

Penny sighed. "This is your cookbook, your recipes,

your disaster. Ultimately, it's your decision. I'll do what I can to get the fairies to release the spell." She disappeared into the kitchen.

Nobody spoke for a while.

Then Fionna said with a small voice, "Here's the thing. I'm pretty certain that Magnusson's father didn't come into possession of the cookbook by accident. There's more to it. I'm sure my mother knows him. This isn't just about the cookbook."

Abbey nodded. "I had that impression from our visit at the Thistle Inn, too. I didn't know what to make of the conversation between Mrs. MacDonald and Magnusson, but now that you say it, it also seemed to me as if there was some long-standing feud going on." Abbey shook her head. "Magnusson greatly underestimated Mrs. MacDonald, though. That doesn't quite fit."

Fionna shook herself out of her thoughts. "Abbey, I want to hire you as a private investigator."

"You want to hire me?" Abbey repeated in surprise. "For what, exactly?"

"I want you to find out who Magnusson Senior is. Where did he get the cookbook? How is he connected to Tarbet?"

When Abbey didn't reply right away, Fionna pleaded. "I can't ask my mother or Mrs. M. for help with this. I just can't. It's dangerous to involve Magnusson in covering up my blunder, I know. I'll have to pay a price. It's like getting into bed with the enemy. I realize that. But I don't want to hide from this. I have to figure it out on my own, and for once in my life, I need to take the bull by the horns."

Her gaze went to Andie. "I know nobody trusts me to handle this situation, and I don't even know if I trust myself. But I have to at least try."

"Oh, Fionna." Andie hugged her friend. "I'm sure you

can handle it. You're more capable than you give yourself credit for."

"I agree," Abbey said. "And I don't even know you that well. I'll take you on as a client. Maybe it isn't the worst idea in the world to get Magnusson involved here. You know what they say: keep your friends close but your enemies closer."

Fionna grinned. "Thanks." Then she got serious again. "First things first. Abbey, call Magnusson and ask him if he's capable of what I want him to do. And then he has to agree to come here."

"Oh." Abbey pulled her phone out of her pocket. "He'll be here in a flash. Trust me. He's not going to miss out on this."

CHAPTER TWELVE

FIONNA

Penny came out of the kitchen carrying a tray of desserts.

"Are these the rest of the Fools?" Fionna asked, looking at them dubiously. "Shouldn't we destroy them?"

"On the contrary," Penny replied. "These are for the fairies."

"What do you mean?"

"This recipe features everything the fairies like. In the past, people used to put out a bowl of milk or cream to appease them. Fairies love cream. They also love sweet things like wild strawberries and heather honey. They won't be able to resist. Offering them this food, we can round them up and put them in a gracious mood. Then we'll ask them humbly to dissolve the enchantment."

"And you think that will work?" Fionna was skeptical. "Sounds a little too easy."

Penny nodded. "Fairies are mischievous folk. They aren't mean; they just like to have fun. Using the result of the recipe as a cure to stop the magic is sort of fitting."

Penny set the tray on the bar. "There's no guarantee,

though. Fairies are also notoriously unpredictable. But does anyone have a better idea?"

Nobody spoke up.

"All right. Let's hurry," Fionna said. "It would be nice if the spell was already reversed when Magnusson gets here."

Penny's eyebrows shot up. "Magnusson?"

Fionna explained to her what she had already told the others. "So Abbey called him," she concluded. "And he agreed to come. Hopefully, he can hypnotize everyone to forget everything."

"Wow, Fionna, you're playing with fire." Penny shook her head, but there was also admiration in her eyes. "But I can understand why you want to handle this mess on your own, without running to your mother or the coven leader. You're taking responsibility, and I respect that."

"Thanks." Fionna was glad for the support. She had originally been sure about involving Magnusson, but as soon as Abbey had confirmed that he was coming, a dark feeling had settled in her belly.

"Okay," Penny said, lining up the dessert glasses on the counter. Then she called out, "Fairy folk at The Kirk. Greetings. We bow down before you. We have a gift for you. Enjoy. With this gift, we beseech you to lift the spell. If you accept it, we'll know you've heard us and will help us."

Almost immediately, the giggling rang out again.

The air stirred.

Then it was silent.

Everyone waited with bated breath, and it really felt like they were in a church.

After a while, Fionna heard soft whispers. It was difficult to locate where they were coming from. First it seemed from the nave, then by the organ, then from the far corner of the restaurant. Finally, there was a whisper right next to her ear. Fionna flinched and turned around. There was nobody. The others kept turning their heads, too, as if they were having the same experience.

Well, everyone except Abbey. The private investigator just watched the witches with interest. She didn't seem to hear anything, even when the giggling got very loud.

Abbey's eyes widened, though, when she saw what was happening with the desserts. She had to see, just like the others, that the invisible creatures were feasting on the Fools.

As the fairies giggled and slurped, the contents of the dessert glasses slowly but surely disappeared. Cream and fruit compote dripped on the counter. Then the nearly empty glasses appeared to dance in the air, tipping over. The last of the cream ran over the rims of the glasses and disappeared into thin air.

There was soft laughter and lip smacking, the glasses descended, and one fell on the floor, smashing on the tiles.

Then complete silence reigned in the restaurant again. The atmosphere changed. Fionna only now realized how charged with magic it had been.

"They're gone," Andie breathed. Her eyes shone.

"Were you able to see them?" Fionna asked.

"Not really. Just a flicker now and then. I thought I saw them, and then I didn't." She shook her head in disbelief. "It's crazy. They seem so delicate, but they're strong in magic."

Fionna wanted to know more about the fairies, but a loud knock at the door made her flinch.

She went over to let Magnusson in, just as Abbey asked, "How do we know if the fairies did as Penny asked?"

"We won't until the binding spell is dissolved," the herb witch answered.

When Fionna opened the door, Magnusson stood there

with a self-satisfied smile. He strolled in, and Fionna quickly locked up behind him.

The feeling of dread in her stomach got worse.

"Well, isn't this interesting?" Magnusson said with a smug voice as he circled the tableau of frozen people holding the string. He hadn't even acknowledged Abbey and the other witches. "What happened here?"

"They fell victim to a spell from my cookbook," Fionna said coolly. "That's all you need to know."

"I'll be the judge of that." Magnusson sounded downright happy. He clearly reveled in having the upper hand. "What type of spell?"

Fionna sighed. "It's a love spell, I guess. Those affected made their affections known in a...let's say, scandalous manner. The women were just witnesses. We put a binding spell on them, and hopefully we also reversed the enchantment, but...we need them to forget the entire thing."

"Very interesting," Magnusson said again. His beady black eyes were fixed on Fionna. "Didn't you tell me you don't have the cookbook anymore, you little witch?" His voice now sounded much more menacing. "Have you been lying to me?"

"No." Fionna tried to remain calm and suppressed the instinct to back away. "But I did make copies. You never asked about that." She lifted her chin, forcing herself not to break eye contact.

A slow smile spread across Magnusson's handsome, if slightly long, face. "Excellent. You've just told me about your bargaining chip. You have copies of recipes from the cookbook. I'll help, but only if you give them to me."

"I expected that. I wouldn't have mentioned them otherwise. This should be a fair price. What I don't want is to be in your debt."

Magnusson laughed. "Oh, what an honorable little witch you are!"

Fionna didn't reply but held his gaze. Finally, Magnusson counteroffered. "You give me the copies, and you get me the book."

"I couldn't, even if I wanted to." Fionna swallowed. "The book is at Mrs. MacDonald's. She would never hand it over to me."

"Then come up with a way to get hold of it."

Fionna shook her head. "You know what a powerful witch Mrs. MacDonald is. If she doesn't want me to have the book, there's no way."

Magnusson stared at her. Fionna spread her hands.

"Look. I could easily say that I'd try to get the book back and promise to give it to you. Instead, I'm being honest and telling you it won't be possible. The deal is erasure of their memories in exchange for recipe copies. I can't agree to anything else."

It was dead silent in the old church while they waited for Magnusson's answer. Fionna felt like she couldn't breathe.

Magnusson finally said, "Fine. But I want to see the copies first."

Fionna nodded in Penny's direction. The herb witch retrieved the stack of recipes from the storeroom.

Magnusson leafed through them. He really took his time, and Fionna couldn't stand the wait any longer. She needed him to agree to the deal, and soon.

"I've tried a couple of the recipes, and they worked. Although it could well be that only powerful witches like us can tap into their magical power." She tried to bait him. "The recipes might be useless to you, since—"

"I'm a lot more powerful than you," Magnus hissed, then quickly regained his composure. "Don't you worry your little head about this, witch."

"Then we have a deal?" Fionna held out her hand to him.

He took it with an amused look. "We do."

They shook on it. Fionna was relieved, but also badly nauseated.

Magnus turned to the tableau of frozen people. With a businesslike voice, he said, "I'm going to release them one by one from the binding spell and put them into a trance. I assume all it takes is to disconnect them from the string?"

Fionna nodded.

"Good. I'll take the person in a trance aside and erase their memories. It would be good if they aren't wondering how they got to the place they're in when they wake from their trance. They'll be slightly dazed and confused, but the more natural the transition, the better. Let's see." He pointed at Milton. "That boy has a chef's jacket on. I guess he belongs in the kitchen? I'll start with him and bring him there."

Fionna took Andie by the arm, and they followed Magnusson as he led a robot-like Milton to the kitchen. She wanted to be there when Magnusson erased the young chef's memory, just to make sure he kept his word—and didn't do anything to Milton that wasn't in keeping with their deal. After all, Fionna only trusted Magnusson as far as she could throw him.

In the kitchen, Magnusson put his hands on Milton's shoulders and locked eyes with him.

Not paying any attention to Fionna and Andie, Magnusson talked in a quiet voice. No matter how hard Fionna strained her ears, she couldn't understand all the words.

Milton woke up slowly from his trance. He nodded a few times. When Magnusson pointed at the back door, Milton turned his head in that direction.

Magnusson let go of Milton, and the young chef went to the storeroom. He soon returned with his coat, nodded at Fionna and Andie, and left through the back door.

The whole thing had taken longer than Fionna had hoped, but at least Magnusson seemed to be able to deliver.

Whether Milton's memory was completely erased, they would only find out in the future.

Since she hadn't been able to hear everything that Magnusson had said to Milton, Fionna asked, "What does he think happened here? I mean, the memory of tonight is erased. But what did you replace it with?"

Magnusson shrugged. "Nothing but an ordinary work-day. He'll just think the evening was so uneventful that nothing stood out for him. His brain will compensate for it, probably replace it with the memory of another dull shift."

Next, Magnusson worked on the four female guests. He instructed Fionna to pick up their jackets and bags and deposit them outside. Then he took one after the other outside, did his hypnosis, and had them pick up their bag and coat and go home.

Fionna just watched from the door they had left ajar. She wasn't too worried about the four women. They could blame excessive alcohol for the gaps in their memories of the evening.

Next up was Drew. Magnusson led him into the kitchen. Fionna followed and propped herself up against the counter, ready for another hypnosis session. However fascinating Magnusson's skill was, the procedure was tedious, and Fionna had seen quite enough of it. She yawned.

Then she suddenly remembered Sally.

The waitress was still at the back of the restaurant.

Fionna quietly left the kitchen to check on her.

When she mentioned to the others in passing what she was doing, they followed.

Sally was lying exactly where they had left her. Her eyes

were closed, and the wet washcloth on her forehead was still in place.

"Sally?" Fionna said cautiously. "Are you awake?"

A barely perceptible nod of the head told them that Sally was conscious.

"How are you?"

With a shaky voice, Sally answered, "Not good. I'm not doing so well. What happened?"

The women exchanged a glance. "Um, you collapsed," Fionna replied. "You passed out. The EMT will be here any minute and he's going to ask you a couple of questions, okay?"

Sally tried to remove the washcloth. "You called an ambulance? I'm sure that's unnecessary, I—"

Fionna pushed her back down on the bench. "Don't get up, Sally. You may have hit your head when you fell. Better be safe than sorry."

"Oh, yes," Sally complied. "I saw and heard some weird…um…it must have been hallucinations, right?"

"Yes, probably from a concussion." Fionna saw Magnusson enter the restaurant and waved him over.

"Sally, here comes the EMT now. Please pay attention to what he says and answer his questions, all right?"

They let Magnusson through and then had to retreat to the nave as it became too crowded for the hypnotist to do his job.

In front of the bar, there was only Mr. Dudley left standing frozen with the yarn in his hand.

Magnusson led Sally to the kitchen. The waitress looked confounded when she saw the health and safety inspector, but Magnusson whispered something in her ear that made her not pay any more attention to what was going on in the restaurant.

They disappeared, and a few minutes later, Magnusson

returned. Presumably, he had encouraged Sally to take her things and leave.

Magnusson looked fairly worn out. His complexion was pale, and there were beads of sweat on his forehead.

Fionna worried he had overestimated what he could do and that the hypnosis might not be as effective anymore.

But he managed to get Mr. Dudley into a trance. The health and safety inspector left the restaurant in a daze shortly afterward.

Fionna should have been relieved, but the feeling just didn't want to come.

Magnusson's efforts seemed to have been successful for now, but there was no guarantee that the memories of the enchanted people or the witnesses wouldn't come back.

There was nothing she could do about it now, however.

Fionna passed the copies of the recipes to Magnusson, and he disappeared without a word of goodbye.

Now that he was gone, Fionna felt a lot lighter.

She turned to Andie. "Would you do me a favor and walk Abbey to the B&B? And can you stay there? Maybe stay the night in her room, if she's okay with it? I don't like the idea of either of you walking around by yourselves, especially since Magnusson is also staying at the B&B."

"Sure, but what about you? I don't want you walking home alone, either."

"I thought Penny could help clean up in here, and then she can drive me home."

The others agreed to the plan.

Everyone seemed exhausted and just glad that the night was over.

After Andie and Abbey left, Fionna and Penny cleaned up in silence.

Finally, Fionna came out with what was on her mind. "My mother was probably right. That cookbook is dangerous. I'm not responsible or mature enough to have it. She was right to take it away from me."

"What a load of bollocks," Penny said, scrubbing the champagne-covered bar. "You were just trying to help. This could have happened to anyone. Why be so vague about the descriptions of the recipes? There should have been instructions regarding their purpose. Or, if your mother knew about them, she should have taught you." Penny looked up. "That's so typical, and it pisses me off the most. We younger witches are always admonished. We have to do everything according to the book and mustn't make any mistakes...but the older witches can do whatever they want and shroud everything in secrecy. It's only natural that we get curious and want to try things out. How can you learn without making mistakes? Instead of teaching us, they treat us like naughty schoolchildren."

"Hmm, you might be right."

"Of course I am," Penny cried, waving the wet cloth in the air. "And you know why they do that? Because they want to keep their positions of power, that's why. I'm sorry to be so blunt, but your mother has done this to you your entire life. You are a much more talented witch than she is, and she doesn't want you to best her. So she made sure that you feel small. She wanted you to depend on her so she can keep her power over you. And then she's surprised that you act irresponsibly or immaturely!"

"Hmm," Fionna said, the mop forgotten in her hand. "There might be some truth to that."

"Come on, let's finish up here," Penny said, suddenly deflated, as if her little speech had taken the last of her energy from her. "I'll tidy and clean up the kitchen."

"Okay," Fionna agreed and resumed mopping the floor.

Penny came back a little later with their coats and bags.

"Um, Fionna." She showed her a piece of paper.

It was the Fool recipe. "You didn't give it to Magnusson?"

"I honestly forgot about it. I just grabbed the stack of recipes from your bag. This was still in the kitchen, next to the rest of the ingredients."

"Don't worry, I can still give it to Magnusson tomorrow, if he even notices it's missing. I didn't copy every recipe from the book, but he is aware we had this, since he knows about the effects of the Fool recipe. It was an honest mistake, so don't beat yourself up."

"That's not it. Look at the title."

Fionna squinted her tired eyes. "Yes, Fool with Rose-Tinted Spectacles."

"No, there is no 's' at the end. You must have misread it the first time, and now it's stuck in your mind, so you automatically add it. But it says Rose-Tinted Spectacle. Singular."

Fionna clapped her hand against her forehead. "Oh, my god. I can't blame my mother or Mrs. M. What did you say about making mistakes earlier? Well, here's one. I should have studied the recipe titles more carefully, as the purpose is clearly always in the name. And this one didn't promise too much. Drew, Milton, and Mr. Dudley well and truly made spectacles of themselves."

CHAPTER THIRTEEN

ABBEY

Abbey glanced down at the brunette head next to her as they walked from the restaurant to the B&B.

It was actually a little ridiculous that Fionna had named Andie as Abbey's escort. How was this petite young woman going to be of any help if they were attacked?

She, the private detective with martial arts training, would probably have to look after Andie in that scenario.

Still, Abbey had to admit that she was glad not to be walking alone in the dark.

She had witnessed a lot of crazy and scary things today, and the thought of fairies or other invisible creatures buzzing around her made her nervous.

Abbey was usually a rational person, and the new information about all the not-so-rational things going on in the world didn't sit well with her. She liked to feel like she was in control, but after a day like today, was there any hope of keeping up that illusion? It felt like her world had tilted.

That Andie, who was used to all these paranormal goings-on, didn't seem to feel much different was no comfort. They had discussed Andie staying at the B&B but had agreed to have Andie's father pick her up with his car instead.

They hadn't talked about the cookbook at all; maybe Andie had forgotten she was supposed to tell her about it. Abbey cleared her throat to ask a question, but the B&B was just around the corner, and a car was waiting in front of the sprawling cottage.

"That's my dad. But I'll walk you inside, make sure you're locked inside your room…"

"I'll be all right." Abbey's phone rang. The melody of *"Je ne Regrette Rien"* told her it was her mother. "It's my mom calling." She fished the phone out of her purse. "Get home safe and sleep well."

Andie hesitated.

"I'm going to take this." She gestured toward the car. "Really, it's fine."

"Okay. Goodnight."

Abbey was already on her way to the front door as she pressed the button to accept the call.

"Hi, Mom."

"Hi, honey. I know it's late, but I had a feeling you'd be up. I just read your email. Finally, you've come to your senses and quit that awful job."

"Um, kind of…" She hadn't told her mom she'd been fired, only that she no longer worked for Sly Investigations. Over the years, she had perfected the art of being vague when it came to talking to her mother. She really didn't plan on informing her mom about the details of how her employment had ended.

Her mother, Xenia, had left her country of birth, Greece, at a young age in order to embark upon a very successful modeling career.

She had no understanding of her daughter's career aspirations at all.

Abbey's father, a British photographer, had passed away a few years ago. Since then, her mother had tried to get closer to her, probably because she was lonely.

"Are you still in Scotland?"

"Yes. I have plans to stay for a bit—"

"Why don't you come back to London? I can line up some modeling jobs for you." Abbey pulled a face and stuck the phone between her chin and shoulder while she looked for the key in her purse. Her mother was always on her about getting into modeling, and Abbey had learned to let her rant on and give the odd noncommittal reply. Otherwise, they'd just get into an argument.

"I don't know why you ever thought it would be a good idea to choose this masculine and dangerous profession," her mother went on. "You're so pretty. If you'd just make a little more effort...but don't worry, that's what the make-up people and stylists are for. Although I could get you an appointment with a style and beauty consultant to decide on a look. It would be good for your headshots."

Abbey sighed, locked up, and turned on the hallway light. "Even if I had any interest in modeling, Mom, I wouldn't have what it takes. You're my mother, so you're not an objective judge."

"What are you talking about?" Xenia's Greek accent reappeared, as always, when she got riled up. "I don't want to hear that from you. Confidence is everything in this line of work. Besides, I'm objective. I know what works and what doesn't after so many years in the industry. Trust me, that gritty look is in again."

Abbey rolled her eyes. Her mother thought her features were gritty because she had a deep chin dimple and slightly protruding sharp canines.

She didn't want to worry about her looks, which was why she had never shown any interest in the beauty industry, let alone modeling.

"I have no plans to change careers, Mom." When Xenia tried to object, Abbey cut her off. "Listen, it's really late. Let's discuss this when I get back to London, okay? I'll call you then."

She purposefully did nothing to correct her mother's assumption that this would be really soon, so Xenia agreed and said goodnight.

Shaking her head, Abbey dropped the phone in her purse and was about to put her room key in the lock when a voice behind her made her flinch.

"Well, if it isn't Little Miss Private Investigator."

Abbey whirled around.

Magnusson.

And he was much too close to her for the encounter to feel anywhere near comfortable. She backed up against the door.

"Oh, wait a minute. You aren't a private investigator anymore, are you? When I told Ken Sly that you were in my way, he quickly got rid of you."

Abbey couldn't get a word out. She hated that she was overwhelmed by this situation, but she didn't want to show Magnusson that she was afraid of him. He clearly enjoyed these sorts of power games, and she didn't want to give him the satisfaction. She had to get over her fear.

"You've made fast friends with the women in town." Magnusson clicked his tongue. "One could almost suspect you've been in cahoots with that red-haired witch for some time. Did you maybe warn her about our little visit this morning? Are you responsible for the fact that the cookbook disappeared just in time?"

Magnus's voice sounded menacing, and he came even closer.

Abbey made a quick decision.

Yes, she had always hated such tactics when she'd worked at Sly, but now she was her own boss. It was up to her to decide where her boundaries were and what she would be willing to do.

Instead of backing further against the door, Abbey took a step forward, right into Magnusson.

He flinched a little, clearly not expecting that.

"Yes, I can be pretty friendly if I want to be," she purred, forcing herself to look straight into his creepy black eyes.

"But I take my job seriously. This morning, I was absolutely loyal to Sly. I didn't warn Simmonds, and I had nothing to do with the disappearance of the cookbook. When Sly fired me, I realized I had to do something to prove my worth, so I quickly endeared myself to the witches. Of course, I knew what they were. They trust me now. I'll get the cookbook, and then I'll get my job back."

Magnusson's expression gave nothing away, so it was impossible for Abbey to gauge if he believed her. Even his eyes stayed exactly the same.

Abbey had no choice but to continue on her course. In for a penny…

"But you know what?" Abbey put on a seductive smile. "Not being employed by Sly right now also has its advantages. You're no longer a client I work for. We don't have a business relationship. So if you want to take me out on a date, I can accept that invitation."

There. An eyebrow went up a fraction of an inch. Magnusson's lips parted, and Abbey could feel his breath on her face.

She did her very best not to show how much it repulsed her and slowly breathed through her nose.

"Wonderful," Magnusson said. A wolfish grin spread across his face. "Let's have lunch tomorrow. I'll pick you up at noon."

"Perfect. I'll see you then." Abbey turned the key in the

door behind her, mustered up one last smile, then turned around and disappeared into her room.

With a racing heart, she locked the door, quickly went to the bathroom, locked that door too, and then propped herself up against the sink, gripping it with both hands.

She tried hard to control her breathing so she wouldn't develop a full-blown panic attack.

Then she splashed cold water on her face and looked up at her reflection in the mirror.

"Keep it together, Fine. You can do this."

CHAPTER FOURTEEN

FIONNA

F ionna was completely exhausted by the time Penny dropped her off at home. When she got out of Penny's car, her legs buckled. She barely made it into the house.

All she wanted to do was collapse in bed, but she really needed a shower first. The sour smell of champagne was still sticking to her.

The sound of water in the pipes must have woken Rosa up, because she knocked on the door just as Fionna was putting on her pajamas.

"What are you doing? It's the middle of the night."

"Sorry, Mom," Fionna replied wearily, slinking past her mother. "I've had a long and tough evening."

"I told you this job wouldn't be a walk in the park," Rosa called after her. "Why did you have to get involved with such a stressful profession? You, of all people?"

Fionna stopped. "What's that supposed to mean?"

"Well, you're not suited to it. You're one of the most sluggish people I know. A part-time office job would have been a better choice. You know I told you that before."

Fionna closed her eyes. She didn't want to let herself be pulled into an argument with her mother. Not tonight. "Mom, I really had a difficult evening, and I can't talk to you right now."

"Oh no, what did you do?"

"Nothing, I...I just need to go to bed." Fionna tried to leave, but her mother grabbed her by the sleeve.

"Fionna! You didn't try one of the recipes from the cookbook again, did you? Did you memorize one of them? Tell me you didn't make copies!" Rosa's face looked as if it had only just occurred to her that this was possible. Her voice lowered. "Fionna? Give them to me right now."

When Fionna didn't respond right away, Rosa stamped her foot. "Don't you ever learn?"

Fionna stopped trying to get out of her mom's grip and turned around.

"I am learning. That's exactly what I'm doing. Through my own mistakes. Please let me. And by the way, I feel bad enough about myself. You don't always need to tear me down."

"Tear you down?" Rosa sounded astonished. "What are you talking about? I'm protecting you."

"I don't need to be protected, Mom," Fionna said through clenched teeth. "I'm not a child, damn it!"

Rosa crossed her arms in front of her chest and peered at her daughter over the rims of her glasses. "Then why are you always acting like one?"

Fionna sank down on the bottom step. The wood was cold under her thin pajama pants, but she didn't care. She was too exhausted. So much had happened in the last couple of days that she didn't even feel like herself anymore.

The old Fionna wouldn't have let herself be provoked into an argument. She would have meekly agreed to anything Rosa said—and then quickly gone to bed. Though maybe she would have made short work of an emergency Snickers bar before going to sleep.

It might have been the events of the last couple of days or just the fatigue that made everything seem slightly unreal, but Fionna just couldn't go on any longer without speaking the truth to her mother.

Granted, the middle of the night wasn't a great time to open a discussion on something that had been plaguing her since childhood…but when would there ever be a time to talk about this horrible secret that had been unspoken between them forever?

"Mom, I know why you treat me like that. You don't trust me to act like a normal person because I…" She clutched the wooden railing until her knuckles turned white. "Because I'm not human. That's why you're always so harsh with me on the one hand and lenient on the other. You think I can't do anything."

Fionna closed her eyes. "You created a monster. Now you have to take care of me, whether you like it or not. But…I'm not a freak, Mom…no matter who my father is." She fought hard against the tears. She needed to get this out in a halfway coherent manner. "I may not be entirely normal, and something sets me apart from the other witches, but in my heart, I am human, and I can act like one. I can learn like one."

Annoyed, she wiped away the tears that she couldn't hold back any longer.

Rosa just stared at her. "What...what are you talking about?"

Fionna jutted her chin out and looked her mother right in the eyes. "You don't have to pretend anymore, Mom. Grandma told me the truth many years ago. I asked her why I don't have a father. Haven't you ever wondered why

I never ask you about him? Grandma explained it to me. You made a deal with the devil when you couldn't have a child. My father is not human. I'm the devil's offspring."

CHAPTER FIFTEEN

ABBEY

"I don't understand. Wouldn't you rather go to Glasgow? I can get us a reservation anywhere you want. Somewhere much more...classy." Magnus scrunched his nose as he opened the door to the Fisherman's Café.

Abbey shook her head. "No, thanks. I prefer this. It's not going to win any Michelin stars, but it's charming. Since we're in a small Scottish village, it's good to get an authentic experience, don't you think?"

Magnusson looked around in disgust.

The Fisherman's was a typical old-fashioned Scottish café that served large portions of hearty food with no consideration of health concerns or food intolerances. Customers sat on wooden benches or plastic chairs. The place smelled like a deep fryer. Which was no surprise, because most dishes came with something fried, and the all-day fry-up breakfast options were the most popular items on the menu.

"Charming?" Magnusson sneered. "I think you and I define that word differently."

Abbey quickly hid her grin behind her long dark curls

when Magnusson took a handkerchief out of his pocket and wiped down the bench before taking a seat.

"Is that starched linen?" she had to ask. "I've never seen anyone under the age of sixty carry around a handkerchief like that. And monogrammed? M. M. M. What does the third M stand for?"

"That's private," Magnus replied, sounding rather piqued.

Abbey grabbed one of the laminated menus. "I think I'll actually try haggis. Here it is, haggis, neeps, and tattis. It doesn't get more Scottish than that."

Magnus didn't look at the menu. Abbey assumed that he'd picked one of the specials on the board above the wooden counter.

But when a middle-aged man came over to take their order, Magnusson said, "I'll have a sandwich. Avocado, smoked salmon, and watercress on rye. No mayo, just a spoonful of Dijon mustard."

The man stared at Magnusson. "Um, we don't serve that."

"Nothing on your menu appeals to me. That's what I want."

The man scratched his head with the pencil. "We have brown toast, avocado, and smoked salmon. But watercress? Is that cress? We serve egg-cress-mayo sandwiches. It's a filling we get pre-made. Shall I put some of that in?"

"Good gracious." Magnus's face distorted. "Don't."

"What was the other thing? Dee…"

"Dijon mustard."

"Right. We have regular mustard."

Magnus snorted.

The man waited but didn't get a different order. Abbey looked at the tabletop, feeling more embarrassed by the minute. The guests at the other tables had stopped their conversations and were staring at Magnusson.

He finally deigned to respond. "Fine. Brown bread with avocado and salmon. No mayo, no mustard. Just slightly buttered toast. And a bottle of mineral water, unopened."

An awkward silence settled between them until their drinks arrived.

Abbey silently told herself off. She needed to make more of an effort; otherwise, she could have saved herself the pain of going on this "date."

She raised her glass of Diet Coke. "Here's to our new friendship," she said. "You must call me Abbey from now on. I'm sorry that my choice of restaurant doesn't appeal to you. I know you're used to something different." She forced a smile. "I hope my company makes up for it."

Magnusson's face took on a slightly less sour expression. "Only if you call me Magnus. And yes, I just think life is too short to put up with poor quality, in all walks of life. I'm only interested in ..." He gave her a meaningful look. "Excellency." His lips twisted into that big smile that he probably thought was charming but always reminded Abbey of a predator.

"Well, Magnus, I'm sorry we got off to such a bad start. Let's start over, shall we? Why don't you tell me a little about yourself?" She leaned forward, propped her chin on her hand, and looked at him admiringly. "You must have an incredibly interesting life, as cultured as you are."

Magnus laughed. "Do you mean cultured...or wealthy?"

Abbey tried her best to look a little abashed, but also a little hungry for attention from a rich upper-class man.

It worked. She'd been right to assume this sort of thing flattered him. He liked to represent himself as wealthy and distinguished, and he used it to pick up women. It clearly didn't bother him that women would be interested in him because of his wealth instead of his personality. It was probably all the same to him.

Most of what Magnusson said disgusted Abbey, but luckily, she just had to focus on nodding and smiling. She didn't have to say much at all. Magnus liked talking about himself. A lot.

He hardly touched his sandwich after he had made such a fuss about it.

Abbey learned that Magnus had grown up in a mansion in London's posh Knightsbridge district. He now had a luxury penthouse in trendy Canary Wharf.

He had studied at Oxford, although he remained vague about what his degree was in.

Magnus's father was a vastly successful businessman. A mother was never mentioned. Magnus worked for his father. He was learning the business from the ground up so that he could one day take over.

Since learning about his father was the entire purpose of this "date," Abbey managed to get a question in. "Growing up in Knightsbridge must have been awesome! Does your father still live there in that mansion?"

"Oh, yes. It's a very impressive building. Tudor style, and architecturally striking. It's close to Harrods. I'd be happy to give you a tour someday soon, and then I can take you shopping, get you some decent clothes that show off your great body a little more." He winked at her.

"Oh, that would be fantastic," Abbey gushed. "Tell me more about that important job of yours. What line of work are you in?"

"Let's just say we're an investment company."

Abbey tried to prod further, but he remained vague. All she got was that it wasn't stocks or anything like that. She wasn't sure if he didn't want to talk about it or if he thought she was too pea-brained to understand. Maybe it was simply boring, and he preferred to remain mysterious.

"Is it antiques or collectibles, like the cookbook?" He frowned, and Abbey knew she had gone too far. She quickly tried to make up for it. "I love antiques. Or vintage dresses! They can be valuable sometimes, right?" she squeaked.

"Dresses?" Magnus laughed. "No. It's special collectibles." He looked around. "You told me last night you knew what your new friends were. I assume, then, that you're also familiar with the…let's call it underworld, ruled by people who distinguish themselves from mere mortals by being…special?"

Abbey's breath caught in her throat. She was so close to finding out something important. She just had to keep a poker-face. Talking proved difficult in this situation, but she was spared giving an immediate answer when Magnus's phone rang. He picked up right away, without apologizing to Abbey for the intrusion.

"Hello, Father."

Abbey pretended to turn her attention to the last bites of her lunch, but she tried to listen in on the conversation.

"I sent the recipes by express this morning," he said with a smug face. "You should—"

Magnus Senior had such a booming voice that Abbey could understand snippets of his part of the conversation. "…abundantly clear…good for nothing…cookbook… useless…loser…"

Magnusson's neck turned bright red. He let the tirade wash over him without saying a word. As usual, he didn't let his emotions show on his face. But his small dark eyes glittered dangerously.

"I will get the book, Father," he finally said, sounding like a little boy who had just been reprimanded. "The mission has been a success so far—"

It sounded as if Magnus Senior had interrupted again,

but this time in a calmer voice, so Abbey couldn't hear what he said.

"I understand, Father," Magnusson finally answered meekly. "I'll try harder." He hung up.

As if suddenly remembering that Abbey was there, Magnus attempted a smile, but it wasn't as convincing as usual. "He's not an easy boss. He's not happy unless he gets the results he envisioned. That's what makes him so successful."

Magnus lifted his chin and squared his shoulders. "I specifically told him to treat me like any employee. He's strict, and that's a good thing. I wouldn't have it any other way. This is how I'll become his successor."

"I admire ambitious men." She gave him the answer he wanted to hear.

But she was a little absentminded for the rest of the conversation because a new plan was forming in her head.

After hearing Magnus interact with his father, Abbey doubted that he even knew what the cookbook was about. He had no actual power or knowledge; his persona was just smoke and mirrors.

No, she wouldn't get much out of him.

What she needed to do was to get this date over with as smoothly as possible—and fast, because she planned to hurry to London.

Straight into the lion's den.

Abbey had an idea of how to gain the trust of Magnus Magnusson, Sr.

CHAPTER SIXTEEN

FIONNA

After the exhausting evening, Fionna woke up late. Her mother had long since left for work.

Fionna made herself something to eat and then went for a long walk. She wasn't one for strenuous hikes, but she enjoyed the occasional stroll along the loch shore. Now and then, she would take a break in one of the small sandy bays, sit down on a fallen tree trunk, and enjoy the scenery.

This was exactly what she needed right now.

Fionna didn't mind that it was windy and wet. It decreased her chances of running into other people, and she preferred to be alone.

Besides, this was how she liked Loch Lomond best: when the usually smooth surface turned into choppy gray waves that merged with the cloudy horizon.

There was something melancholic about it, but Fionna also felt the strength of the forces of nature. She drew on that.

Today she hardly noticed the scenery, since she was so preoccupied with her own thoughts.

Countless times, Fionna had played out different

scenarios in her head, imagining what would happen when she finally confronted her mother with the unspoken secret of her paternity.

Not one scenario included the reaction Rosa had shown when Fionna had finally come out with it the previous evening.

Her mother had laughed.

"What nonsense is that?"

"Nonsense?" Fionna was incredulous. "We both know it's not nonsense. You don't have to pretend anymore. I've known since Grandma told me many years ago."

Rosa waved it off. "My mother became more and more senile in the last couple of years of her life, you know that. She clearly wasn't in her right mind when she told you that. Or she was pulling your leg." That cold laugh again. "Your father certainly isn't the devil."

Fionna stared at her. Then she shook her head. "No. You're lying. I know the truth. I *feel* the truth. I don't even feel right in my body—" She looked down at her belly when she said that.

"Of course you don't feel comfortable. You're overweight. The devil has nothing to do with it, although it's just like you to blame someone, anyone, for your shortcomings. If you'd have the discipline for a stricter diet—"

"No, Mom! That's not what I mean," Fionna cried out in frustration.

"Well, what then?" Rosa now looked impatient herself.

Fionna swallowed. "I have no periods. I've never started menstruating. Grandma told me that's because I'm not a real woman. I'm unnatural in that way." Fionna pressed her lips together when she saw Rosa's face.

Her mother looked relieved.

"Jesus, Fionna, that doesn't have to mean anything. I'm sure there's a very simple medical explanation for it. Most likely to do with hormones. Didn't you learn anything at school? Why would you believe in this hare-brained super-stition my mother gave you instead of getting your problem checked out by a medical expert? You've clearly tortured yourself with this for years. And you probably blamed me all this time. That explains why you're always so hostile, even though I have your best interests at heart and am nothing but supportive." Rosa shook her head. "Blaming the devil instead of taking responsibility…so typical! Have you mentioned this to any doctor at all?"

Fionna gave a barely perceptible head shake.

"Then go and have it checked out." Rosa sighed. "I guess I need to make you an appointment, since you don't seem to be—"

"No, I can do it myself," Fionna quickly interrupted. She pulled herself up with the railing to a standing posi-tion. Her legs were shaking.

"If what Grandma said isn't true, how come you never told me who my father is? You could have told me his name long ago."

"No, I'm afraid not. I only ever knew his nickname, not even his first name. He was a tourist, just passing through. I'm not proud of it, but it was a one-night stand. He was long gone by the time I found out I was pregnant. I never told you about him because there isn't anything to tell."

Fionna didn't know what to say to that, so she just turned around to walk up the stairs. "Good night, Mom," she whispered.

Her legs had felt like they were made of jelly, but she'd tried not to show her mother how weak she felt.

Upstairs, she had fallen into her bed and let sleep take over.

Now, walking along the shore of Loch Lomond in bright daylight, yesterday's conversation seemed so surreal. She wasn't actually sure it hadn't been a dream.

But it had happened.

Fionna didn't know if her mother had told her the truth or not. But Rosa had certainly made her feel like a naive little child who still believed in the bogeyman. Her mother had succeeded in ridiculing her for this dark and heavy burden Fionna had carried on her heart for years.

It was enough to make her doubt what she had always known to be true.

Is it really possible? Fionna thought to herself, as she stopped in one of the sandy bays and let her eyes roam over the gray-on-gray scenery.

Could her grandmother have played a very nasty trick on her?

CHAPTER SEVENTEEN

ABBEY

A bbey had tried to pump Magnusson for as much information as possible, but she couldn't get the name of his father's company.

She'd searched the internet but wasn't altogether surprised nothing could be found. Whatever Magnus Senior's mysterious business was, he wouldn't be advertising it in the Yellow Pages.

Magnusson had rambled on about the mansion in Knightsbridge, so Abbey had a pretty excellent description. She would just have to walk around the Harrods neighborhood and hope to find it.

The previous evening, Abbey had returned to London. Her sparse two-bedroom apartment in Stepney Green seemed strangely stark and real compared to all the fantastic things she had experienced in the Highlands.

After only a few hours of sleep, Abbey set off to Knightsbridge in the early morning hours, afraid that her belief in everything she had vividly seen in Tarbet would fade over time the longer she was in her reality again.

She had been walking around Knightsbridge for hours, trying to spot the striking architectural features Magnusson had mentioned. She'd thought she had found the right house twice. The first time, she'd naively rung the doorbell. A butler had opened the door and treated her like a vagrant begging for a handout. He'd threatened to call the police before she could even explain herself.

Abbey's black leather jacket and faded skinny jeans clearly made her stand out as not belonging in this district.

The second time, she'd gotten smart and checked the address on her phone. The house was listed on a realtor's website. It couldn't be the Magnusson residence. Besides, the interior images didn't match Magnus's description.

Discouraged, she walked back to Brompton Road, where she recharged with a cappuccino and blueberry muffin at a café.

Ignoring her sore feet, Abbey set off again. When she spotted the spiraling chimneys, she walked faster. She turned the corner and saw the blue half-timber and red brick towers. The distinctive bay windows also matched Magnusson's description.

Abbey took a deep breath and dug out her phone. She couldn't find any information about this address.

This had to be it.

The feeling of relief or even accomplishment that she expected didn't hit. Even though she had been looking for this place all morning, and had formulated a solid plan, her steps slowed as she approached the front door. Something told her to run.

She pulled herself together and tapped the heavy brass ring with the lion's head to knock at the door.

After what seemed like an eternity—and a real struggle not to listen to her intuition and run away—a butler in livery opened the door.

Abbey explained who she was, and the man let her in.

He asked her to take a seat on one of the chaise lounges in the big hall and then kept her waiting for a good half an hour. The antique furniture looked delicate, and Abbey didn't trust the spindly legs. She hardly dared to move once she was seated, for fear that the chaise lounge would collapse under her.

Just when she thought she couldn't take it any longer, the butler returned with a tray of coffee, cream, sugar, and biscotti. He set it down on a side table.

Even though the butler was not very forthcoming, Abbey assumed the coffee meant that she would have to wait a little longer. She couldn't take sitting still any longer and jumped up as soon as the butler disappeared through the doors again.

She didn't drink any of the coffee, either.

Knowing what games Magnus Junior was capable of playing, she didn't want to underestimate the master who'd taught him. Making Abbey stew here, in the large, opulent, antique-filled hall, where she clearly didn't belong, had to be part of his game. Abbey didn't want to take her chances with food and drink, not before she had a chance to meet Magnusson Senior face to face.

Instead, she inspected the enormous hall. The amount of antique furniture could have filled a whole auction room, but it looked forlorn. The pieces were all classy, but the combination of marble flooring, walnut wood panels, and gold on anything that could be gilded seemed ridiculously ostentatious, and yes, even tacky, to Abbey.

The butler finally returned and led Abbey through a corridor where wooden panels and mirrors overlapped in some kind of infinity loop effect. It reminded her of fun house mirrors at the carnival. To say it was disorienting was an understatement. Abbey didn't know how the butler managed. After a few twists and turns, she couldn't have found her way back to the entrance hall if she had to.

Just when the unsettling feeling of being trapped in the

mansion got to be too much, the butler opened a door and asked Abbey to step in.

She found herself alone in a study, the door now closed behind her.

Abbey fought the urge to check if it was locked.

Ornately carved wood panels on the one wall without floor-to-ceiling bookshelves drew her attention. The depictions seemed medieval and turned Abbey's stomach. But they weren't as bad as the fireplace the size of a walk-in closet. The thought of standing upright in it made Abbey dizzy. She really didn't like this room and wanted nothing more than to escape it.

She focused on the most ordinary features of the study: two dark-green Chesterfield sofas and a large desk. The desk was tidy, with no revealing personal items except for a row of framed photographs.

Abbey bent down to examine them. They were black-and-white pictures of a traveling circus.

A dark, gravelly voice made her flinch and nearly knock over one of the frames.

"Miss Fine. How nice to make your acquaintance."

Abbey slowly turned around.

Magnus Magnusson, Sr., looked younger than she had imagined. She guessed him to be in his mid-fifties. There were very few lines on his attractive face. It was rounder than Magnus Junior's, but the resemblance was definitely there. The father had a stockier build than the son, and his eyes were not small and black; they were piercing blue. The color almost seemed unnatural, and Abbey wondered if he wore tinted contacts.

The only thing that made him look older was his hair. It was full and thick but stark white.

Magnus Senior was a few inches shorter than Abbey but still a very imposing figure.

His charisma filled up the entire room, drowning out the unease she had felt in here until now.

Abbey told herself to be careful.

She put on a smile, stepped forward to shake Magnusson's hand, and said, "It's nice to meet you, too."

Magnusson pointed to one of the Chesterfields, and Abbey took a seat.

"Can I offer you something to drink?" he asked, walking over to a large old globe that turned out to have a hidden bar inside.

"I'll have the same as you," Abbey replied sweetly, and then took the glass of cognac he passed her.

Magnusson took a seat opposite her, his own glass in hand. "Let's talk business," he said.

"I'm here to offer you my services as a private investigator."

Magnusson pursed his lips. "What makes you think I need one?"

"You want the cookbook back. Your son won't be able to get it."

Magnusson gave a short laugh. Abbey flinched but met his mocking gaze.

"You already had the job of retrieving the cookbook. You failed. That's why Sly let you go."

"Ken Sly insisted on tactics I didn't agree with. Your son is using the same method right now, and I can guarantee that he won't get anywhere with it."

Magnusson leaned back. He looked relaxed, almost as if he was enjoying the conversation. "And your approach would be different how?"

"I have a long-term plan. Sly wanted to handle the case quick and dirty. With force. Your son is using the same intimidation techniques. The owner of the cookbook has a whole community of women behind her. They're closing ranks against anything that is perceived as a threat. And they have a vested interest in keeping the book and their secret safe. You should know that."

She watched Magnusson's face closely.

Abbey suspected that he knew the women of Tarbet, or Mrs. MacDonald at least. The old lady had played her games with Magnus Junior because of her history with his father. Andie had told her that Fionna's mother reacted as if she knew Magnusson, too.

But Magnusson's expression gave nothing away.

"What's your plan, then?"

"The opposite of hostile aggression. I'm gaining the trust of the younger women in the Tarbet community. Your son can confirm that they've already revealed their secret to me."

An instant later, Abbey knew where Magnus Junior had gotten his predatory smile from: his father. Only the older man looked more like a wolf, with his glinting blue eyes.

"So I've heard. My son reported this to me. Unfortunately, he has fallen short of telling me more about those young women. Maybe we can remedy that." Magnusson tapped his fingers on the green leather of the couch and pursed his lips.

Eventually, he said, "I'm going to test your knowledge. If you pass the test, I'll hire you."

Abbey swallowed. Her mouth felt dry. She took a sip of cognac, letting the liquid burn down her throat, making the feeling worse.

"Deal," she croaked.

First, Magnusson asked her to describe the prominent women of the Tarbet community in detail. Abbey had to tell him names, ages, where they lived, what they looked like.

Abbey watched Magnusson like a hawk, but neither her descriptions of Mrs. MacDonald nor any of the other women elicited any visible emotions.

139

Until she got to Fionna. His eyes narrowed a little when Abbey told him Rosa's daughter was in her mid-twenties. He asked a few questions, then told Abbey to move on to the next woman.

But Abbey had the feeling he wasn't really paying attention anymore.

She was in the middle of describing Penny when Magnusson interrupted her.

"What magical powers does Fionna Simmonds have?"

Abbey was caught off guard and took a moment to collect herself. So far, she had avoided describing magic or magical talents. Magnusson had given nothing away, either. That he didn't mince his words now was a little startling.

Abbey cleared her throat. "She can enchant objects."

"Have you seen what she can do? Is she very talented?"

Abbey answered in the affirmative. She only had to think of the surreal evening in The Kirk. "She has performed magic with the recipes from the cookbook, and I don't have a lot of comparison, but—"

"Did she use the cookbook?" Magnusson interrupted.

"What do you mean?"

"My son sent me copies of pages from the book." Magnusson sounded impatient. He leaned forward. "Were those the copies Fionna used to do the cookbook spells? Or did she need to use the book?"

Suddenly, it dawned on Abbey what Magnusson was getting at. Fionna had assumed that the cookbook was such a powerful enchanted object that it wasn't needed directly. What had Andie told her when she'd explained the whole thing to her? Fionna's grandmother had to have been so gifted that she could not only enchant the cookbook but allow the magic to transfer from the cookbook to the person performing the recipe rituals.

They had been wrong about that.

The cookbook wasn't that powerful.

Fionna's grandmother hadn't been so gifted.

It was Fionna who was immensely powerful and gifted.

She could perform the recipe rituals successfully without the cookbook. The way Magnusson now looked at Abbey, she had to assume that nobody else could do it.

It now made sense why Magnusson wanted the actual cookbook back so desperately.

They would have to test that theory and have another witch try out a recipe.

Abbey wasn't sure if she should reveal that important bit of information to Magnusson. If it was true, this was… huge. Fionna probably didn't even know.

She didn't want to tell this dangerous man.

But in the game she was playing with Magnusson, it was Abbey's turn.

And she had to make a big move if she wanted her plan to work out.

"No," she said. "Fionna doesn't need the cookbook to perform the magic."

CHAPTER EIGHTEEN

FIONNA

Fionna started talking as soon as Andie's alarm clock went off. "Oh my god, you won't believe what happened yesterday."

Andie yawned, sat up, and stretched. "You're awake? And dressed? Put the mattress away?" She rubbed her eyes. "Wait, did you even sleep here?"

"Yes, but I woke up early." Fionna waved it off.

She was staying at Andie's because she didn't want to be around her mother right now. Last night, she had come in late after her shift at the restaurant, and Andie had already been asleep.

Fionna had been very close to waking her up to share her news with her.

Now Fionna was excited she could finally do that.

Pacing the small space between bed, desk, and closet, she ran her fingers through her hair.

"When I got to the restaurant yesterday, I was so nervous. I had no idea if our plan had worked, if Magnusson had done what he promised. The night before, when he put them in the trance, they just walked away—

but he had done *something* to them. I was afraid they would wake up the next morning and remember everything after all."

Andie nodded. "I was afraid of that, too. So did Drew say anything? What about Sally?"

"It was Sally's day off yesterday, and Milton wasn't there, either. So it was only Drew who could give me any indication if he remembered and…" She stopped in her tracks and looked at Andie in horror. "Right after I walked in, he took me aside and apologized to me."

Andie's eyes widened. She suddenly seemed very much awake. "Whaaat? Then he did—"

"No. No, wait. He apologized for the kiss."

Confusion was written all over Andie's face.

"He said he was terribly sorry he kissed me the night before, after the restaurant closed. He really likes me, but he has to put his feelings aside, because he's my boss, and that's just unprofessional. He didn't know what came over him, but he deeply regretted it."

"Wait, so…he apologized for something he didn't do? But he didn't remember what actually happened?"

Fionna nodded, still a panicked look in her eyes. "I tried to gloss over the fake kiss thing and asked him if he remembered anything else from that evening, any other odd behavior. He just looked at me disconcertedly and said no. I really believe he doesn't remember that crazy night. Unless, you know, him thinking he has feelings for me is some sort of residue of that." She gave a nervous laugh. "It looks like Magnus stuck to our deal…but he must have implanted another memory."

"Not just an ordinary, uneventful workday, like he told us. Something that didn't happen at all. Why would Magnusson do that?"

"Because he wants to harm us! This is bad, Andie.

Who knows what he planted in the heads of the others? I haven't heard anything yet, but I expect the worst. That's why I didn't get a wink of sleep."

"I understand. But calm down." Andie kept a level head as usual. "If he had done something really bad, we would have heard by now. Magnusson probably just took the opportunity to mess with us a little."

Fionna exhaled and dropped down on the bed. "Yes, you're probably right."

She sat up and grabbed her purse. "There's something else." Fionna pulled out a small, folded piece of paper. "Here, take a look at this."

Andie put out her hand, but Fionna hesitated.

"What is it?" Andie asked impatiently.

Fionna unfolded the recipe and handed it to her.

"I thought you gave Magnusson all the copies?"

"The Fool recipe was still in the kitchen. Penny forgot to grab it. So I still have that one. And this..." She pushed her hair out of her face. It probably resembled a bird's nest by now. "This was never in the stack of copies. I had it in my purse...and I looked at it so many times, folded and refolded it, that it got smaller and smaller. It..."

She broke off. Fionna wanted to tell Andie about it, desperately wanted to tell someone about it, but she lost her nerve.

"The Devil's Children," Andie read out loud and skimmed the recipe. "Sounds like this is from the Specialties section?"

Fionna nodded, still pulling on her hair.

"Rub with moor butter. What the heck is moor butter?"

"Read on," Fionna whispered.

"Tadpoles. A cat queen? Calf in its early stages. A squab fresh from the nest." Horrified, Andie looked at Fionna. "Is this supposed to be a sick joke? What's a cat queen?"

"A pregnant cat. It gets worse."

"Worse than throwing animal babies into a cauldron?" Andie looked back down at the recipe again. "Alive! This is horrendous!" She quickly read a few more ghoulish ingredients.

Then she folded the recipe back up to a small package, as if that would undo reading the nausea-inducing list of ingredients. "It's just—"

"Sick. Like you said, it's sick."

"Whoever came up with this definitely wasn't right in the head. I mean, I'm sorry to say this about your grandma. She might not even have come up with the recipe herself, but she included it. Why would she do this?" Andie shook her head in disgust. "Anyway, let's hope nobody ever puts that into practice."

Fionna dropped her head. "I'm afraid someone did."

"What do you mean? Why would anyone do that? Nobody in our coven could be that…depraved—"

"You're wrong. It was someone in our coven. At least one person. My mother. And I can't believe that Mrs. MacDonald wasn't involved. Someone with a lot of power had to have helped her with this. My grandmother, too, probably."

Andie looked at her as if she didn't know if she should be outraged or laugh out loud. "What…what makes you think that?"

Fionna forced herself to sit up straight and look Andie right in the eyes.

"I have a feeling…a very bad feeling…that I was made with this recipe."

Andie just stared at her, openmouthed.

Fionna took a deep breath to say what had been heavy on her heart for years. She needed to tell her best friend. And she just wanted to get it out, however ridiculous it sounded. Because with all the evidence in front of them, it didn't appear to be ridiculous at all anymore.

"They made me with it. My mother. The coven. With this recipe. My father isn't an ordinary man. My father isn't any man, but an evil entity. I'm the child of the devil."

CHAPTER NINETEEN

ABBEY

W hen Abbey got home from her meeting with
Magnus Magnusson, Sr., she was exhausted.
Her whole body ached, as if she'd physically
as well as verbally sparred with Magnusson all afternoon.

But the effort had been worth it. She had passed the
"test." After answering his questions for hours, she'd been
hired by Magnusson to retrieve the cookbook for him.

In her apartment, Abbey flopped down on the bed.
However tired she was, her brain wouldn't switch off. The
conversation with Magnusson looped in her head.

Finally, she jumped up, grabbed her phone, and called
Fionna.

She explained what had happened to her actual client.
"Listen," she concluded. "I'm pretty sure Magnusson
would need the cookbook itself to do any of the recipes.
Same with anyone else who would want to use them.
Anyone but you."

Fionna remained silent.

"Do you understand what I'm saying?"

"Yes. Yes, it means only I can do magic with just the
copies instead of the enchanted book."

"Why do you sound so down about that? Doesn't it mean you're incredibly powerful?" More powerful than Magnusson—or whoever he had in the wings to do magic for him. Abbey was still too new to the world of witchcraft to know if men could be witches. Was Magnusson one?

"That's not necessarily a good thing," Fionna said quietly.

"Why not? You're very special in a community of already special women. Which brings me to the next point. You hired me to find out what's so important about the cookbook. We know that now. But you also wanted to know why Magnusson, in particular, wants it so badly. I don't know about you, but the answer, that he can do magic with it, doesn't seem enough for me. The way he's been going about this…I think there's some personal connection. I'm pretty certain he knows Mrs. MacDonald."

Abbey wasn't sure if she should say how Magnusson had reacted when she told him about Fionna, so she left that part out. "Could he be a witch himself and know the coven that way? Is there such a thing as a male witch?"

"I honestly have no idea. I've never heard of any other people like us. The Tarbet coven is the only one I know. But I recently met someone else with…let's say supernatural abilities of a kind. Pari, a girl from Hunza, turned up at Penny's, and Penny took her in. I would say that Pari and her grandmother are also witches. Not in the same sense as we women from Tarbet are, but they have their special gifts. In their case, the gift is passed from mother to daughter, too, just like in Tarbet. Male witches? I've never encountered one."

"But maybe you have. What Magnus Junior can do with his hypnosis…don't you think that's a kind of supernatural ability, too? Magnusson Senior could have that power, and more."

"You might be right." Fionna sounded gloomy. "And

148

even Magnus's talent might be more dangerous than we knew. He implanted a false memory in Drew's head. Drew thought he'd kissed me. That's not what we agreed upon with Magnus. I'm really worried he could have implanted even more harmful false memories in the others."

"That's a whole other caliber than just putting someone in a trance and making them forget something." Abbey shuddered at the thought of what Magnus Senior would have been able to do her earlier—if he had the same talent as his son. "So we definitely want to find out who or what the Magnussons are exactly, right?"

Fionna agreed. "Do you have a plan?"

"I've already looked up Magnusson on the internet, but he's a ghost. It's strange, since he's supposed to be a successful business owner, so he should be listed somewhere, but he might hide behind a shadow corporation. Who knows? Whatever he does, he doesn't want the public to know. But his mansion is really ostentatious, so he makes money. It could be family money... Then again, he might use his talents to gain wealth, whatever they are." Abbey paused. "With the coven...I had the impression that you rarely use your talents to get rich, do you?"

"It's against the rules. But some of us do make money with our gifts, at least tangentially. We don't openly sell our services as witches."

"Well, Magnusson, at least, doesn't seem to either. He's secretive about what he does. But you said you don't know what else is out there in terms of a community of magic practitioners. It could be that he has dealings in that community and makes his money that way. Anyway, I'm going to dig a little deeper. I have other methods than simple internet searches, of course, and I love a challenge. I aim to find out *something* about Magnusson. I just have to get creative."

"All right, keep me updated," Fionna said. "And Abbey?"

"Yes?"

Fionna hesitated, and Abbey looked at the phone display to check if the call was still connected. Just then, Fionna started talking. "I have a feeling Junior shouldn't be underestimated. But he's probably nothing compared to his father. Who knows what Senior is capable of? What kind of impression did you get from him?"

Now it was Abbey's turn to pause. "Yeah," she finally agreed. "I got the feeling he's very dangerous."

"I want you to figure this out," Fionna said. "But I don't want you to…I don't know, get hurt or anything—"

"It's okay, Fionna. I'm a professional. This is my job."

"Just…promise you'll be careful, all right?"

"I will. I'll be careful."

ABBEY RUBBED HER EYES. After many hours in the British Library's newspaper archive, she was losing heart.

Her research into Magnusson kept hitting dead ends. Yesterday, she'd searched the land registry database and found out that he'd bought the house in Knightsbridge in the early eighties. So the mansion wasn't a family home. It didn't seem as if he'd owned a house before that. A contact at a local brokerage firm working with high-end estate agencies told Abbey that Magnusson had paid cash at the time.

Normally, money trails led her somewhere, but in this case, there was no bank account data she could follow up on.

There weren't any other titles or deeds with Magnusson's name either, so Abbey had to assume he hadn't owned property before his purchase of the Knightsbridge home.

After a short night, she had gotten up early to search genealogy sites for a history of the Magnusson family. She'd come up with nothing.

It was almost as if Magnusson Senior had been a ghost before 1982.

Out of sheer desperation, Abbey was now following a trail that could only be vaguely referred to as such.

On Magnusson's desk, she had seen pictures of a circus. On one of them, the name had been visible: Ashfield Circus.

The people in the pictures were mainly dressed in costumes, so it was a little difficult to guess the time period.

Abbey had started with the 1950s and was going backward. She was now at the beginning of the nineteenth century, and she kept looking for the name, even though she was pretty certain the photos had been taken later than the Victorian era.

Frustrated, she sat back and closed her eyes.

If the circus had performed in Great Britain at any time, she should have found the name by now. Maybe the photos were staged to look old. Just because they were sepia-colored and people had old-fashioned clothes and hairstyles, that didn't mean the photos had to be historic. She'd searched the internet, of course, and if Ashfield was a contemporary circus, she'd have found it. But there were other possibilities...

During her training as a private investigator, she'd had the warning drilled into her that appearances could be deceiving. A good investigator always looked behind what seemed obvious.

She'd taken the photos at face value, and it had gotten her nowhere. So Abbey tried to think of other possibilities.

The images could have been staged, maybe for a party. Ashfield Circus could be completely fictitious. But they really hadn't looked like the sort of photo booth pictures with fake props that were fashionable at weddings. The clothes hadn't seemed like cheap and cheesy Halloween costumes.

It could have been something a historical society had set up. But Abbey's instincts told her the photos were authentic and really from the past.

She could usually trust her gut.

What else had she been missing, then?

Abbey tried to visualize the pictures again. But she didn't have a photographic memory, and only bits and pieces would come back to her. The small details she'd paid attention to at the time. She wished she could examine the photos in their entirety again. It occurred to her that the pictures themselves only showed parts of the scene. Like a puzzle that only had very few pieces left. She would never know what the complete picture looked like.

Then it hit her.

The name she had read on the photo was Ashfield Circus, and she'd assumed it was complete. What if it was only part of something else, too?

Abbey tried several letters that could have been cut off at the edge of the picture.

Finally, she found it.

Washfield Circus had performed in England and Scotland from the 1920s until the 1960s.

There wasn't a lot of information in the newspapers, but Abbey felt that she'd finally picked up a trail.

She tried books about circuses next. In one of them, she found a poster advertising Washfield Circus for a 1935 performance.

Some of the circus's most popular attractions were featured on the poster.

Abbey shivered when she read the name of one of them.

Magnus the Great.

A magician.

CHAPTER TWENTY

FIONNA

A few days had passed since Fionna's revelation of her big secret.

Andie still seemed in complete disbelief.

"I really don't know why your grandmother would tell you something like that," she kept saying. "But in this case, I have to agree with your mother. It's nonsense. Of course you have a father. Your conception has nothing to do with this disgusting recipe."

But Fionna kept insisting that it wasn't all in her head. "I remember my grandmother talking about some ritual in the basement. And she said exactly those words: The Devil's Child. It cannot be coincidence that there's a recipe called something very similar in the book that she wrote. I know how it sounds. That's why I never told anybody. I tried to repress it. Who wants to deal with the fact that they're the result of a Frankenstein experiment? I don't want to be a monster, believe me. But I've always felt different. I've felt it, Andie! Like my grandma said, I'm unnatural."

No matter what Fionna said, Andie insisted that it simply wasn't possible, particularly after Fionna's gynecologist appointment. "The doctor would have said if there was something visibly different. We'll wait for the test results. But mark my words, there'll be a scientific explanation as to why you haven't gotten your period."

"Maybe." Fionna didn't want to argue anymore. And who knew, there might be a medical reason, too. Deep down, she knew her grandmother had been right, though.

Fionna had moved back home. The few times she'd run into her mother, they'd just pretended the conversation in the stairwell a few nights ago hadn't happened. They'd had years of practice of leaving things unsaid, so they just had to get back into their old habit of living in the same house without talking to each other.

The past few days had been uneventful, almost back to normal, and Fionna didn't trust it.

She was glad when she heard Abbey had returned from London the previous evening. Finally, there were developments in the case.

Rosa was at work, but Fionna preferred to meet with Abbey anywhere other than her house. Who knew what her mother was capable of when it came to sticking her nose into Fionna's business—all in the interest of looking out for her, of course.

Fionna arranged to meet Abbey for breakfast at the B&B.

The private investigator was already waiting for her and waved her over to her table. Abbey's cheeks were flushed, and her brown eyes sparkled with excitement. She seemed almost giddy. Fionna eyed Abbey's coffee cup suspiciously.

"How many of those have you had?"

Abbey smiled. "I'm just high on new information. I have an exciting update."

Dessie came to the table and served them coffee and scones.

155

Fionna didn't want to be impolite, but she was glad when the B&B owner was gone again. "What is it? What did you find out?"

Abbey pulled a folder out of her bag. Inside, there were notes and photocopies. Abbey pulled out a few pages.

"In Magnusson's office, I saw old photos of a circus." She explained how she'd found out more about the Washfield Circus. "I believe his father or grandfather must have worked there. What do you think his act was?"

"I don't know." Fionna shrugged impatiently.

"A magician!"

"Oh. Of course." Fionna thought for a moment. "If there is a magical talent that gets passed down from father to son…a little like our magical gifts…then it would make sense that Magnusson has use for a witch's cookbook. It would also explain Magnus Junior's hypnosis abilities. Maybe magicians are the male counterparts to us witches, and it all works in a similar way. Or are we jumping to conclusions?" She took another long look at the color copy of the poster. "All we have is a name, right? Can we be sure this is Magnusson's ancestor?"

"This is just what got me started," Abbey said, triumph in her voice. "I then found photos of the circus and its employees in a book. There's a picture of Magnus the Great. And he looks an awful lot like Magnusson Senior."

"Really? Show me." Fionna held out her hand for the photocopy.

"Wait. I have to prepare you for something. In the photo, there's a woman next to Magnus the Great. According to the caption, it's his wife and glamorous assistant, Flame Hair Zelda."

"Flame Hair Zelda?"

"Yes. I have to assume it's because of her red hair. The photo is in black and white, of course. But even without seeing the color of her hair…the resemblance is striking."

Abbey held up the copy.

Fionna sucked in a sharp breath. Shocked, she looked up at Abbey, then at the photo again. "That's…that's me."

Abbey smiled. "No. But it looks an awful lot like you. This really is Magnus the Great's wife. Magnusson Senior's mother or grandmother, I assume. The photograph is from the thirties. Fionna, do you know what that means?"

Fionna's eyes had caught a detail on another photograph in the open file folder.

"Fionna?"

She pulled the copy out. "Oh my god!"

Turning the photo around so Abbey could look at it, she said, "Did you see this?"

"Um, that's Magnus the Great again. What—"

"Not him! The woman."

"The woman with the dark hair? What about her?"

"It's Mrs. MacDonald!" Fionna shouted. She caught herself and looked around. But they were alone in the breakfast room.

Abbey bent forward to examine the image more closely. "That can't be."

"It's a younger version of her, I'm sure. I know it's hard to imagine Mrs. MacDonald young, but I saw a picture in her bedroom once. I'm telling you, this is Mrs. M."

Abbey shook her head. "Do the math. She can't be that old."

"Okay then, maybe like with Magnusson, this has to be her mother or grandmother. The resemblance is too strong for this to be a coincidence. Look at the eyes. And the shape of the face. The hairline."

"You're right. Now I see it, too. What can that mean?"

"It must be an ancestor of Mrs. MacDonald's. And Flame Hair Zelda must be an ancestor of my mother."

Abbey stared at her. "Oh. I thought…But…maybe."

"Well, it would explain the connection between Mrs.

157

MacDonald and Magnusson, and why I had the impression my mother knew him. Many years ago, their ancestors worked at a circus. Magnus the Great and Zelda could be my grandmother's parents." Fionna's eyes widened at the thought. "Maybe this is why Magnusson is so interested in the cookbook."

"How could we find out more about this connection?" Abbey asked. "I don't imagine your mother or Mrs. MacDonald would be willing to talk about this to me, do you?"

"Tomorrow, the coven is meeting for a spring equinox ritual. We'll be in the forest until after midnight. I think you should take a look around Mrs. MacDonald's house."

Abbey's eyebrows rose. "You want me to break in?"

"This is a good opportunity. It won't arise again soon. Maybe you'll find more evidence that connects Mrs. MacDonald to Magnusson."

Abbey sighed. "All right. I'll do it."

FIONNA SHIFTED the willow basket to her left arm so she could more easily pick dandelions from the side of the path with her right hand.

She added the dandelions to the other plants in her basket, careful not to crush the crocuses. Then she hurried to catch up with the others.

It was spring equinox, a traditional festival for the Highland witches.

Walking the bounds was one of the customs they upheld. In the past, the coven members would have walked the boundaries of fields and pastures. Nowadays, very few inhabitants of Tarbet lived off the land, so it was more of a symbolic walk.

Every once in a while, Mrs. MacDonald would beat a

boundary marker with her willow wand, muttering some-thing under her breath.

Fionna couldn't hear what she said. The coven upheld a strict hierarchical structure during the walk.

The older witches led the way, Mrs. MacDonald in the front. Next came the younger witches, like Fionna, Andie, and Penny. Their task was to find edible plants like dande-lions and nettles for a spring salad and to gather the first flowers of spring for decorations.

Trailing after them were the children. They were singing songs and dancing.

Right now, there were only three children; the Rivers brood, weather witch Jem Rivers's little sisters.

Fionna had never questioned the way things were done during these sorts of rituals. But a comment from Penny, that the older witches wanted to maintain their position of power and thus took care not to reveal too much knowl-edge to the next generation, had stuck with her.

Now, for example, it struck her as a genius move to have the younger witches occupied with tasks so they strug-gled to keep up and couldn't observe the walking the bounds ritual closely.

After the walk, it was customary to stop at a witch's house for refreshments before they made preparations for the feast.

This year, it was Tara Baird's turn to host. The young witch was about Andie's age and lived on the same street as the MacLeods. Another thing they had in common was that the gift had skipped a generation in both of their families. Neither Tara's mother nor Andie's had a magical talent. Still, they were privy to the secret of the local "women's club" and helped out during such occasions.

Tara's parents had made space in their house and garden for the big group. Fionna suspected that Tara's mother had prepared the refreshments, too, even though it should have been Tara's job.

Andie and Tara had been friends by default when they were younger, but they stopped hanging out so much when they were teenagers. The two of them couldn't have been more different.

Tara was mainly interested in boys, partying, clothes, and make-up. The more earnest and quieter Andie had become friends with Fionna.

Since Penny had also become part of that friendship group, Tara must have felt more and more left out because she'd been trying to push her way into their little clique.

Tara probably thought Jem Rivers was a lost cause. The weather witch worked as a park ranger and was passionate about nature and the environment—something that Tara had absolutely no interest in. Besides, Jem had always been thick as thieves with Petunia "Birdie" Peters.

Tara clearly looked down at Birdie for being so nerdy and unattractive. Birdie did look like a disheveled baby bird fresh out of the nest, which was where she'd gotten her nickname from. The young woman was an easy target for Tara's bitchy gibes.

Jem wasn't the type of friend to stand for something like that.

So if Tara wanted to have friends in the club, Andie, Fionna, and Penny were her only options.

That day, Tara did her usual dance around the three of them, which annoyed Fionna. She wanted to bring the others up to speed on Abbey's investigation, but she couldn't really talk in front of Tara.

Penny noticed Fionna's dilemma. With a mischievous grin, she called over to Tara.

The bubbly blond happily bounded over.

"What's up?"

"You want to know what we're talking about, don't you?"

Tara looked down at the piece of sponge cake in her hand, clearly uncertain how to respond. "Um…I don't really care."

"It's okay. We'll tell you."

"Really?" Hope shone in Tara's eyes.

"Yes."

Fionna jabbed Penny with an elbow. The herb witch whispered. "I want to ask if she knows anything about magicians. What's the harm?"

"Tara? She's bound to gossip about this," Andie put in.

"What am I gossiping about?" Tara asked, who was now right beside them.

"Nothing." Fionna gave her a hard look. "You won't gossip about this if we ask you not to, right? Otherwise, we'll never tell you anything again."

Tara took a bite of her cake. "Sure," she mumbled.

"Let's not make it a big deal," Penny said. "We just wanted to ask if you've ever heard about magicians."

"'Course I have."

Fionna rolled her eyes. "She means in real life. Have you ever encountered…or heard of…a magician? Not someone who does tricks, but, you know, someone like us."

"Oh. Nah. Do they exist?"

"Forget it," Fionna waved it off. "Come on, let's go ask Jem and Birdie," she told the others.

Jem had also never heard of men with magical abilities.

But Birdie at least knew that the Highland witches weren't the only ones in the world.

"There are other people with our abilities. I once heard from my great-grandmother that covens all over Britain meet every thirty years for a big festival."

Birdie pushed her thick glasses up her nose and looked around. In a quieter voice, she continued. "I don't think

161

this is supposed to be common knowledge among all the coven sisters. Or at least we younger ones aren't to be told about it. The older witches must know, if it happens every three decades. My great-grandmother told me all sorts of stuff like that when she got older and confused me with my grandma or my mom." She hesitated. "Hang on, I do remember her saying something about a mage. But she also told me about fairies. I'm not sure what was real and what was a fairy tale, actually. I was quite small."

"It doesn't matter," Fionna said. "Tell us what you remember, anyway."

"Hmm, let's see. In Grammy's stories, mages were like Travellers. They didn't live together in a community like we do. They didn't have any roots. So they traveled. In caravans and so on."

"Highland Travellers. Travelling shows," Fionna said, more to herself, but Birdie nodded. "Exactly. Oh, and in the stories, they weren't ever nice. They were pretty nasty, in fact. Used magic to con people out of their money and stuff."

Fionna pulled a face. "That's what I was afraid of." She sighed. "I don't think it's a fairy tale, Birdie. I think these mages exist. And I think they want to play one of their nasty tricks on us."

CHAPTER TWENTY-ONE

ABBEY

bbey nervously shifted from one leg to the other and pulled the visor of her baseball cap farther down over her face. She had the feeling she was being watched while she waited in front of Mrs. MacDonald's inn, even though not a curtain twitched in any of the windows of the neighboring houses.

She heaved a sigh of relief when she finally saw Penny come around the corner and approach her.

They just nodded at each other and quickly ascended the steps to Mrs. MacDonald's front door.

Penny pulled out a little bag of dried herbs and sprinkled them on the doorstep, muttering a few words. She went to the window and repeated her little ritual.

Abbey was too anxious to be curious about the herb witch's spell. She kept looking around to make sure nobody was watching, but that wasn't what worried her the most. The Thistle Inn was a B&B, and the neighbors had to be used to strangers hanging around the place.

No, Abbey was more concerned with the level of magical alarm system Mrs. MacDonald had installed to keep anyone unwanted from entering her home. There was no guarantee that Penny's spells could counteract that.

Abbey only had Fionna's word that Penny was a capable herb witch.

Oh, and she had the enchanted cloak.

Fionna had given it to Abbey with the promise that it would make her immune to spells and protect her.

Abbey was torn between wishing that it would be a proper invisibility cloak—unfortunately Fionna wasn't that powerful—and doubting that the flimsy thing would work at all.

"All right," Penny said, when they were behind the house and at least out of sight of any potential onlookers. "I'm done. See that window there? That's the bathroom window Andie rigged this morning when she helped Mrs. M. with the preparations for the spring equinox celebration. You should be able to pry it open from the outside. Technically, you can now get in and out wherever you want. If Mrs. MacDonald has any magical alarms, they won't be triggered. I hope. Fingers crossed." Penny smiled confidently, but Abbey's stomach did a nervous flutter.

"You have the cloak and…oh yes, rub oil on your hands before you go in there." Penny handed her a vial. "That way, she won't notice if you touch anything. Questions?"

Abbey tried to remember one of the hundred concerns that had been running through her head since the conception of the plan, concerns that had prevented her from sleeping a wink last night. Before a single question could come to her, though, Penny had already said, "Okay, I've got to run. Good luck."

Abbey followed Penny around the house and down the street. "Um, wait…"

The herb witch turned around and said with a reassuring tone, "You'll be fine. Remember, you have all night.

Don't rush it. If something seems funny to you, observe and reassess. It's going to be all right. I really have to go before someone misses me."

With one last skeptical look at the innocuous-looking house looming above her, Abbey returned to Dessie's B&B.

She passed the time until nightfall with research on Magnusson. But Abbey could hardly concentrate.

She'd never been this nervous doing this sort of thing as a PI for Sly Investigations. But then, none of her previous cases had ever involved the powerful leader of a coven of witches.

When Abbey finally returned to the Thistle Inn after nightfall, she was sick with nerves.

Her heart pounded in her chest as she hurried up the steps and walked around the house. All the windows were dark. The dark woods behind the house would have seemed eerie to anyone else, but Abbey would have preferred to be entering them right now, instead of Mrs. MacDonald's house.

In fact, she would have liked nothing better than to disappear among the trees and get as far away from the witch's property as possible.

Abbey told herself that she was a grown-up and that she had a job to do.

She gathered all her courage and approached the bathroom window. With a little effort, she managed to pry it open.

Pulling herself up and squeezing through the narrow opening was no small feat, but Abbey managed.

She slowly slid through and landed on the toilet. Abbey was about to exhale in relief when a loud tearing sound made her wince.

She paused and tried to listen, even though her own pulse was pounding loudly in her ears. No other sound penetrated. When she slowly tried to move again, she realized she was stuck.

Was she caught in a binding spell that prevented her from entering the house? Panicked, she frantically pulled herself forward, and the same sound as before, only louder, rang out again. But she had managed to move, ending up in an awkward position on the bathroom floor.

After catching her breath, Abbey rolled her eyes at her own stupidity. She knew now what the sound had been. Her cloak had caught on the window frame. She'd torn it, and then made it much worse by throwing herself forward in a panic.

She struggled to her feet and pulled the cloak around so she could survey the damage. There was a long rip almost through the entire length of it. It was probably useless now.

"Great job, Fine," she muttered to herself. Abbey decided to keep the cloak on, just in case.

Then she took out her flashlight, careful to keep the beam of light directed at the floor, and slowly opened the bathroom door.

The house was dead silent.

According to what Abbey remembered from her previous visit, she was in the front hallway. There was the front door and two other doors. According to Fionna, they led to the guest rooms.

Abbey ignored those for now and went into the kitchen.

It didn't seem anywhere near as disgusting and dingy as it had when she was here with Magnus. Maybe Mrs. MacDonald had just cleaned—it seemed like the right thing to do around spring equinox.

It was now an ordinary kitchen, and Abbey was tempted to start with this non-threatening room.

Instead, she forced herself to go through the other

kitchen door into the second small hallway. There were two doors. One led to the living room.

Abbey slowly pushed open the other door, the one that was supposed to lead to Mrs. MacDonald's bedroom, according to Fionna.

The hinges creaked, almost giving Abbey a heart attack.

"Get a grip," she told herself. "It's just a house. The house of a witch, yes. But really, just a house."

Her hand trembled as she shone the flashlight around the room.

There was a large loom with colored threads interwoven with ribbons in every hue.

Windowsill and dresser were littered with candles, oil lamps, and crystals.

That was the only indication that this was a witch's bedroom. Everything else seemed downright austere, especially the old-fashioned wooden box bed.

Abbey told herself the reason that she wasn't rifling through any drawers yet was that she wanted to search the room systematically. In truth, she was a little scared of what she would find.

There were a few framed photographs on the whitewashed walls. Abbey took them down to remove them from their frames.

The most interesting to her was the sepia picture of a young woman with dark curls. It was the same woman Fionna had discovered in the circus photo with Magnus the Great and his wife, Zelda. It looked like a young Mrs. MacDonald. But it could also be her mother, grandmother, or another female relative.

There was nothing written on the back of the picture, not even a date. There was also no stamp or sticker from a photographic studio, as was often the case with portraits from an older time period.

An old photo of Mrs. MacDonald's house was equally blank on the back.

Then there was another picture that hung next to a painting with an aerial view of Loch Lomond.

It was a group portrait of the Tarbet coven. Abbey recognized younger versions of Andie, Fionna, and Penny. She guessed the photo was only a few years old. She didn't bother to take that one out of the frame.

But she checked the other two framed photographs. There were people in very old-fashioned-looking clothing in them. Again, nothing on the back.

Abbey took pictures of all the images in the room with her phone.

Next, she dared to open the closet.

There was a row of the type of dresses she had seen Mrs. MacDonald wear. Black, baggy, with layers of heavy fabric.

The closet reeked of mothballs…and something else Abbey couldn't immediately bring to mind. Maybe camphor? Whatever it was, it gave her a headache.

Impatiently, she pushed the dresses to one side and discovered a whole second row of clothes behind them. These dresses were old fashioned but not quite as tragic as the front-row ones.

The closet was much deeper than it appeared from the outside; it had to extend into the wall or something.

It made Abbey think that there could be further hidden compartments. She tapped the walls on the inside of the closet, but there were no hollow sounds.

Disappointed, she straightened the clothes. That's when she discovered that they were all from different eras. Even though Abbey knew little about fashion, these clothes didn't seem like cheap costumes. One of the dresses, in midnight blue velvet with a beaded bodice, was downright stunning. Abbey could imagine Scarlet O'Hara in that thing, but not Mrs. MacDonald.

The young woman in the photograph came to her mind. Maybe she had worn this dress.

Abbey was about to close the closet door when her eyes fell on the hat rack. It was quite high up. The small, frail-looking Mrs. MacDonald wouldn't be able to reach up there, and the hats looked dusty.

In order to be thorough, Abbey grabbed the stool from in front of the loom and climbed up to see the back of the hat rack.

She discovered two hat boxes and took them down.

Abbey coughed when the dust swirled into the air.

One box contained a velvet top-hat.

With the other, Abbey finally hit pay dirt.

It was filled with the hodgepodge assortment of things people kept as mementos.

Abbey's heart beat faster as she carefully spread the contents on the bed.

She took photos of all the items individually. There was a snow globe with the Tower of London inside, a gold pendant, and three rings with Gaelic engravings.

Next came a bunch of postcards, all from British seaside resorts. The squiggly writing on the back was so faded that it was almost impossible to decipher.

At the bottom, Abbey found a small illustrated book on Scottish plants. It seemed very old. And then there was what looked to Abbey like an old autograph book. The small volume featured poems and well-wishes from various people as well as pasted-in pictures of flowers and little drawings.

Abbey quickly took pictures of a couple of pages with her phone but then moved on to the stack of photographs.

Some were black and white, others in color. Abbey identified fashions and hairstyles from various distinct eras.

Buildings and vehicles also gave her clues as to what decades the photos might be from.

There was only one common denominator in most of the pictures.

The dark-haired young woman was in them—the same woman Fionna had spotted in the photo with Magnus the Great, and the same woman who was in the portrait on the wall.

At least, it looked as if it was always the same woman, in all the pictures from the turn of the century to the 1980s.

The only logical explanation was that Mrs. MacDonald's female ancestors all looked very much alike.

Abbey's heart stopped for a moment when she turned over the next photo.

She stared at it, trying to find a logical explanation for what she was seeing.

She couldn't come up with one.

CHAPTER TWENTY-TWO

FIONNA

Penny's absence went unnoticed, and she was back before the coven set off to Cruach Tairbeirt. Compared to the mountains surrounding Loch Lomond, Cruach Tairbeirt was a mere hill, but it was a special place to the Tarbet coven. The spring equinox festival was traditionally held there.

The witches hiked up the trail through Argyll National Forest. After passing through the dense forest, the climb got steep quickly.

Fionna, who carried a heavy load, just like most of the others, began to perspire. Her breathing became heavy. But she wasn't the only one, and the chatter that had accompanied the hike so far now died down.

They all stopped and rested for a moment at an outlook. Fionna soon breathed easily again and enjoyed the view of Loch Lomond between the conifers. They didn't linger long. Onward they went for the last stretch of the hike.

Mrs. MacDonald, Rosa, and two other witches of the older generation had set off earlier to take their time with the climb. The advance party had already been busy building the fire and preparing everything for the rabbit stew they would serve later.

Relieved to have finally arrived, Fionna set her backpack down next to the white stone that marked the summit. She looked around.

It was a clear, sunny day, and from up here they had a magnificent view of the lochs and mountains.

Fionna could easily identify the Cobbler by its shape: a cobbler bending over his last. She also recognized Beinn Narnain. On one side, she could make out Loch Long, and behind it the Firth of Clyde. On the other side was Loch Lomond, with Ben Lomond towering above it.

Fionna looked forward to the sunset, expecting it to be spectacular in this weather.

A few of the women were already busy preparing the feast with everything they had brought in their backpacks. Fionna quickly joined them.

Before they sat down to eat, however, it was time for an ancient pagan ritual that was nowadays integrated into modern Easter traditions: they exchanged colored eggs.

After everyone had marked their egg with their initials, they bowled them down a heather-covered slope. The owner of the egg that rolled the farthest had the honor of distributing the bowls of spring flowers in a circle on the summit.

A small jug of heather honey was placed next to each bowl. It was food for the fairies. Fionna had never thought about this tradition much, but now she knew that the custom was more than a symbolic gesture. She shivered and looked around furtively. It was a bit creepy to think that those little invisible creatures might be hanging about, watching them all the time.

Then it was finally time for the feast.

Fionna was starving and happily tucked into the rabbit stew, spring salad, and small cakes shaped like mountain hares. She also enjoyed the honey wine, a version of mead the witches brewed themselves.

After sunset, the women were supposed to put on their hooded cloaks and perform the spring equinox ritual around the fire. They would stay here until sunrise, until the fire went out.

But it didn't look as if that was going to happen this year.

It was Rosa who noticed the group ascending the hill first. "Be quiet. There are people coming."

Soon everyone saw the flashlight beams dancing. Fionna held a hand over her eyes so she wouldn't be blinded. It was hard to make out faces.

They were already pretty close when Fionna realized the group was led by a very gung-ho-looking Sally. The waitress from The Kirk—what was she doing here?

A few villagers were accompanying her. Fionna almost had a heart attack when she recognized the mayor, Chief Inspector Declan Reid, and Drew!

Fionna was still searching for a logical explanation as to why this group had decided to climb Cruach Tairbeirt together, tonight of all nights, when Sally's screeching voice sounded through the darkness.

"There they are. Witches! All of them, witches! I told you."

Fionna flinched. She looked around and saw some worried faces. She just hoped everyone could hold it together.

When she turned her attention to the mob again, she was a little reassured.

The mayor—a very sensible man—looked sheepishly at the ground. Declan, who was Penny's brother and knew about the coven, had established eye contact with his sister, slowly shaking his head. Most of the others—curious villagers, most likely—had their eyes trained on Sally.

173

The usually shy and unremarkable young woman was unrecognizable. Her eyes were ablaze with a passion Fionna had never seen in her. And she had managed to stir up a couple of her followers. They raised their fists and shouted "Heathens" and "Witches."

"They're witches, and this is where they perform their satanic rituals," Sally exclaimed. "I've heard them talk about it. I've seen them cast spells. You didn't believe me, but now we have proof!"

Mrs. MacDonald stepped forward. Her walking stick wobbled, and she suddenly looked a lot frailer than she had all evening.

"What are you talking about, Sally?" she asked in an appeasing tone. "You all know we uphold old Highland traditions. I'm sure some of you saw us walking the bounds today. We do it every year. It's no secret. And this festival, too. You know that, Craig. After all, we obtained the permit from you, as usual."

The mayor squirmed under her look.

"Well, yes, the traditions are pagan, if you want to call it that," Mrs. MacDonald went on. But to call us witches? I think you're overreacting a little, Sally."

"You are witches!" Sally cried, even more hysterical. "I saw what they did." She waved the beam of the flashlight in the direction of Fionna, Andie, and Penny. "At The Kirk. They were talking about their devilish activities. Fionna cast a spell on the guests, and they were frozen for hours, couldn't move an inch. And it wasn't just the guests. There was Milton, the health and safety inspector, and Drew. Drew, you were there. Tell them!"

Fionna had the strong urge to hide somewhere. But of course she stood rooted in place. With a pounding heart, she forced herself to look at Drew.

"Sally…I told you, I have a different memory of that evening. Nobody talked about…witches or magic. Or

Satan. There were no…spells. You got dizzy, and you laid down. Maybe you were dreaming this."

Fionna exhaled slowly. Apparently, Magnusson really had erased Drew's recollection of that evening. Even if he'd implanted a new fake memory of a kiss.

But he didn't seem to have upheld his side of the deal in Sally's case. Had he done that intentionally, in order to get the witches into trouble? Or had he been too drained from hypnotizing all the others that he hadn't been successful in Sally's case?

Fionna's knees went weak with relief when Drew continued. "Milton said the same thing, Sally. And your other so-called witnesses didn't know what you were talking about, either. Don't you think that at least one of us would have remembered something like that happening?"

"Because there was a man…a man who made you forget. Now you have the proof." Sally gestured at the witches. "They're performing a pagan ritual, worshipping Satan."

Sally had a wild look in her eyes. Fionna didn't even recognize her colleague anymore. What had Magnusson done to her?

"Worshipping Satan?" Mrs. MacDonald asked calmly, without any mocking undertones. It made her response even more effective in making Sally sound ridiculous. "We aren't doing anything like that. Please, feel free to have a look around. We're celebrating spring equinox, eating and drinking. It couldn't be more harmless. Please, Declan, Craig. You know all of us. We're a small community. We have nothing to hide."

The mayor finally stepped forward. "Of course, Mary. We know that." The mob behind him had gone quiet. Nobody shouted "witches" anymore. "Sally here insisted, and since she wouldn't calm down, we agreed to come up here…" He broke off. "Please, go on with your little celebration. I'm sorry we bothered you. Come on folks, let's leave."

Most of the group turned around, but some stayed when Sally shouted. "Wait, no!"

They had probably expected more for their trouble of hiking up the hill and weren't ready to give up just yet.

Fionna and the others followed Mrs. MacDonald's lead and continued to eat and drink and talk as if nothing had happened. Soon, every one of the villagers had departed. Only Sally still stood there, eyes blazing, shouting insults.

In the end, she didn't seem comfortable being by herself in the coven's company.

"I'll prove it," she yelled before she left. "I'll make sure you witches burn on the pyre."

Mrs. MacDonald didn't make a move to carry on with the ritual. She acted perfectly calm, but Fionna knew appearances were deceiving. She hardly dared look up as she pretended to drink her cup of mead. Some of the other witches carried on with what seemed like forced conversation. The tension was palpable. When the last of the cakes had been eaten, Mrs. MacDonald got up.

"Unfortunately, we won't be able to finish the ritual. It's too risky." After a brief pause, she continued. "Needless to say, I'm not happy about this. There will be consequences for those responsible."

Fionna kept her eyes trained on the ground. Thankfully, it was too dark for anyone to notice how red her face was.

She helped pack everything up, carefully avoiding Mrs. MacDonald and Rosa.

On her way back to Tarbet, Fionna mulled over what Magnusson's goal had been in making Sally a crazed witch-hunter. Had it been a spur-of-the-moment thing with the intention of stirring up whatever kind of trouble he could?

Or did Magnusson have a plan?

Surely, he would have known that the craft and knitting club had a long-standing reputation in the community. And Mrs. MacDonald, too. He must have realized that it wouldn't do her much harm to have one hysterical person accuse her of being a witch.

But Mrs. MacDonald and the older witches would hear about what Fionna, Andie, and Penny had done in The Kirk. If Magnusson had intended to drive a wedge between the young witches and the leaders of the coven, he had certainly succeeded.

It was particularly annoying because Fionna had been willing to pay a high price to hide what she had done from Mrs. MacDonald, namely involving Magnusson.

Fionna had almost reached Tarbet when she remembered something else. She had been so worried about what Sally's accusations meant for her and what they revealed about Magnusson that she had completely forgotten Abbey.

Abbey was in Mrs. MacDonald's house, under the impression that she had all night to search it.

But it wasn't even midnight, and Mrs. MacDonald would be home any minute now.

Fionna tried to reach Abbey by phone, but the call went straight to voicemail.

She furtively sent her a text message while she tried to keep up with the others and not stumble on the forest path in the dark.

Abbey didn't answer.

CHAPTER TWENTY-THREE

ABBEY

The photo Abbey held showed Magnus the Great and the woman who looked so much like Fionna, the magician's wife, Flame Hair Zelda.

It resembled the picture Abbey had found in the book from the British Library, and she assumed it had to be from the same time. In fact, it might have been from the same photo session.

Only in this picture, Mrs. MacDonald didn't look like a young woman at all. She was older. Not quite as old as the Mrs. MacDonald of Abbey's own time, but close to it. And it was definitely her.

Abbey told herself that it couldn't be the present coven leader, no matter what it looked like. Mrs. MacDonald couldn't be in a photograph from the 1930s, especially not looking the same age she did today. It had to be an ancestor. Just like in the case of Flame Hair Zelda and Fionna.

But her whole body was tingling, and a voice inside her head told her she was deluding herself. The goose bumps wouldn't go away, even after she put the photo back in the box.

Distracted, she looked through the rest of the photos.

She didn't find anything else interesting, and she didn't find the cookbook, either.

After putting everything back the way she'd found it, Abbey left the bedroom to have a look around in the living room, but it was pretty bare. There was an old wing chair facing the TV and several bookshelves.

There were no pictures on the walls. Abbey tapped until her knuckles were raw, but there didn't seem to be any hidden closets in the wall or other places where Mrs. MacDonald could have hidden the cookbook, or anything else revelatory.

Next, she checked out all the books. No tomes on witchcraft or the cookbook. Abbey even checked to see if innocuous-looking dust jackets were hiding something more interesting.

Frustrated, Abbey surveyed the room one more time, then pulled out her phone to check the time. Her phone was turned off—maybe it had happened accidentally when she'd crawled through the bathroom window.

Abbey turned it back on and winced when she saw Fionna's missed call. She checked her text messages, and her heart started racing.

It had been half an hour since Fionna had sent the warning that Mrs. MacDonald would be home any minute.

She had to get out of the house right now!

Abbey quickly headed for the bathroom window. That way, she was sure not to trigger any magical alarm. It would be easier to get through from the inside, as she just had to climb onto the toilet. And she would come out behind the house and could slink off via the footpath that led along the edge of the forest to the train station. If Mrs. MacDonald arrived on the street in front of the house, she wouldn't see Abbey.

She started to dart through the kitchen, but the beam

of the flashlight hit the kitchen table, and Abbey stopped in her tracks.

She was pretty certain the table had been empty earlier, when she'd passed the kitchen on her way to the bedroom.

Hadn't it struck her how ordinary the kitchen looked?

Now, a deck of large cards was spread out on the surface of the table.

Abbey lifted her gaze and looked around.

She was definitely alone in the kitchen.

It was dark, and it was quiet.

She forced herself to calm down so her heavy breathing and the blood rushing in her ears wouldn't drown everything else out.

As if the cards drew her to them, Abbey slowly approached the kitchen table.

It looked as if someone had just carelessly thrown a stack of cards face down on the table.

Abbey switched the flashlight to her left hand and stretched out her right to turn a card over.

The cards weren't ordinary playing cards but had colorful pictures on them. They were worn and yellowed, as if they were ancient.

Abbey's eyes widened when she understood she was holding a tarot card.

The image showed a young man with a crown on his head on top of a horse-drawn racing cart. It reminded her of Greek mythology illustrations or that old Ben Hur movie.

"The Wagon," a voice said behind her.

Abbey dropped the card.

Her heart skipped a few beats, and she didn't dare breathe as she slowly turned around.

A figure stood in the doorway to the kitchen.

With a shaking hand, Abbey lifted the flashlight.

It was a petite woman.

"Interesting. It represents success in your chosen career."

The woman didn't have Mrs. MacDonald's raspy voice. She sounded younger.

Abbey held the hand with the flashlight a little steadier. The woman looked more youthful, too. She held up her hand to shield her eyes from the blinding beam, but Abbey could make out that she had dark curly hair.

"It's not surprising, considering you seem to go the extra mile to solve the case. Who are you working for now? Fionna or Magnusson? Who will you give the cookbook to? Oh, but you didn't find it, did you?"

Abbey swallowed. Then she moved the flashlight beam a little to the right.

There was a light switch next to the door frame, just as she'd hoped.

Determined, she took two steps toward it and flipped the switch.

Abbey now stood right in front of the young woman, who had dropped her hand.

It was the face from the photo on Mrs. MacDonald's bedroom wall. The same one Abbey had seen in the picture of Magnus the Great inside the British Library book and in the photos in the hatbox.

It was the woman who looked so very much like a youthful version of Mrs. MacDonald.

"What are you doing here?" Abbey spoke aloud the first question that popped into her head.

The woman's lips quirked into a smile.

"I live here."

CHAPTER TWENTY-FOUR

FIONNA

Fionna waved to Andie sitting in the waiting area of the doctor's office as she made a follow-up appointment at the reception desk.

She slipped into her jacket while Andie got up from her seat.

"And?" Andie asked, as she held the door open for her friend. But Fionna waited to answer until they were down the flight of stairs and outside on the street.

"Okay, so what I have is called amenorrhea. It's not that rare, actually. In my case, the cause is a thyroid problem. The tests results were quite clear."

"There you go." Andie seemed relieved. "I told you there would be a rational explanation."

"The doctor scolded me for waiting so long to have it checked out. The thyroid problem has other consequences for my health. He prescribed me pills I have to take to restore my hormone balance. The doctor also mentioned…" She hesitated, stuffing her fists deeper into her jacket pockets. "He said that what I have might be hereditary. He asked if any of my family members had similar diagnoses. I told him I only know about my mother's side, and nobody had anything like it as far as I'm aware. After admitting that I don't know who my father is, the doctor advised me to have genetic testing done. They would check for certain genetic markers, whatever that might mean. Hey, there's a pharmacy." Fionna pointed at the building across the busy Glasgow street.

Andie nodded, crossed the road with Fionna, and waited outside while Fionna had her prescription filled.

On their way back to the car, Andie said. "As you know, I've had a genetic profile done."

Fionna nodded. "When you did an internship at the genetics lab?"

"Yes. I'd be really interested to find out if there is anything in our genetic make-up that differentiates us from normal people."

Fionna scrunched her nose. "You mean like a witch gene?"

"Kind of. That's what got me interested in studying biotechnology and genetics in the first place. Anyway, my profile is pretty useless on its own. None of you wanted to get tested. But if you did, we could compare and see if anything similar stands out."

"Don't you think that's a bit…creepy? What's the point? So you can single out the gene and then create magically gifted children in the lab?"

Andie remained calm. "Of course not. But knowledge is power. That's what science is all about. Who knows when it might come in handy to have a scientific explanation for our gift, instead of shrouding it in superstitious secrecy? Oh, wait—it would have already come in handy, many years ago, when witches were persecuted because of super-stition."

"All right, all right, you have a point," Fionna grumbled.

"Anyway, I have a good relationship with the company

I did my internship with. We can go there right now and do a simple test. It's just a buccal swab, and it doesn't even hurt. You can also do an ancestry test. It's not going to tell you who your father is, but it might provide some answers."

When Fionna didn't reply, Andie continued. "Comparing your test results with mine could give you peace of mind. It would show you that you're not that different from me."

Fionna's heart beat faster, and her palms got sweaty. She really didn't want to do this. She was scared the results would prove the complete opposite.

But she had to get over that fear.

Andie was right. This was an excellent opportunity to get answers to her questions.

Fionna had hidden from the truth about what she was and where she came from for far too long.

Where had it gotten her? It had turned her into a timid, insecure, antisocial person.

She didn't want to live that life anymore.

Besides, Magnusson and his son weren't going to just go away.

Fionna needed to arm herself with something, and Andie was also right when she said that knowledge was power.

It was high time Fionna faced this.

"Okay," she said with a shaky voice. "I'll do it."

CHAPTER TWENTY-FIVE

ABBEY

"**D**o you know Maryanna? The young woman who lives at Mrs. MacDonald's?" Abbey asked and set her cup of coffee down.

She'd met the young witches at Penny Reid's house, an old, picturesque cottage between Tarbet and Arrochar, to discuss the previous night's events.

Fionna drew her brows together. "What do you mean? Is she a guest at the Thistle Inn?" She clapped her hand over her mouth. "Oh my god, is someone staying there? We didn't even consider that. Mrs. M.'s rooms are so rarely occupied…"

"No, she isn't a tourist. She must be related to Mrs. MacDonald. A granddaughter maybe? Or a great-niece? Something like that."

Andie, Penny, and Fionna exchanged worried glances.

"She looks just like the young woman in the circus photo," Abbey explained. "And in the photo in Mrs. MacDonald's bedroom. You thought it was a young Mrs. MacDonald, but it could easily be a relative. The women in Mrs. MacDonald's family must look very much alike. That also explains why I saw her in pictures from different eras. It isn't her, but different relatives. Like that Maryanna."

Penny shook her head. "Mrs. M. doesn't have a grand-daughter, or a great-niece, or anything like that. We surely would have heard of her."

"Yes," Fionna agreed. "Especially considering that magical gifts run in the family, and Mrs. MacDonald is a powerful witch. Any female relatives of hers would have been at coven meetings at some point."

Abbey shrugged. "I don't know what to tell you. You said this magical talent can skip a generation, didn't you? Maybe that's the case with Maryanna. Or Mrs. MacDonald fell out with her family and didn't have much contact apart from the pictures. Happens all the time. All I know is that Maryanna caught me in the Thistle Inn yesterday. I accidentally turned my phone off, and when I saw your text was half an hour old, Fionna, I bolted out of there. Suddenly she was standing at the entrance to the kitchen."

Andie sucked in a sharp breath. "Oh my god, it must have scared you half to death. She must have come from one of the guest rooms. That's weird. When we got stuff for the spring equinox ritual out of Mrs. MacDonald's house, the doors to the guest rooms were open. They looked unoccupied."

"I could have sworn there was no one in the house when I did my spells," Penny said.

"Well, it didn't seem to me as if someone was there when I got in through the bathroom. The windows were dark. Maryanna must have been out and came in later, when I was busy searching Mrs. MacDonald's living room. It was all a bit strange."

Abbey told them about the tarot cards on the table.

"It didn't surprise Maryanna to see me. I mean, she didn't act like a person would who'd just caught a burglar in their home. And she knew everything. About the cookbook. That I work for you. She even knew Magnusson Senior had hired me. She called me a double agent and asked if I'd hand the cookbook over to you or him."

Fionna got up and paced the kitchen. "I don't like this one bit. Are you even sure this woman resembled Mrs. MacDonald? You said it was dark. It could have been someone else. A person hired by Magnusson, maybe?"

"No, no, I switched on the light. I got a good look at her. She must have been a relative of Mrs. MacDonald." Abbey broke off. "Although… It doesn't mean she couldn't be connected to Magnusson. I'd already had a strong feeling that Mrs. MacDonald knew Magnusson, remember? When I was at the awkward meeting with Magnus Junior at her house? It isn't too far-fetched to think that her whole family might have a connection to Magnusson's family. Maybe from the time some of them were in that circus together." She told them about the photos she'd seen in Mrs. MacDonald's hat box.

"Did you take pictures on your phone?" Penny asked. "I'd love to see some of them."

Abbey sighed. "I did. But unfortunately, Maryanna took care of that before she let me go."

Fionna stopped pacing. "What do you mean?"

"I had to empty my pockets, and then she asked for my phone. She deleted all the pictures, even from the cloud."

"And you let her?" Penny asked incredulously.

"What would you have done? I was just glad she didn't call the police. When she told me I could go, I just high-tailed it out of there."

Penny got up to refill their coffee cups, even though Fionna's was still full. The red-haired witch was clearly much too agitated to drink it.

"Don't you think her reaction was strange?" Penny asked everyone. "I mean, aside from the fact that

Maryanna knew all about the cookbook and Abbey's case. Whoever this chick is, she should have been more ruffled about Abbey breaking in and searching the house, right?"

Fionna agreed. "Yes, it would have made sense for Maryanna to detain Abbey until Mrs. MacDonald got there. If this was half an hour after my text, she couldn't have been far away. In fact," she scrunched up her face, "I only sent that text as we were exiting the forest. Mrs. MacDonald should have been home already."

"Maryanna might not have known the ritual was canceled," Andie put in. "She might have expected Mrs. MacDonald to be gone until the next morning. And considering what this is all about, it isn't surprising that she didn't call the police. Although that would mean this Maryanna knows all about us."

"I told you, she's definitely in the know," Abbey said. "So what happened? Why was the ritual canceled?"

The three witches explained what had occurred the previous evening and why they hadn't spent the entire night on Cruach Tairbeirt as planned.

"That sounds really scary," Abbey said, eyes wide. "If the mob would have had torches instead of flashlights, it could have been a scene from a movie about a medieval witch hunt. Lucky that Sally seemed so fanatic that nobody believed her. Do you think she'll let it go now?"

"She didn't sound like it," Fionna said, clearly worried.

"People won't believe her." Penny waved it off. "You have to remember that our little women's club has been an institution in Tarbet for ages. We've been commended for upholding Highland traditions. Do some of the villagers have an inkling we're doing more than just knitting and crafting? Maybe. But remember where we are. People here are proud of their pagan roots. A certain degree of super-stition isn't uncommon here, in the Highlands, even today. Especially with the older generation. Besides, many of the older witches are also active in the community, like in the church or other clubs. We're too much a part of this community for someone like Sally to do any actual damage. If she'd tried to expose what we were actually doing…but she was talking about satanic rites. It was really over the top. I don't think anyone believed her."

"That doesn't mean there won't be any consequences for us, though," Andie interjected. "We're supposed to keep our activities a secret, and what we did in The Kirk was anything but discreet. Now Mrs. MacDonald knows what happened. Worse, the spring equinox ritual couldn't be performed because of it. I mean, maybe she did some rites herself, to make up for it. That could be the reason she didn't go straight home like the rest of us. But she is going to hold us accountable."

Fionna agreed. "I'm glad I was out of town today for my doctor's appointment, but I've been waiting to be summoned. It's so nerve-racking. I kind of wish it would be done with and over already. And tonight I have to face Drew and Sally at the restaurant. My life well and truly sucks."

Penny got up and steered Fionna to the table. "Here, sit down. I'm going to make you an herbal tea, and you'll drink it. It's for calming your nerves."

"I'm sorry," Abbey said. She felt like she had failed. "If last night's disaster would have at least been productive, if I had found out anything tangible, or even found the cook-book, then it might make up for it."

"But you're not going to give up, are you?" Fionna looked at her with hope in her eyes. "Don't leave me hanging now."

"Give up? Me?" Abbey shook her head. "No, I'm going to find out something. At the very least, I'll figure out who this Maryanna is. It must be possible. She's a person made of flesh and blood, not just someone in a picture.

Don't worry, Fionna," she added with a lot more confidence than she felt. "We'll figure this out."

WHEN ABBEY RETURNED to Dessie's B&B, she was racking her brain about how to proceed with her investigation.

Unlocking the door to her room and pushing it open, she was suddenly shocked out of her thoughts.

A person was sitting on a chair facing the door.

"Hello, Abbey," Magnus Junior said.

"What are you doing here?" Abbey did her best to make her voice sound icy, but it came out a little shaky. She left the door wide open and stepped aside. "You broke into my room? Leave now, or I'll call the police."

Magnus brought his fingertips together and pulled his lips up into his trademark predatory grin.

It should have looked comical, but Abbey's stomach lurched.

"You think you're so smart, don't you?" he said. "Not taking my calls, not returning my messages…I couldn't make heads or tails out of why you were ghosting me. Then I find out that you had a meeting with my father. Our date was just a ruse to find out information about my dear pater, wasn't it?"

Abbey didn't reply. Instead, she pulled her phone out of her pocket. She didn't want to just dial the emergency number, so she called Dessie instead. Hopefully, the B&B owner was close by and could contact her boyfriend, the chief of police, directly.

"You've made a big mistake, sweetheart," Magnus continued, undeterred. "My father is out of your league. Do you really believe he would entrust this case to you? A rookie? Someone who has just been fired from her job for being completely incompetent? You're so naive. My father only pumped you for information. Now he knows all about Fionna."

Dessie picked up.

"Hey, this is Abbey. Magnusson broke into my room. Can you come quickly and inform the police?"

Magnus got up, mumbled a few words, and gestured with his hands. Abbey's phone flew out of her hands.

"Those pathetic, good-for-nothing witches." Magnusson's expression was pure hate. "We don't need them. We're better than them. I don't know why my father wants anything to do with them, but he'll regret it."

Magnusson's face was now inches away from Abbey, who'd backed into the wall.

Abbey tried hard not to flinch or break eye contact. She didn't want to seem afraid.

"And those wannabes will regret ever getting involved with my family, especially that red-haired witch with a 'b.' I'll make sure of it."

Abbey almost sank to the floor in relief when she heard footsteps in the hallway.

Magnusson took a step back but still fixed her with his vicious glare.

"What's going on?" It was Dessie.

"When I unlocked my room, Magnusson was sitting there." Abbey pointed at the chair.

Dessie addressed Magnus with a frown. "You have no business being in here, or even in the B&B. You checked out days ago. What did you do, steal my keys and have copies made?" She didn't give Magnus time to reply. "You know what? You can explain all that to my partner, who'll be here any minute to arrest you."

Magnusson just grinned and made a sweeping gesture with his hand.

Thick smoke came out of nowhere. It completely enveloped him.

Abbey and Dessie started coughing and waving the smoke away with their hands.

But the smoke cleared as quickly as it had come.

Magnusson was no longer in front of them. It was like he had disappeared into thin air.

Dessie and Abbey looked at each other with wide eyes.

Abbey shook her head. "That must have been a trick. He's a magician. They distract, so people can't see what they're really doing, and then it seems like magic."

Even if Abbey couldn't quite convince herself, the explanation seemed good enough for Dessie.

"I'm so sorry this happened, Abbey. I'll have the locks changed. Declan will be here any minute. As soon as Magnusson shows his face in Tarbet again, he'll be arrested. Declan will make sure of it."

"It's not your fault. I don't think conventional methods will stop Magnus. Anyway, I'm not too worried about him trying this again. He's mad at me, that's for sure. But his deepest hostility is reserved for the witches, especially Fionna. I'm not sure why that is. All I know is, in his rage, Magnus showed his true colors. He's consumed with hate. I'm scared for Fionna."

CHAPTER TWENTY-SIX

FIONNA

Fionna had just put her coat on, leaving it to the last minute to set off for work. She really didn't want to face Sally and Drew after what had happened on Cruach Tairbeirt. They were bound to ask her questions she didn't know how to answer. Even if Drew didn't believe Sally, he had to be curious about the women's club, and he would surely want to talk about the entire episode. Fionna didn't trust herself to keep her cool, especially not around Drew.

When the doorbell rang, Fionna caught herself wishing it would be an emergency that would prevent her from going to work.

The saying "be careful what you wish for" popped into her head just as she opened the door.

She looked into the bright blue eyes of an older gentleman. He had a head full of white hair, but that didn't detract from his handsome face. There was also something vaguely familiar about him.

"Hello, can I help you?" Fionna asked.

A smile spread across the man's face, lighting up his eyes. "Fionna!"

"Do we know each other?" She shifted her weight from one foot to the other.

"Not personally, but I know your mother."

"Oh. Okay." Fionna looked over her shoulder. "Mom! There's someone at the door for you." She looked back at the gentleman with uncertainty. "Um. Well, come in."

He confidently stepped in. By the time Fionna had closed the door, he was already heading straight for the kitchen. Her mother was nowhere in sight. "Uh, wait—" She hurried after him. "Mom!" she yelled.

She heard a thump and a clang. When Fionna rushed into the kitchen after the self-assertive visitor, her mother stood next to an overturned chair, a broken mug on the floor in front of her.

Rosa seemed frozen, and fear shone from her eyes.

Fionna looked at the visitor, and it suddenly became very clear to her who he was.

"Leave my mom alone!"

Magnus Magnusson, Sr., just shook his head and said calmly, "I'm not doing anything, Fionna."

"You have her in some sort of binding spell, and I want you to release her right now, or—"

"I don't. She's frozen in fear. No magic required."

Fionna walked up to Rosa. "Mom? Are you okay?"

Rosa's mouth opened and closed, but no words came out. Then she nodded slowly.

"She's paralyzed by guilt." Magnusson sounded cold. "Your mother knows what she has done. She must be aware of the consequences, must know me well enough not to expect me to be lenient. That's why she's scared to death right now. As she should be."

Fionna's throat was dry. She swallowed and put her hand on Rosa's arm. "It's okay, Mom. I'm here. Whatever you did, I'm here. I can help. Don't give him the power."

194

Magnusson laughed. "How sweet. You two must be very close, huh? A regular mother-and-daughter team."

Rosa seemed to have recovered enough to talk, even though her voice sounded brittle. "It's not what you think, Magnus. No, I haven't been honest with you. I've kept Fionna from you. But it's not like I took anything away from you." She took a deep breath, regaining her composure. She looked like the confident Rosa Fionna had always known. "We didn't succeed, Magnus. All we created was…" She looked at Fionna with a mix of disdain and disappointment. "A failure."

Magnusson stepped between the two witches. "I don't think so. Maybe you believe that now, but when you reneged on our deal, you had other expectations of what would become of her, and you knew full well what you were doing. And you're wrong, anyway. That makes it so much worse, dear Rosa," he said with venom. "Because you gave up on her when she could have become all that we hoped for."

Fionna's gaze darted between them in confusion. "What are you—"

Her mother's laugh cut her off. "You actually believe that, Magnus? Then you're blinded by ambition, as usual. I know my daughter. She is nothing. Nowhere near what we expected her to be. Any regular mother would be disappointed in her, let alone—"

"You fool!" Magnusson's voice thundered through the kitchen. "You wouldn't know a magical wonder if it hit you on the nose. You don't have the aptitude. All you have is arrogance, and that's why it is you who failed your daughter. I, on the other hand, have not given up. I have continued with experiments, and I've become an expert. I've developed a nose for this. I can smell it." His nostrils flared as he stepped closer to Fionna. "She is all we wanted to create and more."

Rosa just laughed again. She no longer seemed scared at all. "Really, Magnus, I swear to you, if you would have spent the last twenty-five years with her, you'd know——"

Magnusson didn't let her finish. With a flick of his hand, dense smoke spread through the kitchen. Coughing, Fionna instinctively moved backward, but someone grabbed her arm.

She tried to extricate herself, but the coughing fit made her weak. The smoke made her eyes tear up. Her vision blurred, and then everything went black.

CHAPTER TWENTY-SEVEN

ABBEY

A bbey had tried to call Fionna several times, even left a couple of messages.

When she hadn't heard back from the young witch by early evening, she decided to go to The Kirk. Fionna had mentioned that she'd be working, so she expected to find her there.

The restaurant was empty. It had only been open for half an hour, and it was the middle of the week. An eager waitress greeted Abbey. It wasn't Sally, and Abbey hadn't seen her before. The woman seemed disappointed when Abbey declined to be shown to a table and instead asked to speak to Fionna.

"Oh. Fionna isn't here today."

Abbey drew her brows together. "She said she was working tonight."

"She was supposed to," Drew said. He'd just come through the kitchen door. "Hi, Abbey."

"Hi. Has Fionna called in sick?"

"No." Drew seemed embarrassed. "She just hasn't shown up. It might be my fault...um, something that happened between us. I should really talk to her again."

He ran his fingers through his dark curls. "Anyway. She's not here."

"Okay, I'll see if she's at home."

Drew's expression changed. "You sound concerned. Is everything all right?"

Abbey forced a smile. "I'm sure everything's fine. I'll tell her to call you so you can work this out."

"Thank you, Abbey!"

"No worries. Have a good evening."

Abbey forced herself to leave the restaurant slowly and calmly, but as soon as she was out the door, she started running.

Something was up, she could feel it. Fionna had been apprehensive about facing Drew and Sally, but she wouldn't have played hooky without even calling with an excuse. The job was too important to her.

Slowing her steps a little, she pulled out her phone and tried to call Fionna. When she didn't pick up, she tried Andie, but to no avail.

Abbey sprinted down the road to the Simmondses' house, pressing the doorbell several times.

Nobody answered.

She walked around the back, peering into all the windows. She couldn't spot Fionna or her mother.

When she was back at the front door, her phone rang.

It was Andie.

"Hey, you called—"

"Do you know where Fionna is?"

"She should be at work."

"She never showed up." Abbey quickly told Andie about her conversation with Drew. "I'm at Fionna's house, and it looks deserted. I have a bad feeling about this. Let's talk in person. Can I come to you?"

"Sure." Andie gave her directions, and they hung up.

Andie's house wasn't far, and Abbey arrived only a couple of minutes later.

Just as she knocked on the front door, a car pulled up, and Penny got out.

"Andie called me. Fionna is missing?"

"Yes!" Abbey answered, as Andie answered the door.

In the kitchen, she told the two witches about Magnus Junior's visit. "And now Fionna isn't at home or at the restaurant… She's missing! Do you think she's hiding somewhere? She said something like that…but she'd tell you, wouldn't she? And she'd make up an excuse for Drew, like she's sick or something?"

Penny and Andie looked at each other in alarm. "She didn't say anything to me," Andie said.

"Me either." Penny shook her head. "I think you're right, Abbey. This doesn't make sense. Magnus must be behind this. If he's in Tarbet—"

The sound of a knock at the door interrupted her.

"Maybe it's Fionna," Andie said hopefully.

They all rushed to the front door, but when they opened it, it wasn't Fionna standing there. It was a girl with dyed blond hair and too much make-up.

"Tara?" Andie said. "What are you doing here?"

"I wanted to tell you something. There's—"

"We really don't have time for this," Penny interrupted impatiently.

When Penny tried to close the door, Tara put her foot in the opening. "It's important."

Andie took a deep breath. "Look, Tara. Fionna's missing, okay? *That's* important. Not an outfit decision for a date, or whatever you wanted to talk to me about. So come back another time."

Tara crossed her arms in front of her chest. "Fine, but then you'll have to wait for the information on the mage. It might have something to do with Fionna, but whatever."

She turned around demonstratively.

Penny, Abbey, and Andie looked at each other with wide eyes.

"What mage?" they asked, almost in unison.

"Oh, *now* you're interested. Well, maybe I'm not—"

"Quit playing around and tell us what you know." Penny pulled Tara into the house.

Andie seemed skeptical. "Is this one of those times when you just want attention?" She turned to Tara. "Because, like we said, we really need to find Fionna. So please don't waste our time."

"Let her talk," Abbey said. "Maybe she met Magnus. She'd be just the type he'd chat up. If she knows anything about him, like where he went after leaving the B&B, that would be helpful."

"Magnus, yes!" Tara said triumphantly. "That was his name. Magnus the Great."

Abbey grabbed her arm. "Magnus *the Great*?"

Clearly happy to have their full attention now, Tara seemed to grow a few inches. They had made it to the kitchen, but nobody sat down at the table because everyone was eager to hear what Tara had to say—as eager as she was to tell them.

"At the spring equinox, you asked me about mages. And I…well, I couldn't help but overhear what you were talking about. You know what my magical gift is." Tara turned to Abbey. "Oh, right, you don't. I see things that happened in the past."

"It's similar to mine," Andie interrupted. "Visions…sort of."

Tara pressed her lips together. "Hmm. Sort of. It's a bit different, actually. I never see anything that happens in the future, so I don't get to play hero and warn others."

Andie narrowed her eyes. "If you think I enjoy seeing those things, you're mistaken. I see helping others as my responsibility, but I would have liked my life to go differently, believe me."

Tara rolled her eyes. "Of course, you just hate to save the day all the time. What a burden!"

"Cut it out," Penny said. "That's not helpful. Get to the point, Tara."

"It's kind of relevant. I said you know what my gift is, but you don't, really. I don't like to talk about it because I hate it. When we were still friends, Andie, I guess our talents seemed similar. I'd have vague visions of the past. But like all of you, my abilities got a lot stronger over the years. What I see is history repeating itself, literally. I think sometimes significant events imprint themselves on the places where they happen. Often, these events are charged with emotions. Come to think of it, that's probably what makes them significant. That's what I see."

"Like a haunting?" Abbey asked. "You're not seeing ghosts, but scenes from the past unfold in front of your eyes?"

"Something like that." Tara turned serious. "The problem is, everywhere is haunted. At least in most places where people live. There are these emotionally charged scenes everywhere. They keep replaying, and I can't escape them. It's almost like…they want to draw me in. Imagine being in a surround-sound theater with movies playing twenty-four seven. There's always a soundtrack of emotions playing in my background."

Abbey couldn't really imagine it, but Andie seemed to get it. She looked distressed. "That's…hard. I had no idea. I must be difficult to focus on your actual life. Why have you never told us? Does Mrs. MacDonald know about this?"

Tara waved it off. "I have my coping strategies. I focus on…simple things."

"You mean trivial," Penny said. "Stuff that's so meaningless that it dulls your senses. So you don't get the full emotional broadside all the time. That explains a lot. But listen, we can talk about your talent some other time. Why don't you tell us what you found out about the mage, because—"

"That's what I'm doing." Tara's face showed her indignation. "I have to explain about my gift, because otherwise you won't understand. This isn't easy for me, so cut me some slack. I hate talking about it. If you let me finish, I can get to the important part."

"All right, all right," Penny mumbled.

"My point is that I'm seeing these things all the time. There's no escaping them. Unless I'm somewhere in the woods, in places few people have visited. I can find peace there. I know the woods behind Tarbet pretty well, and I know where stuff has been going on. For example, there's this place where Travellers used to camp. Fairground folk, showmen, a circus, that sort of thing. It's an interesting place. I can tell you stories...but some other time. When you asked me about mages, I remembered something. I went to that place and checked it out. There was a magician among those Travellers, and his name was Magnus. I heard you talking about Magnus, so I figured that had to be more than a coincidence. One thing I can do..."

Tara hesitated. She was clearly uncomfortable talking about her gift. "I can also conjure up events that happened somewhere. I hardly ever do it, because why would I?" She gave a hollow laugh. "I already see enough. But I can, and so I tried it with this Magnus guy."

"Did you see anything?" Andie sounded breathless.

Tara nodded. "Magnus the Great. And his wife."

"The woman who looks like Fionna?" Abbey asked.

Tara nodded. "It was freaky. I thought it was Fionna, at first. But the outfit, the hairstyle...it didn't fit. And she was slimmer than Fionna. But..." Tara closed her eyes, as if she wanted to unsee the event that had played out for her in the woods. "She was murdered. Shot. She was killed right in front of my eyes."

They were all silent.

Abbey was the first to speak. "When? When did all of this happen, exactly?" The private investigator in her needed to make sense of how the events of the past and the present were related to each other.

"I don't know. There isn't a calendar at the events, so I can only guess from the clothes and the surroundings and the overall vibe. These Travellers, they're in costumes, and there are tents, so it's really difficult to tell."

"I really would like to know when Magnus the Great and Zelda lived," Abbey said, dejectedly. "I could search the records if I could narrow it down to maybe a decade. Otherwise it's like looking for a needle in haystack, considering these are Travellers, and I can't exactly add a place name to the search—"

"I'm not finished," Tara interrupted her. "I haven't told you the real shocker yet."

"What?" Penny said. "Spit it out, already."

"I saw the person who killed the Fionna lookalike." Tara smiled triumphantly and made a dramatic pause. However much she suffered from her gift, she was obviously enjoying this moment.

Penny took a step toward her. "Tara, I swear—"

Tara held up a hand. "All right, all right, I'll tell you. The person who killed her? Get this: It was Mrs. MacDonald."

CHAPTER TWENTY-EIGHT

FIONNA

The first thing Fionna noticed was the cold. It was the sort of clammy chill that penetrated deep into the bones and led to uncontrollable shivering.

She curled up into a tight ball.

Fionna would have loved to sink back into unconsciousness, but aside from the icy dampness, there was an unpleasant musty smell she couldn't ignore.

She blinked and moved her stiff limbs.

Once her eyes got used to the semi-darkness, she could make out her surroundings. She lay in front of an old and crumbling stone wall, partly covered with moss. Fionna lifted her head. Above her, there were slits in the wall, and pale moonlight fell in, streaking the stone floor.

Scrambling up, Fionna pulled her coat tight around her. She still couldn't stop shaking and almost slipped on the slick stones in an effort to reach the open side of the stone alcove that lay in the shadows.

When she got there, though, she realized iron bars blocked her exit.

She touched the old, rusty bars with a sense of incredulity, then wrapped her fingers around them. No matter how much she pushed and pulled, those bars were solid.

The cold suddenly didn't bother her so much anymore.

Fionna slowly turned in a circle.

It looked as if she really was confined to an old dungeon.

"Hello?" she called out. "Hello? Is anybody there?"

Her voice sounded weak and ineffective, as if it was swallowed up by the thick stone walls.

She got no answer, but she tried calling for help until her throat was hoarse, pacing her cell and pulling at the bars periodically. All to no avail.

Exhausted, she sank to the floor. Her gaze fell on something in the dark corner. She slid across the floor to see what it was.

A thermos, sandwiches in a plastic container, a bucket, and a roll of toilet paper.

Fionna started to cry.

She wasn't meant to escape this dungeon. Whoever had brought her here had planned for her to stay.

Whoever?

Fionna had been too preoccupied with escaping her prison to think clearly, but now the fog in her brain lifted.

She knew who'd brought her here.

Magnus Magnusson, Sr.

He had come to her house, forced himself inside, and then…she just remembered the dark fog, nothing else.

He had kidnapped her.

Fionna's despair slowly gave way to rage. How dare he do that to her?

She didn't even care about why. Well, okay, she wanted to know why.

But right now, what she cared about most of all was getting out of this awful dungeon.

She resolved she wouldn't be reduced to a whimpering victim, no matter how grim her surroundings.

At least Fionna assumed that Magnusson's choice of cell was designed to make her desperate and plead for mercy. She didn't know what his endgame was, but she could only assume this was about power.

Even though she didn't feel at all brave, and in fact would have loved to curl up in the corner and cry, Fionna was determined not to give Magnusson the satisfaction.

She just had to hold on to that rage, and she would be fine.

Fionna grabbed the thermos and unscrewed the top. Steam wafted out, carrying the scent of black tea and rum.

She hesitated before drinking. There was a possibility that Magnusson had drugged the tea. But she needed it to fortify herself, so she risked it.

Magnusson clearly was a powerful magician. He could probably do whatever he wanted to her without resorting to spiking her food and drink.

She wolfed down the sandwiches and would have loved to finish the tea that warmed her nicely from the inside. But since she had no idea how long these supplies were supposed to last her, she did the sensible thing and saved some for later.

Fionna wrapped her coat tightly around herself and perched on the driest patch of stones she could find.

Then she waited.

"FIONNA."

She woke with a jolt.

"Fionna!"

Cursing herself for falling asleep, Fionna blinked.

She could only see the silhouette of a person standing

in front of the iron bars of her cell. He held a burning torch in his hand. It had to be Magnusson.

Fionna shifted slightly and could now make out that the person was shrouded in a dark cloak.

She got up and stumbled toward him.

"Let me out. Right now!"

The flames of the torch flickered and illuminated Magnusson's face. He studied her with apparent fascination and acted as if he hadn't heard her speak.

"I said, let me out!" Fionna cried. "If you think you can make me tell you where the cookbook is, it's not going to work. I don't know where it is!"

Magnusson smiled. "This isn't about the cookbook anymore. I don't need it. I have you. And don't worry, I've come to let you out."

He lit what looked like oil lamps in wall sconces, extinguished the torch, and walked to the edge of Fionna's cell. He did something to a heavy padlock Fionna hadn't even noticed in the dark before now.

"I'm not going to release you," Magnusson continued in a tone that implied they were just having a pleasant chat. "We're on an island, and it's entirely under my magical influence. You won't be able to escape, so don't bother trying."

The lock clicked open, and the bars slid to the side without so much as a creak. Fionna looked at the bars skeptically. There definitely had to be magic involved. Magnusson was probably telling the truth, and he had put supernatural fortifications in place that wouldn't let her escape.

Still, she had to make an attempt.

She rushed past Magnusson, frantically looking for the exit.

"What was I thinking?" her captor's perfectly calm voice echoed behind her. "Of course, you'll try."

Something wrapped around Fionna's middle, and a violent jerk stopped her in her tracks. The air left her lungs with a whoosh, and she bent over to get her breath back.

When she groped for whatever was holding her in place—a rope, or something, wrapped around her torso?—she felt nothing.

Fionna tried to lurch forward again but felt some sort of restraint preventing her from doing so.

"It's an invisible leash. Neat, isn't it?"

Fionna grunted.

"Now be a good girl and stop struggling. You're just going to hurt yourself."

Fionna pulled and tugged, but in the end she didn't have a choice but to follow Magnusson as he led her down the corridor.

In the light of the wall sconces, she saw her cell was just one of many in this dungeon. She winced when she made out a dark figure in one of them. It was a woman, huddled on the floor.

"Mom!"

No response. Fionna's gut wrenched.

"Mom!"

"Don't worry, she's just asleep. I even put a blanket over her. She'll be fine."

Magnusson's reassurances did nothing to ease Fionna's worries. She had no reason to believe anything he said.

Her captor dragged her up a flight of crumbling stairs and then threw open a heavy wooden door.

The chilly night air hit her, but Fionna much preferred it to the dank dungeon. She was almost dizzy with relief at being able to breathe fresh air again.

It wasn't as dark, either. The full moon shone above the walls of the ruins of a castle.

Fionna briefly wondered which island they were on, but even if she could figure it out—they were in Scotland,

and there were stone ruins everywhere—it wouldn't really help her right now.

The mage led her to a circle of torches, much like the one he had carried into the dungeon. It looked as if Magnusson had set them up to provide him with an illuminated space for whatever his plans were for Fionna.

Fionna shuddered and quickly suppressed any surfacing nightmarish ideas of what those plans might be.

Magnusson pointed at various objects strewn inside the circle. "Show me what you can do."

Fionna looked at him in confusion.

"Okay." Magnusson led her to a cauldron on top of a pile of stones. "There's water in it. I want you to change its state of matter. For instance, can you turn it into ice?"

Fionna folded her arms across her chest. "You're confusing me with my mother. She does that sort of thing, not me."

Magnusson eyed her. "Are you telling me you've never tried this before? It's Magic 101. It's called elemental magic."

"I know what it's called," Fionna scoffed. "I read books."

"So you know about it in theory. Still, nobody ever tried this with you?"

"I don't have to. Like I said, it's the sort of thing my mom does. It's her gift."

Magnusson nodded patiently. "Yes, it's her gift. And you, as her daughter, inherited it. She should have trained you to do the same. If your gift stretches beyond that, which I imagine it does, you would have moved on to other things. But this is…elemental." He laughed at his own joke.

"My mother didn't have to train me. This is…I do other things."

"To properly develop your talent, you need to master

the basic things first. So go ahead. Freeze the water in the cauldron."

Fionna huffed.

She hated that she didn't know where this was leading, but freezing the water wouldn't hurt anyone. She might as well get it over with.

"All right, tell me how to do it."

Magnusson gave her instructions and taught her a spell that would help her focus her effort.

Fionna pointed at the cauldron, said the words, and peered inside. The water was still liquid.

"Focus." Magnusson sounded disappointed.

She tried again, without success.

Magnusson sighed and shook his head. "Witches. Typical."

It raised Fionna's hackles again, which she thought was a good thing. As long as she was angry, she could keep fear at bay.

"Witches are taught that magic comes from your gut. That its intuitive. That's not wrong, exactly, but there's also an element of learning involved. At least if you want to step out of your comfort zone and develop your gift. It might not be intuitive from the beginning, and the only remedy for that is practice. The thing about magic is that you can't think about it too hard. You need to get to a place of high confidence, where there's no doubt in your mind that you can do it. Practice makes it so it eventually seems natural. We need you to learn to believe in yourself. I have a feeling that could take a while."

Fionna wanted to be annoyed by that character evaluation—this man didn't even know her! But she secretly had to admit that he was right.

All her life, her mother had been hard at work undermining her confidence. She had certainly never encouraged her to learn magic or develop a talent. It was more like Rosa had expected her to be supremely gifted—and had then been disappointed before Fionna even knew what she was supposed to do.

Magnusson also seemed to know quite a lot about witches. A magical talent was acknowledged, but nobody really learned magic. You either had it or you didn't. There was a sort of moral code, rules around what you could do and what you couldn't do. Everything else was learned by doing, especially in a group setting. In a coven, younger witches learned by observing or doing spells with older witches.

It interested Fionna that Magnusson talked as if he was familiar with witches in general, not just her coven. That had to mean there were other witches, maybe even other covens. Fionna was curious about that.

Of course, she didn't ask. She also didn't share her thoughts about Rosa and her own coven. She didn't want to give her kidnapper the satisfaction, and she didn't want to appear weak.

"So, you believe in me, or what?" she said with all the spunk she could muster.

"Yes," he simply said.

The irony wasn't lost on Fionna that this stranger who had kidnapped her and was holding her captive had more faith in her than her own mother.

She quickly hardened her heart. Clearly, she was vulnerable to such manipulations and had to be more careful.

Fionna squinted in his direction. She should really figure out what his plan was, but the man was giving nothing away.

She told herself to get these Magic 101 games over with. Magnusson was right, after all. She was capable of much more powerful magic, so she should be able to do this.

Her next attempt resulted in a thin layer of ice on the surface of the water. Fionna tapped her finger on the cold surface. A grin spread across her face.

This was actually fun. And once she got the hang of it, it felt natural. As if she'd done it her whole life.

She turned the contents of the cauldron into a solid block of ice, then melted it again. On a whim, she modified Magnusson's spell, and the water began to boil.

Fionna could hardly hide her sense of triumph when she looked at Magnusson.

"Wonderful," he said, equally thrilled. "Let's move on."

His enthusiasm put a damper on Fionna's mood again. Why on earth would he be interested in teaching her this?

"Let's talk about what you're capable of," Magnusson said, as he opened a thermos and poured the steaming liquid into a cup. "You said earlier that this isn't the kind of thing you do. Give me an example of what you can do."

He passed her the cup.

Fionna hesitated. She could smell that there was no rum in the tea this time.

She was cold, and the hot drink would be welcome, but she didn't want to trust her captor too easily.

Again, she reassured herself that he didn't need to resort to drugging her, considering the powerful magic he was capable of.

Besides, drinking the sweet, hot tea gave her time to think about what she was going to reveal to Magnusson.

"Elemental magic is the gift passed down in my family, like you said," she began carefully. "In essence, it means manipulating objects, changing their make-up, I guess." She shrugged.

"But you have much more advanced capabilities than your mother," Magnusson encouraged her. Fionna nodded. "Give me an example of that."

"Hmm, in the coven, my gift is used to enchant

objects. I basically enhance what we create with certain traditional methods. We waulk tartan cloth, and I can enhance its protective qualities. I also make talismans from stones and other natural materials. The coven has a secret meeting space, and a while ago we decided we needed to hide it better. We came up with a spell to make it invisible, and I was instrumental in that, too."

Fionna couldn't help but sound proud of these accomplishments. But she stopped herself because she didn't want to reveal too many coven secrets.

"All I hear is 'we.'" Magnusson's eyes glittered silver in the moonlight. "Are you telling me you only ever perform magic within the bounds of the coven?"

Fionna felt heat creep into her cheeks and hoped Magnusson wouldn't notice the telltale blush. "Most of the time, yes."

"And the other times?"

Fionna shrugged.

"Come on, Fionna. You've never tried to experiment by yourself? As a teenager, when you came into your powers? I can't believe you weren't curious. And with all those books you collect…you must have tried things out."

"Okay, yes, sometimes."

"Tell me about that."

Fionna rolled her eyes. "As a teenager? I don't know… I once enchanted a pen that wrote on its own and did my homework for me. Satisfied?"

Magnusson nodded. "You used your magic to make life easier for yourself."

When Fionna wanted to protest, he said, "That's only normal. Who wouldn't do that if they were able to? I'm sure you've done more than that little homework trick. Come on, tell me something that you wouldn't admit to anyone because you feel guilty but that you secretly feel very proud of. That's the kind of thing I'd like to know. Your greatest accomplishments."

Fionna didn't want to tell Magnusson, but the part of her that had been bursting to tell someone for a long time somehow won. Her lips moved as if they had a mind of their own.

"At my driving test, I was so nervous I was sure I wouldn't pass. So I enchanted the car to drive as instructed and according to all the traffic rules and regulations. I even got it to parallel park perfectly."

It was as if something had lifted from her shoulders, and Fionna could suddenly expand. She was always making herself small, trying not to be noticed, because she worried people thought negatively about her. Hiding her accomplishments under a bushel because she was so scared she'd never be able to meet anyone's expectations, having heard all her life that she wasn't good enough.

She certainly could never have told her mother these things. And her friends… Well, for a long time, Andie had pretty much been her only friend. Andie was such a stickler for moral boundaries, Fionna never felt she could admit these things to her.

Andie's gift was all about helping others.

Fionna was different, and she liked to help herself from time to time. She still had her own honor code, though, she liked to think.

The others sometimes joked that Fionna could use her gift to just accumulate a lot of money; for example, with a piggy bank that replenished itself or an enchanted slot machine. The possibilities were endless.

But that was never something Fionna had considered. She didn't really care about money. In fact, she had more than enough of it without trying very hard. With her talent, she helped other people who were more than happy to pay her. Plus, where was the fun in just generating money for money's sake?

If she was honest with herself, she enjoyed coming up with clever ways to use her talents.

As if Magnusson could read Fionna's thoughts, he asked, "I bet you use your magical gift in your antiquarian book business in some inventive ways, don't you?"

Fionna narrowed her eyes and handed Magnusson the now empty mug. "I don't know what you're talking about."

"I know you do. I've asked around and heard some pretty amazing things about your books. Rare books, indeed. There's nothing wrong with making a profit with that, you know."

Fionna said nothing, just pulled her coat closer around her. She suddenly felt cold again.

"I'll say it if you don't want to. You enchant books. So that the content is transferred to your customer, for example. I heard from someone who bought an old book on gardening from you and suddenly became an amazing gardener. Then there was the person who paid you a lot of money to make the dragons in a fantasy novel come alive right in front of their eyes, as if they were in a 3D movie. It's those sorts of custom orders you use your gift for, isn't it?"

"Now and then," Fionna whispered. She straightened up and said in a louder voice, "Mainly, I just buy and sell rare books."

Magnusson was silent for a moment. Then he implored her, "Fionna, do you have any idea what it means that you can do these things? Think about it. You don't simply change the make-up of objects, manipulate them so they take on other properties. You extend your spells so the enchanted objects affect other people. You can transfer your magic onto them. That's a pretty strong power. I've

215

only known a few witches who were capable of something like that. One of them was your grandmother, Matilda."

"The cookbook." So it came down to Matilda's skills, after all.

"Yes. But Matilda couldn't transfer the magic of the recipes to an ordinary person. Not even an ordinary witch. It takes someone with spectacular powers to perform these spells off book, so to speak. Someone like you."

Fionna shrugged.

"I want you to understand that you're even more powerful than your grandmother. Think of the powers that lie dormant inside of you. Your possibilities are limitless. It's a crime that Rosa and your coven have neglected you like this, deprived you of developing your full potential. Here, I want to show you something."

Magnusson pulled a wooden staff from the folds of his cloak. "Do you know what this is?"

Fionna raised an eyebrow. "Looks like a wand to me."

"Don't sound so contemptuous. It's more than just a prop in a movie or magic show. Just because witches don't use them, they're not something to scoff at."

It was the first time that Magnusson's voice sounded sharp, and Fionna wondered if he was revealing some of his own insecurities to her. Magnusson clearly was proud to be a magician. But if Abbey's research was anything to go by, he came from poor Traveller stock. His ancestors probably had had little choice but to use their abilities to make a living, and they had to work with the cliché.

Magnusson clearly had ambivalent feelings about this. He was convinced that there was nothing wrong with making a profit from his talent, but he also didn't want to be reduced to a sideshow act.

Fionna kept silent, hoping Magnusson would reveal even more.

It worked.

"Yes, magicians sometimes need magical objects like wands. But one of their strengths is that they can learn magic. They train and practice from a young age, instead of coming into their powers with a sort of poof"—he made an exaggerated gesture, underlining his mocking words—"dropping a talent in your lap, like with you witches. They use any help they can. Wands, illusions, distractions, tricks...Everything plays together. The result is what counts. And in the end, after many years of practice, the wand can still help us do this."

He pointed it at a stone, said a few words under his breath, and in the blink of an eye, the stone disappeared.

Fionna went over to the spot where the stone had been. She suspected some sort of invisibility spell, but when she tried to touch the stone, it definitely wasn't there anymore.

With a questioning look, she turned back toward Magnusson.

Nonplussed, he pointed the wand to another spot, said his spell again, and the stone reappeared.

Fionna grabbed it and weighed it in her hand.

She couldn't be sure that it was the same stone. She hadn't paid enough attention to it before it disappeared. It looked the same size.

She still had the feeling Magnusson was somehow tricking her.

Again, Magnusson pointed at the stone, and it disappeared right out of her palm. The mage let it rematerialize in thin air, and she quickly caught it before it fell to the ground.

It definitely felt like the same stone.

"A wand is nothing but a tool to focus and direct energy. Here, try it."

He threw the wand, and Fionna instinctively caught it. She could feel the power coursing through it. It felt like holding an electrical wire.

"But I can't make objects disappear and reappear. That's not part of my magical gift."

"Not exactly. But it's close enough for you to learn it."

"Witches don't learn other talents. They either have a talent or they don't."

"I know that. But you aren't an ordinary witch. I'm positing that you can learn. If you want to prove me wrong, be my guest."

Fionna bit her lower lip. She wanted to refuse. On the other hand, she knew Magnusson wouldn't leave her alone until he proved his point, whatever that was.

She also couldn't deny that he had hooked her. She wasn't simply curious. It was the first time in her life that someone believed in her. It was too enticing.

"All right," she sighed, and followed Magnusson's instructions.

It took her longer than changing the state of matter of water, but the first time the stone disappeared for just a fraction of a second, Fionna's ambition awakened.

She tried again and again, until beads of perspiration formed on her forehead.

In the end, she managed to make the stone disappear and then reappear somewhere else, but she had to act fast. If she left the stone in "the void" for more than a few seconds, it would just reappear of its own accord.

But Magnusson seemed to view her efforts as a tremendous success.

He spurred her on like a tireless cheerleader until Fionna said she was simply too exhausted. The arm that was holding the wand was shaking uncontrollably. She felt feverish and couldn't stop shivering.

Magnusson spread out a blanket and told her to sit down and rest. He gave her more tea and sandwiches.

She scarfed the first couple of sandwiches down ravenously, but then slowed down a little. Chewing, she looked around.

There were some objects in the circle they hadn't even touched. Something square covered with a cloth. Candles. A small pile of what looked like scrap metal. Three small balls.

Fionna had the bad feeling that her lessons were far from over.

She put the half-eaten sandwich aside.

Why was Magnusson doing this? Why would he want her to learn all those things—things a mage was trained in?

Magnusson was already continuing with his lesson. "Here's the wonderful thing about your gift. You can enchant objects. That means you can turn any suitable object into a wand, a tool to bundle and focus energy. Then you can use it to perform the magic I'm teaching you. You could pick a twig from a tree, if you wanted to, and turn it into a wand. Amazing, isn't it?"

Fionna shook her head. "Why are you telling me all this? I'm a witch. You're treating me as if I'm a magician."

"Yes, it certainly looks like that, doesn't it?"

Fionna and Magnusson turned around.

The mage seemed as startled as Fionna when Magnus Junior stepped through a hole in one of the ruin's walls.

"I'm happy to answer your questions, Fionna, even if my father prefers to stay cagey. He's treating you like a magician because that's what you are."

CHAPTER TWENTY-NINE

ABBEY

Tara was obviously pleased to have everyone staring at her in disbelief. The young witch was basking in the attention.

Abbey was the first to speak. "How do you know it was Mrs. MacDonald?"

"What do you mean?" Tara's brow furrowed.

"What makes you sure it was her?" Abbey rephrased her question impatiently.

"Duh—I know what she looks like."

"Yes, you know what she looks like now. Old, with a lot of wrinkles. The person in your vision was exactly the same?"

"Well, not exactly the same," Tara answered, her tone suggesting she didn't appreciate being treated like a child. "It was a scene from the past. She wasn't as old then, so she had fewer wrinkles."

"So it could just be someone who looked a lot like her?"

Tara folded her arms. "Why are you giving me the third degree? I know what I saw. How many women out there look an awful lot like Mrs. M.?"

Abbey sighed. "An ancestor of hers, for starters." When Tara started to interrupt, she cut her off. "Hear me out. The woman who was killed, the mage's wife, who looks like Fionna? Her name was Flame Hair Zelda. I saw her in a photo, together with her husband, Magnus the Great. The photo was from the thirties. Zelda would have been killed ninety years ago. The killer can't be Mrs. MacDonald."

Tara screwed up her face but seemed placated when Andie said, "What you saw is still really important, Tara. Let's unpack it more, though. You said you saw the scene in the woods. A woman who looks like Mrs. MacDonald kills a young woman in a circus costume who resembles Fionna. How did you know she was the wife of Magnus the Great?"

"Because I had seen other scenes before that, where it was evident that they were married."

"Like what?"

"Like what led to the murder," Tara said, evidently pleased that she had a captive audience again.

"This magician, Magnus the Great? I had seen him around before. He was an intense dude, so there are quite a few emotional scenes on repeat around the campsite. Get this. He met in the woods with a beautiful woman. Natural beauty, not made up. No costume or anything. Young, dark curls. I don't think she was from the circus, but I'm not sure. Her accent was from around here. And she said she was a witch, so I thought she might be from Tarbet or thereabouts. In any case, the woman practically begged Magnus to impregnate her. It was embarrassing. She kept saying that it would be the most amazing child, the child of a mage and a witch. Magnus was having none of it, though. He kept saying, 'I love my wife, Maryanna. I already have a child with her.'" Tara changed her voice to a deeper tone to impersonate Magnus the Great. "'I have a family. That's all I want.'"

Tara looked at the others expectantly.

"And then?" Penny asked. "What happened then?"

"The young woman, Maryanna, threw a tantrum and stormed off."

"Wait, back up," Abbey said. The blood was rushing loudly in her ears, and the hairs on her arms stood up. "Maryanna? The woman's name was Maryanna? And she was a witch from Tarbet?"

Abbey made Tara describe Maryanna in such detail that the blond young woman rolled her eyes.

"What is it, Abbey?" Andie asked. "You look really pale."

"Yes, you'd better sit down," Penny suggested, and took Abbey's arm.

Abbey sank down onto a chair. "I just…" She rubbed her temples. "It's just all a bit much. Witches, fairies, magicians…it's a lot of belief to suspend, but this… Maryanna is the name of the woman who caught me searching the Thistle Inn. She looked exactly like what Tara described." She shook her head and took a deep breath. "There has to be some sort of explanation, even if it's not a rational one."

She looked up at Tara. "Okay, so are you a hundred percent sure this was a scene from the long ago past? Maryanna begging Magnus for a child, that was during the same time period as Zelda's murder?"

"Well, I didn't think the murder happened that long ago, a younger Mrs. M. being the killer and all. You questioned the timing of that, remember?" Tara was now defensive. "All I can say is that it felt like both scenes happened close together. The magician, Magnus, he looked the same. The clothes they were wearing…" She shrugged. "I don't know. Like I said, if there's no calendar lying around, I can't know for certain. It felt like this was what led to the murder," she said again. "I can only trust my feelings."

"You think Zelda was killed because Maryanna wanted Magnus for herself," Andie deduced.

"But it wasn't Maryanna who killed Zelda," Penny put in. "It was someone older, someone who looks like Mrs. M."

"The photos I found at the Thistle Inn showed that same young woman with the black hair in several eras," Abbey said. "The only explanation that makes sense is that they're different women. All of Mrs. MacDonald's female ancestors looked a lot alike. And it wasn't uncommon to pass a name on in the family, too. There might have been Maryannas in Mrs. MacDonald's family in the past. I mean, Mrs. M. herself is called Mary. It might be a family name."

Penny nodded. "Yes, you must be right. The woman who killed Zelda, the one who looked like a slightly younger Mrs. MacDonald? She had to be the mother or grandmother of the Maryanna who quarreled with Magnus the Great, who asked him to have a baby with her."

Abbey nodded vigorously, relieved to finally be able to make sense of all this. "That tracks. Magnus the Great has to be an ancestor of the Magnussons. He talked about a child he had with Zelda? That's likely Magnusson Senior's grandfather."

Tara pulled a face. "You completely lost me."

The others didn't pay her any heed because they were all coming to the same conclusion.

Abbey jumped up, Andie grabbed her arm, and Penny shouted, "Zelda isn't Rosa's ancestor. She must be Fionna's paternal great-grandmother or something!"

"I had a feeling, but I didn't want to say it to Fionna before," Abbey agreed. "It all makes sense now, why

Magnusson Senior was so interested in the cookbook, why he shifted his interest to Fionna. Why Rosa knew him, and Mrs. MacDonald…"

Tara stamped her foot. "What are you talking about?"

The others still didn't give her an explanation.

Abbey, Andie, and Penny stayed quiet for a moment, contemplating the staggering truth, while Tara was huffing with indignation.

Finally, Abbey said it out loud.

"Magnus Magnusson, Sr., is Fionna's father."

CHAPTER THIRTY

FIONNA

"What…do you mean?" Fionna looked at Magnus in bewilderment.

"He means to say that I'm your father, Fionna," Magnusson said in a soft voice.

Fionna shook her head. "No, I…" She closed her eyes and swallowed. "It doesn't matter, and it makes no sense. Magical abilities are passed down the female line. I inherited my gift from my mother and my grandmother and all the women who came before them. That's who I am. A Tarbet witch. No magician could have passed any abilities down to me."

She opened her eyes again and dared to meet the senior Magnusson's icy blue stare. "Besides, you aren't my father. My conception involved…evil forces or something. Anyway, I don't have a father."

"Everyone has a father. I am yours. But you're right, a higher power was summoned to aid with your conception. Some might call it evil…or black magic, but I don't find that sort of distinction useful."

Fionna lifted her chin. "Like I said, it doesn't matter if you're my biological father or not. We don't have anything in common. And I don't have mage abilities. That's not possible."

"Apparently it is, in the child of a witch and mage," Magnusson explained patiently. "That's what makes that sort of child special. The trouble is that they rarely exist, so we have very little knowledge. Nature has a way of keeping power in balance, and it almost seems that the combined power of witch and mage has to be negated in some other way. Let's just say those children don't come out right most of the time. I have experimented a lot with this. Magnus and you are my only successes."

"And here I thought you forgot about me, Father," Magnus scoffed. "You hear that, Fionna? You're not the only special child, so don't flatter yourself. My mother was a witch, too. She could manipulate people and read their minds. What's your mother's ability again? Elemental magic? Changing the state of matter of the elements?" He laughed.

"Why did you come here, Magnus?" His—their?— father sounded tired. "I didn't ask you to come. In fact, I didn't tell you about any of this. This isn't your business."

"I'm not stupid, Father. You think you found someone better than me and can just throw me away like the rest of your failed experiments? Think again."

With a wave of his hand and a quick incantation, Magnus threw his father to the ground.

Magnusson clearly had not expected that. He only came to and reacted when Magnus bent over him, grabbing his arm.

Fire shot from Magnusson's fingertips, causing his son to withdraw quickly. But he deftly dodged the fireballs and took cover behind one of the ruin's half-crumbled walls.

Father and son didn't speak anymore, as they were too busy fighting each other with everything they had in their magical arsenals.

Fionna backed away quickly until her back was pressed against a wall. The opening Magnus had come through was only a few yards away, but she didn't dare run in that direction, afraid to get hit by the fireballs, ice arrows, stones, and whatever else was flying through the air.

She was stuck watching the impressive demonstration of magic skills in front of her. Magnusson was clearly more accomplished, but his son had youth and agility on his side.

Magnus managed to jump on top of his father, once he had him prone on the ground. He shouted a spell that sounded to Fionna as if he planned to immobilize him by magic.

Magnusson struggled, but then moved less and less until he seemed completely paralyzed. Only his eyes were alive, blazing at his son with a blue fire.

Magnus met his father's gaze, staring into his eyes and mumbling something under his breath.

Fionna saw her chance and dashed to the opening in the wall, but she was suddenly pulled back against her will. Invisible ropes twined around her body. Fionna fought them with all her will but in the end had to admit defeat.

When she turned around, she expected to face Magnus, but it was his father restraining her with his invisible leash.

His eyes were dead.

It seemed that Magnus had managed to put his father into a trance. Magnusson acted like a robot as his son told him to bring Fionna to her cell.

"Oh, how the tables have turned, Father," Magnus said with glee. "What a shame you won't get to remember what it feels like to be under someone's thumb." He laughed. "But what matters is that I'm in control now. You completely underestimated me, as usual. I knew you were up to something. All it took was a little snooping around in your office. I found your journals where you recorded all your plans for designing a magic cell that even a powerful witch like Fionna couldn't escape."

Magnusson, who dragged Fionna down the stairs to the dungeon, was deep in a trance and didn't appear to hear any of what his son said to him.

Magnus evidently didn't care because he couldn't keep himself from carrying on with his gloating monologue. "A little tip for next time, Father. Don't write everything down in a code that's so easy to crack. But I guess at your age you wouldn't be able to remember otherwise."

Now paying more attention to Fionna, Magnus addressed her. "Come on, get a move on, we don't have forever. I'm sure my father's subconscious is hard at work trying to free him from my influence over his mind."

At the bottom of the stairs, Fionna tried to walk faster, in the hope of not drawing Magnus's attention to her mother. But she couldn't help but cast a quick glance in Rosa's direction to make sure she was all right.

Magnus noticed. "Don't worry, I'm not interested in the old witch. My father's plans for her would probably top anything I could come up with. He has an interest in punishing her for keeping you from him. I'll find out what torture he had planned for her later. It might be fun."

He pushed Fionna into the cell and then told his father to go in, too. After pulling the bars shut and clicking the padlock in place, the younger Magnus regarded both of them for a moment.

"Come to think of it, I might have to kill Rosa, after all. I'm going to make it look like Father killed you, and it would make more sense if he killed Rosa, too."

He sounded so matter-of-fact. An icy shiver ran down Fionna's spine.

There would be no point in trying to reason with Magnus.

Magnusson's reasons for capturing her, she could understand on some level.

Fionna still wasn't ready to believe that he was her father, but that was beside the point.

The man thought he'd found out he had a daughter who had been hidden from him all this time. He had high hopes for Fionna, and in a dark and twisted way had wanted to make up for the lost time with these forced training sessions. She would never have agreed to them, otherwise; would not have wanted to get to know him at all. So he had resorted to designing a prison for her and kidnapping her.

Magnusson was most likely wrong. He'd soon find out that teaching Fionna to become a magician was an exercise in futility. And Fionna still found him scary and abhorrent. But she could muster up a certain amount of sympathy for the old man.

Magnus, though?

Okay, so he was pissed to find out that he wasn't the sole child and only potential successor of the mage's empire. From what Abbey had said, Magnus had been jumping through hoops for his father his entire life. It seemed as if he could never really please him.

Suddenly, a half-sister turns up and commands all of his father's attention. Fionna understood that Magnus wasn't happy about it.

But to resort to this extreme action?

She knew what Magnus was capable of, in terms of magical skills. He'd been nothing but derisive about Fionna and the gift she had inherited as a witch. He couldn't really believe his father could teach her to be a magician, either.

If Magnus would have let this play out, he probably would have had his father back by next month, when Magnusson realized that Fionna was a disappointment— just like everyone else in her life had always said.

Fionna glanced at the younger Magnus out of the corner of her eyes as he observed his captives through the bars. His facial expression showed triumph, but his eyes… there was something missing in them.

Fionna shivered when she realized what it was.

His eyes looked soulless.

CHAPTER THIRTY-ONE

ABBEY

Everyone was talking at once.

"Magnusson must have taken Fionna," Andie said. "Who knows what he'll do to her?"

"Magnus Junior's behavior and his warning make much more sense now," Abbey realized. "He knew Fionna was his sister, and he didn't want his father to know about her. Maybe he's worried about his inheritance. His hatred for Fionna runs deep for some reason, and he could be the one who…did something to her. We need to find Mrs. MacDonald. She can clear things up and help figure out what happened to Fionna."

"No!" Penny disagreed. "We'd better solve this ourselves. We don't even know what her role is in all this. Has she ever been open about anything with us? And she was the one who took the cookbook from Fionna. She's in cahoots with Rosa, who I don't trust at all—"

"And no matter what you say, she was somehow involved in the shooting I witnessed," Tara put in doggedly.

"That's why I want to talk to her," Abbey insisted. "We

need to find out how she's involved. She's the only one who can bring some light to the situation right now."

"No, listen to me!" Andie made herself heard. "It's Magnusson we need to find. He's dangerous, and if he really is Fionna's father…" She took a shaky breath. "Fionna thinks she's the product of dark magic. There's a recipe in the cookbook called the Devil's Children, and she's convinced that's what…cooked her up. I was always sure that she had to have a biological father, and that seems to be Magnusson. It means, though, that he was involved in that ritual. It's ghastly. If he had any part in that—if he went that far to make a child—then he's dangerous."

"Rosa clearly had a part in it, too," Penny said. "Don't forget that. And Mrs. MacDonald, most likely. She knows about all of this, and it takes a powerful witch to pull something like this off."

"We can't be sure of that," Andie said. "Maybe the cookbook was already in Magnusson's possession at that time, and he was doing this by himself, and…I don't know, somehow involved Rosa…"

"And got her pregnant remotely?" Penny raised her eyebrows. "That doesn't seem very likely. Whatever the magic ritual, there must have been a very natural conception, and unless it happened in a Petri dish, Magnusson and Rosa must have been together during the ritual."

"And think about the scene I saw, where the young witch begged Magnus the Great to give her a baby," Tara squealed.

"Well, yes, in the past, someone in Mrs. MacDonald's family must have thought it a good idea to produce a child from a witch and a mage. They wanted it so much that they killed Magnus the Great's wife to get to their goal. It wasn't the magician's idea at all."

"Do you really think the coven wanted to…cook up

someone like Fionna?" Andie sounded skeptical. "Mrs. MacDonald is against black magic, remember? It doesn't seem like something she would do. Not voluntarily. I think Magnusson must be behind it."

Again, everyone talked over each other.

"Guy, guys!" Tara shouted, until the others were quiet. "I can help. This black magic ritual, it was supposed to have happened in the Simmondses' basement, right?"

When Andie frowned, she added, "Okay, I admit I was eavesdropping on the conversation Fionna and Andie had at the spring equinox festival. You can be mad at me about that later. But listen, why don't we go to the basement and find out exactly what happened there?"

Andie's eyes widened. "Are you saying you might be able to see what happened there over twenty-five years ago?"

Tara grinned. "Even better. I can make you guys see it, too. My grandmother taught me how to work with other witches, to conjure up a scene so that it's visible to everyone in the circle."

When everyone just stared at her in disbelief, she shrugged. "All right, I admit, I haven't done it since then. You know, with other witches but Grandma. It's just that I don't like to see these scenes myself, so why would I also share them with others? But I know how to do it in theory, so it's worth a shot, right?"

Penny was the first who got her voice back. "I'd say so. If we can figure out how exactly Magnusson, Rosa, and Mrs. M. were involved in the ritual, then we'll hopefully know who's involved in Fionna's disappearance and who we can trust. But we need to be quick. Fionna might be in danger. What do you need for the ritual, Tara?"

∾

ABBEY, Penny, Andie, and Tara's first port of call was the Simmondses' house. They broke the patio door to get in. In the kitchen, they discovered signs of a scuffle.

Andie insisted on involving the police. "There's real evidence that Fionna and Rosa have been taken. Whatever we can do—we owe it to Fionna to have as many people looking for her as possible. And contacting the authorities is the right thing to do."

Penny was against it. "But they might cordon off the house and station someone here. We might not get to see what happened in the basement then. I vote we wait until we see what happened, and—"

"And if something happens to Fionna in the mean-time? Can you live with that?"

"Andie's right," Abbey agreed. If Magnus Junior is involved, we have a genuine reason to be scared for Fionna. There's no telling what he might be capable of."

"Okay, fine, but let's call my brother." Penny got out her phone, found Declan in her contacts, and pressed the call button.

Andie held out her hand. "I'll liaise with Declan. You go and get all the stuff Tara needs for the ritual."

"Abbey, you can come with me to get Jem and Birdie," Tara suggested. "The more witches involved, the better."

Abbey would have rather gone with Penny, but the herb witch was already out the door, and there was no time to argue.

When everyone was back together in the Simmondses' basement, it was almost midnight.

Andie had remembered the Devil's Children recipe in Fionna's purse and had found the purse next to the hall closet.

Tara said the recipe would help access the right event. Shivering, she looked around the basement. "Because a lot of stuff happened down here, and I'd much rather not see it all."

Tara instructed the witches to stand in a circle and hold hands.

Abbey had no role in this, so she stood outside the circle. She felt useless and a little impatient. But since they had had no update from Declan Reid, this strange ritual seemed their only recourse.

Abbey watched as the witches closed their eyes and murmured the spell Tara had taught them. The room filled with the scent of the burning herbs in bowls that Penny had arranged in an outer circle together with different-colored candles. They were the only source of illumination.

Tara instructed the witches to release their hands and take a step back into the circle of herb bowls and candles.

Tara was in her original location, a little inside the now wider circle. She focused on the piece of paper with the recipe, then stared into the middle of the circle, muttering words under her breath.

It took a while. Eventually, the air inside the circle seemed to flicker. A 3D image materialized, out of focus at first, but then it became sharper.

It looked a little like a hologram in old sci-fi TV series, but coming out of nowhere, here, in the Simmondses' basement, it sent a shiver down Abbey's spine.

Abbey had already been witness to pretty far-out stuff in The Kirk the other night, but this topped everything.

She couldn't believe that an actual event that had happened a quarter of a century ago was replaying right in front of her.

A fire was burning in the center of the room, and a brew was bubbling in a cauldron. The image was superimposed over the actual, still-existing fireplace with the old cauldron hanging above it.

Abbey had been told about the horrific ingredients of the potion, and she was relieved she wouldn't find out what the cryptic phrasing really translated to, as everything seemed to be already inside the cauldron.

She didn't know what she would have done if the witches had thrown an animal into the boiling potion, dead or alive. So she just hoped whatever had sounded so terrible had just been symbolic.

Abbey pushed away any further thoughts about the unappetizing ingredients floating in the broth and focused on the woman in the black cloak instead.

The gold metal of a brooch with a purple stone reflected the flames of the fire as the woman stirred the potion with a long staff.

Her face was pulled deep into her hood, and Abbey could only see her lips moving as she recited the spell.

When the woman straightened up, Abbey could tell it was Mrs. MacDonald.

She looked a little younger, but it was unmistakably her. The same warts and wrinkles, the same pink lipstick.

Abbey looked around to observe the reactions of the young witches. She saw their attention was caught by something else.

The circle was suddenly overpopulated. Where the witches of the present stood, there were also the coven sisters from the past, having formed a similar-size circle twenty-five years ago.

They were easy to differentiate, though. The women from the past were all stark naked.

As they had to be the present witches' mothers and grandmothers, it was no wonder everyone seemed a little mortified or amused.

Only Penny's expression was different. She stared at a woman across from her who looked very much like the pretty blond herb witch. It had to be her mother, who had died in Penny's childhood.

The witches of the past had jars filled with a thick, opaque paste in front of them. They were rubbing the stuff onto their naked bodies. The heat of the fire melted it pretty quickly, so it ran down their skin in thick drops.

Suddenly, two people entered the circle, commanding everyone's attention.

Abbey recognized Magnusson right away. Twenty-five years ago, he had looked a lot like his son. Abbey's throat tightened with fear, and she had to remind herself that this was not real, but only a replay of the past.

The woman was in her forties, and it took Abbey a moment to identify her as Rosa Simmonds. She was so used to Rosa's grandmotherly look; it was difficult to reconcile her with the slim woman with long dark-blond hair.

Magnus and Rosa were also naked, and their bodies glistened with the same fatty substance the others had rubbed on themselves.

They stepped up next to Mrs. MacDonald.

Rosa fidgeted a little, which could have indicated that she was nervous. But her face showed sheer determination. It mirrored Magnusson's expression.

Mrs. MacDonald removed her hood and began to speak.

"We are gathered here today to unite witch and mage. It's not the first attempt, as some of us know. Innocent souls died because they stood in the way of fanatics who wanted to make this happen."

Mrs. MacDonald seemed sad, but Abbey thought she saw something else in her eyes. Was it shame?

The coven leader looked at Magnusson, who would not return her gaze.

His tightening jaw muscles were the only visible reaction to her words.

"There have been recordings of what happened to children of witches and mages in the past. Unfortunately, they were mentally and physically disabled. But we also heard of one success story. A witch gave birth to a most powerful being, neither man nor woman, with unimagined magical capabilities. This being devoted themself entirely to their calling and completely renounced all worldly needs. The records describe it as an amorphous creature, pale as the moon, who lived in a cave and only came out at night."

Abbey saw all the witches—from present and past— look horrified at Mrs. MacDonald's words. She felt the same. It sounded as if such a union was incredibly risky, and completely irresponsible if one had any respect for human life.

Mrs. MacDonald cleared her throat. "We don't want to leave anything up to chance. This is a controlled experiment, and we feel more prepared for success than anyone else in history who has ever tried it. Matilda has dedicated her life to this task, and she has developed magical recipes that have led us here. Recipes that allowed her to transfer her magical power to other witches, so we can conjure up a healthy child together. Matilda's efforts have culminated in this one perfect recipe, the Devil's Children. Please don't be scared, sisters."

Mrs. MacDonald addressed the witches of her coven. Some of them did look ready to run away, and Abbey couldn't blame them.

"Matilda had to record this recipe, but she took the precaution of letting the ingredients sound very…unappetizing. The name, too, is designed to discourage anyone from trying it, should the recipe book fall into the wrong hands. The recipe is embedded in other, more enticing recipes for a reason."

Someone from the past dared to ask, "It's still dark magic, though, isn't it?"

238

"Yes. Yes, we are crossing a line here, into a territory that we usually avoid. Sometimes it is necessary."

A low murmuring came from the witches in the circle, but Mrs. MacDonald talked loudly over it, until it died down. "Together we can control these dark forces and harness only what we need from them. Show no weakness or doubt now, my sisters, because one weak link in the chain could be our downfall. You don't want to be the one who is responsible for this going horribly wrong, do you?" Her piercing eyes went from person to person.

"We need your courage and conviction. Take Matilda as an example. She is so convinced that the recipe will work just as it is designed that she volunteered her own daughter, Rosa, to be the bearer of the child."

The older woman who had to be Fionna's grandmother looked proud.

"Let's be bearers of hope, right here and now, sisters. A son for the mage and a daughter for the witch. Both of them the most powerful magical beings known in supernatural history. Our future leaders, who will rule amicably and unite witches and mages in harmony."

Once Mrs. MacDonald finished her speech, the ritual began. The witches chanted, Magnusson and Rosa drank from the brew, and then, to everyone's horror, Magnusson and Rosa began to have sex.

"I think we've seen enough," Andie shouted.

Tara dissolved the scene with a wave of her hand.

The witches from the past faded away.

What remained was the unused fireplace and the old cauldron: silent witnesses to the ritual from twenty-five years ago.

It was bizarre, and everyone seemed to need a bit of time to process what they had seen.

Penny was the first to speak.

"No, we haven't seen enough, actually."

When some of the others started to protest, Penny cut them off. "I don't mean here. I mean, we need to go upstairs, and you need to conjure up what happened in the kitchen, Tara."

Now everyone understood what Penny was getting at, and they all ran up the stairs.

"Do you think Magnus Junior is Fionna's twin brother?" Andie asked Abbey, out of breath.

"No, that doesn't add up," Abbey answered. "Magnus is younger. And what he said in my room in the B&B...it sounded as if Magnusson didn't know that Fionna existed. Magnus didn't want his father to know about her. If this experiment would have been a success...and he would have gotten the son and the witches the daughter...he'd know about Fionna, right?"

"Maybe there was no son," Penny put in. "Only a daughter. The witches must not have told Magnusson about her. Maybe they told him the Devil's Children ritual was unsuccessful."

"You might be right," Abbey agreed. "And only when he was looking for the cookbook in Tarbet did he learn about Fionna. But there's one problem with our theory. Fionna isn't some sort of magical genius, an all-powerful being. She's a talented witch, for sure, but... Unless I'm understanding this all wrong. I'm new to this, after all."

"No, you're right." Penny called a spade a spade, as usual. "The strong, powerful leader who brings harmony to the supernatural world? I love Fionna, but she doesn't quite fit the bill. I mean, you can kind of understand Rosa. How could Fionna ever have lived up to her expectations?"

"Hey, it's not Fionna's fault." Andie crossed her arms in front of her chest and glared at Penny.

The herb witch raised a hand. "I didn't mean it like that. Fionna is fine just as she is. I'm just saying, that's what

Rosa and Mrs. MacDonald must see her as. A failed experiment."

"Hey, are we doing this or not?" Tara interrupted their discussion. They were all gathered in the kitchen by now.

"Of course," Penny said. "I think you should try and see the scene for yourself, Tara. If we all join in, like in the basement, it takes too long and requires too much energy. We just need to know what happened."

Tara nodded.

She knelt beside the broken mug on the floor, picked up a shard, and looked around.

Just a few minutes later, she straightened up again.

"It was Magnusson Senior," she said. "At least I think it was. He resembled Magnus the Great. An older man with gray hair and piercing blue eyes?" She looked at Abbey for confirmation, who nodded.

"Fionna didn't understand that he's her father. What he said makes sense once you know that little fact, though. He accused Rosa of hiding Fionna from him, so I think your theory is right. Rosa tried to make him understand that she didn't hide anything important, because Fionna failed to turn out like they'd hoped. Magnusson didn't listen to her."

"What did he do?" Andie interrupted. "Did someone get hurt?"

Tara shook her head. "I didn't see anything like that. Rosa jumped up and dropped the mug when she saw Magnusson come in. I'm not sure, could be that he froze her with a binding spell, but she could still talk. He also froze Fionna, it seemed. At least she didn't move. And then…they just disappeared." Tara shrugged.

"What do you mean, disappeared?" Abbey wanted to know more.

"There was some sort of fog. They disappeared in it, and when the fog cleared, they were gone. That's all I saw."

"But—"

"Well, well, well, what do we have here?" A voice sounded behind them.

They all turned in unison.

In the doorway stood Mrs. MacDonald.

CHAPTER THIRTY-TWO

FIONNA

F ionna thought feverishly. She had to find a way out of this dungeon.

At first she had paid attention to what Magnus was saying, but now he was just repeating himself and talking himself into a frenzy.

She had gleaned all the information he was willing to tell her, and she really didn't want to know the myriad ways he planned on hurting her.

Letting her know the details was probably meant to be part of the torture. So she blanked out what he was saying and pushed the fear of him putting his plan into action deep down inside herself. She couldn't let the fear get to her because she needed to think as rationally as possible.

All her life people had given her the feeling that she was a disappointment. It turned out, though, that she wasn't the failure everyone, especially her mother, thought her to be. The truth was that she had powerful magic inside of her. Fionna had let the magic lie fallow—no, the other witches in her coven were the reason her magic had never developed to its full potential.

From what Magnusson had told her, witches had an

intuitive magical gift. When a witch came into her powers, she received that gift, and then she developed it. If she was lucky to have a witch with the same gift mentor her.

Most of the time, that was supposed to be a mother or a grandmother with the same talent. The witch's gift would also be fostered in the coven. It was the community that made the witch stronger, not her individual talent.

When Fionna didn't exhibit the incredible powers that had been expected of her, the witches had simply thought the Devil's Children ritual hadn't worked properly.

Mages had a gift that had to be turned on by learning. They had no special ability that just broke through during puberty. They needed to be taught magic.

A young man could be a mage and never know it—if nobody ever told him where he came from and what he could do.

That wasn't altogether rare, as mages didn't live in communities. They were loners and preferred to travel from place to place. The life of a Traveller, for example as part of a group of fairground folk, suited them to a T.

Nobody had activated Fionna's mage talent. Magnusson seemed to be convinced that she was capable of learning. He had brought her here, onto this island, to train her. The magician seemed to be certain that she was capable of great things. He had seemed pleased earlier when she had exhibited signs of being a decent student.

From Magnus's mad ramblings, Fionna gathered Magnusson had been looking for a worthy successor for many years. His experiments with a variety of witches had produced children, but none of them had measured up. They may have even been differently abled or had special needs, Fionna suspected, because Magnus called them "freaks."

"Nobody is as gifted and capable as me! I've always done everything Father said. I stood by him, no matter what. I learned from him. Still, he always hoped for a better successor than me. He kept going with his experiments, always letting me know I wasn't quite what he had in mind. No matter what he did, I was still the best. I thought he would see, in the end. He'd see that he'd underestimated me. I showed him today! I'm powerful. He always tells me that my talent isn't balanced enough. That I can only do cheap mind control tricks."

Magnus pressed his face to the bars, glaring at his father, who was still prone on the floor. It looked as if he was slowly coming to.

"So what, Father?" Magnus spat. "So what if I can *only* do mind control? I do it better than anyone, and it proved useful enough to overpower you!"

Magnusson shook himself. "What? What did you say?"

Magnus laughed but took a step back. "You didn't expect this from me, Father, did you? Didn't think I had it in me. Am I powerful and strong enough for you? Am I worthy of being a great mage?"

Magnusson blinked, then shook his head. "I always knew you were powerful enough. But worthy? You have the emotional maturity of a four-year-old. You expect to get what you want without putting effort in, and then you throw a tantrum when things don't go your way. *That's* what you've proven again today."

Fionna was fascinated by the exchange between father and son, but she told herself to focus on escaping the dungeon instead.

She rummaged around in the pockets of her coat. She wasn't the tidiest of people, and things tended to accumulate in there. This character flaw now worked in her favor. Her fingers tightened around a pencil.

"Well, Father, it doesn't matter to me what you think. In the end, you'll be stuck with me again. Because Fionna won't exist anymore."

Fionna quickly came up with a plan. She needed to get out of this cell, because all her powers were useless thanks to Magnusson's wards.

But she had a feeling Magnus would take her away from here to the place he planned to torture her. He'd probably waited for his father to wake up because he wanted Magnusson to know what he had done.

Magnus was indeed opening the padlock. Despite her plan, Fionna was scared. The young mage radiated hate, more so than before.

Perhaps there had been a part of him that had imagined Magnusson would finally show him respect.

Magnusson tried to rush at Magnus with a spell, but he was unsuccessful. His own wards worked against him. Magnus, on the other side of the bars, countered with a simple blowback spell, which had his father crashing into the wall of the dungeon.

By the time the older man had picked himself back up, Magnus had grabbed Fionna and pulled her out, shutting the bars behind her.

Fionna didn't put up too much of a fight. After all, she needed to be out of the cell for her magic to work.

Luckily, it was easy for her to turn the pencil into a wand. She'd had enough practice enchanting objects. When she felt the electrical current through the wood of the pencil, she knew she'd been successful.

Magnus warned her not to run away—he still had her on the invisible leash. The young mage felt confident enough that he paid little attention to her. Instead, he took pleasure in watching his father struggle to the bars and try to open them.

The padlock was in place, and Magnusson seemed weakened by the attack, anyway.

Fionna carefully took the pencil out of her coat pocket.

She pointed it at her half-brother and muttered a few words.

Nothing happened.

Magnusson now tried to conjure up some of the spells he had used outside. They were much less effective in the cell and never penetrated the bars.

But at least he kept Magnus preoccupied.

Fionna gave herself a silent pep talk. "Come on, Fionna, you can do this. There's nobody here to help you. You have to save yourself. This isn't about proving anything to anyone. But if you have powers, any powers, you must believe in them now. You must use all you've got."

She tried again, pointed the wand, said the spell.

At that moment, Magnus turned around to grab her.

His hand was already outstretched, his fingers inches away from her arm, when it happened.

Fionna's magic trick worked.

Magnus vanished into thin air.

Fionna was so surprised at herself that she forgot the next step for a second. It was the most important part of the spell, though, so she quickly pulled herself together.

Not a moment too soon.

She pointed her makeshift wand at a spot inside the cell, and Magnus reappeared.

He was far too surprised to understand what had happened right away, but Magnusson's face showed triumph and admiration.

Fionna had turned toward the stairs, ready to make a run for it, when Magnus finally caught on to what she had done.

He shouted after her, "You'll pay for this! You think you're so clever. But I'm getting out of here, and you just wait and see what I'll—"

Fionna was already out the door, letting it fall shut behind her.

For a moment, she thought with regret about her mother, who was still in one of the cells downstairs. But she couldn't take the time to figure out how to break Rosa out of there.

Magnusson's wards might hold—but then again, they might not. The old mage had been able to do some magic in the cell, and Magnus might try the same. Maybe they were specific to Fionna's magic. In any case, she couldn't risk it.

She had to get away.

Somehow, she needed to get off the island, get help, and then retrieve her mother.

CHAPTER THIRTY-THREE

ABBEY

"We saw everything that happened twenty-five years ago in the basement." Penny took a step forward. "Tara showed us."

Mrs. MacDonald gave Tara a surprised look. The young witch sheepishly avoided the coven leader's eyes.

"We witnessed that sick ritual you performed in order to create a powerful witch." There was nothing but contempt in Penny's eyes.

Abbey, just like the other women in the kitchen, remained frozen. She was a little scared of Mrs. MacDonald and was sure the coven leader would reprimand Penny for being so disrespectful.

To her surprise, the old woman gave a sad sigh. "You only saw a snippet of what happened. You don't know the context. Don't presume to judge us. Yes, Magnusson's idea appealed to some of us, especially Matilda Simmonds. She became a bit obsessed, worked tirelessly on her recipes. And Rosa, who had wanted a child for a long time, was overly eager to volunteer. The truth is, there was nobody else who wanted to do it. We had to choose Rosa, even though she was well past prime child-bearing age."

"Don't pretend it was Magnusson's plan," Andie said, with a sad look on her face. "We know it was a witch who came up with the idea in the first place. His family had been opposed to it."

Mrs. MacDonald looked at Tara. "You know that, too?" she said thoughtfully.

Tara blushed, but then she lifted her chin. "I saw it. I see a lot of things."

"It must be a burden. Why didn't you come to me sooner? We could have taught you how to control your gift."

Tara was about to say something, but Penny beat her to it. "Really? Like you taught everyone else? We're all left to our own devices because that's the way you want it. We only know what our mothers and grandmothers taught us, and some of us aren't even that lucky. Tara's and Andie's moms couldn't teach them, and both their grandmothers passed before Tara and Andie came into their powers. My own mother died before she could guide me onto the right path. Only very few of us, like Jem, are blessed with a whole magical family."

Jem pulled a face that suggested to Abbey she didn't feel exactly blessed with her family, but Penny didn't notice and kept talking.

"The rest of us, we were left to our own devices. You never helped us much because you didn't want us to learn too much. You wanted to keep the power balance tilted firmly to your side."

"If there was any truth to that, Penny, why would we have wanted to bring a child into this world whose powers would have far exceeded my own?" Mrs. MacDonald remained calm. "In fact, we were hopeful then to build a new generation that would lead us into a better future. Our hopes were dashed. We learned that being careful had to be our priority."

When Andie opened her mouth, Mrs. MacDonald didn't let her speak. "It's a conversation for another day." She sounded tired. "Let's talk about the current situation, though. It's more urgent."

Nobody disagreed.

"Yes, at one time, someone in my family wanted a mage child so badly that she did terrible things. That was the reason we owed it to Magnusson to comply with his request, to make such a union happen. This coven has his mother's blood on their hands." Her eyes darkened. "I have his mother's blood on my hands."

"It doesn't matter who's to blame," Andie said. "What happened, happened. Now we have to find out where Magnusson took Fionna and Rosa."

"I learned from Declan Reid that they were missing. He questioned me. I came here to see for myself." Mrs. MacDonald turned to Tara. "So you saw it was Magnusson Senior?"

Tara nodded.

"Okay, then I can put your minds at ease. I'm certain he won't harm Fionna. Rosa…now that might be a different story. Magnusson must think that Fionna has a combination of mage and witch powers, that she's the child he's tried to so hard to create. His obsession with making the most powerful progeny is the reason he took the cookbook in the first place, and why he was desperate to get it back. Twenty-five years ago, we told Magnusson the ritual didn't work after we found out Rosa was carrying just one baby, a girl."

"And he just…believed that?" Jem looked skeptical.

The others were disbelieving as well. It didn't seem likely that he would just give up so easily.

"Of course not," Mrs. MacDonald replied. "He came here when Rosa was already seven months pregnant to make sure we hadn't deceived him. Fortunately, Rosa had lost a lot of weight during the first trimester, suffering from extreme morning sickness. We managed to squeeze her into a corset just before Magnusson laid eyes on her. When he saw she didn't have a round belly, he believed her. Rosa was still scared, though, and in her panic to get rid of him, she offered him the cookbook. He left, although he came back twice just after Fionna was born. We hid her, thanks to some pretty powerful spells. Magnusson eventually turned his attention to new experiments, using other witches as surrogate mothers. It's an obsession, and I'm sad to say that the poor mites who survived are paying the price for it. Some of them have to receive twenty-four-hour care. It's not a life…"

Mrs. MacDonald trailed off and stared into the distance. Her eyes teared up, but then she shook her head. "Anyway, Magnus Junior is the result of one of the experiments. He's the only able-bodied son Magnusson has fathered, and he considered him a success. But Magnusson always had the suspicion Magnus was…lacking in other ways."

Andie furrowed her brow. "He feared his son was mentally ill, but he never got him help? Instead, he let him run around and terrorize innocent people?"

Mrs. MacDonald shrugged. "I don't know what he thought, exactly. Maybe he didn't want to see Magnus's… problems, because his son gave him hope that one day he'd succeed and father a truly magnificent magical being."

Abbey shivered, thinking of Magnus's small, pitch-black eyes. It wasn't Magnus's fault—he should never have been born—but she was sure a part of his soul was missing, and she couldn't help but be creeped out by that.

"We were lucky with Fionna," Mrs. MacDonald continued. "She's a healthy girl, in body and mind. For a while we worried she might be on the spectrum. But when the expected powers didn't materialize, I told Rosa not to pressure her. I always thought it was a blessing in disguise for Fionna that she turned out so unremarkable."

When Penny started to interject something, Mrs. MacDonald quickly said, "Unremarkable compared to what everyone expected. I know she's a pretty remarkable witch. Not a mage, but a great witch. Only Magnusson doesn't know that. He needs to believe that Fionna is the child he always wanted. It would make all the horrible things he's done worthwhile."

"Okay, well, you think he won't harm her, but I still say we need to get Fionna back as soon as possible," Penny said. "A man like him probably has a completely different definition of the word harm than we do."

"Yes, how do we find him?" Andie followed up.

"I don't know."

"Come on, the cards, tea leaves, a crystal ball…you must have something you can use to track him down…or to locate Fionna?" Penny looked at the coven leader with a challenging stare, but the mixture of hope and desperation in her eyes betrayed her.

Mrs. MacDonald shook her head. "If Magnusson were an ordinary person, sure. But he has done his best to make sure I won't find him or Fionna."

The young witches all started talking at once, begging her to at least try.

"Stop!" Abbey finally called, waving her hands to draw attention to herself. "Stop talking, everyone."

When everyone looked at her, Abbey said, "Ever since I learned about the witches of Tarbet, I've heard complaints that the older witches never let the younger ones do anything. That their secrets are guarded and withheld from the younger generation. Penny, you accused Mrs. MacDonald of not training witches enough, not developing their gifts. I don't know if this is true. But right now, you're all looking to Mrs. MacDonald to solve this situation. You expect it from her. You can't even admit to yourselves what you're capable of. Take Tara, for example. She can do the most amazing stuff, and none of you knew, not even Mrs. MacDonald."

Everyone was stunned into silence. Mrs. MacDonald crossed her arms in front of her chest and gave Abbey a challenging look.

Abbey felt like a child, reprimanded by a teacher. She swallowed and continued talking. "What I mean is, now is your chance. Show Mrs. MacDonald and the older witches what you can do. They evidently can't help. Why don't you own up to your abilities, band together, and come up with something innovative? Who cares about those old secret rituals? You're all clever, so put your heads together and show those old crones what you're made of."

Abbey dared a look at Mrs. MacDonald's face, but the coven leader didn't seem angry at her description. Her lips twitched.

"You're not wrong, Abbey Fine," she said. "Witches can be powerful individuals, but we are only really strong in numbers. We can achieve remarkable things if we combine our powers. That's what differentiates us from mages."

Mrs. MacDonald looked out the window and sighed.

"Don't forget that we older witches have secrets in our blood. We had to get used to hiding our abilities. And a lot of our knowledge only survived by sticking to old rituals and traditions, since nothing could be written down. Doing things the old way always made a lot of sense. But times are changing. For the first time in a long while, we have a whole generation of strong, powerful, very talented young witches. You might be right in suggesting that we haven't developed your talents enough. I don't usually care for involving strangers in coven business, but sometimes it takes an outsider's view to see things from a new perspective. Thank you, Abbey."

Abbey turned bright red. She hadn't expected praise.

"Okay then." Mrs. MacDonald clapped her hands together. "Let's do what Abbey said. Describe your talents without holding back—nobody is going to be punished for coloring outside the lines today—and then we can discuss how our combined powers can help Fionna and Rosa."

ABBEY SILENTLY WATCHED as the young witches came up with a plan.

She sometimes had to bite her tongue so she wouldn't comment. What she'd seen from Fionna, Andie, and Penny was pretty impressive.

Tara's talent blew her mind.

But Birdie and Jem could do even more fantastical things. Even though the two friends had been standing on the sidelines so far, it turned out that they would be in the best position to help Fionna.

Abbey had imagined Birdie had gotten her nickname because of the way she looked, as the young woman resembled a baby bird. But in actual fact, she had the eyes of a bird of prey. It was a residual from the shapeshifter abilities her ancestors had once had a long a time ago. Birdie was good at spotting things from afar, but to function in a world that relied on seeing things up close, she had to wear special Coke-bottle-thick glasses.

If something or someone could bring Birdie high in the sky, the young witch could scan her surroundings and home in on the details, just like a bird of prey.

Weather witch Jem Rivers was the right person for that job.

According to the other witches, Jem had already

demonstrated her amazing weather witch capabilities during a ritual a couple of months ago. Back then, Abbey learned, a friend of Penny's had needed the coven's help.

Jem had summoned up a storm. For the first time in the young weather witch's life, she had also ridden on the wind.

Unbeknownst to Mrs. MacDonald and the others, Jem had since fashioned herself a special wooden staff that replaced the clichéd broom, and she had been practicing her new skill.

Since Mrs. MacDonald was pretty certain Magnusson couldn't have taken Fionna very far away, it was decided that Jem should take Birdie along for a ride. The witch with an eagle eye could then scan the area for Fionna.

"According to what you told me, Tara, Magnusson used magic to transport Fionna and Rosa away from here," Mrs. MacDonald explained. "I'm familiar with that sort of trick. Mages can beam themselves, others, and objects to another place. It takes quite a lot of control to do it, and even then, the destination can't be terribly far. Magnusson might be powerful, but even he could only have made it somewhere within a few miles' radius from Fionna's house."

"Okay, so that's doable," Jem agreed.

"We still need to come up with a method that would make it easier for me to spot Fionna, though," Birdie said. "Otherwise, it would be like looking for a needle in a haystack. And if she's hidden in some sort of building, I wouldn't see her at all."

"I agree," the coven leader said. "Knowing Magnusson, he has taken precautions. He probably warded Fionna and Rosa's prison. I mean, that's the reason I can't simply look into a crystal ball."

"So how on earth are we going to find Fionna, then?" Penny groaned. "Birdie won't be able to see her in some magical fortress. We're back to square one."

"We need to think of something really simple," Mrs. MacDonald pondered. "Something that wouldn't even enter Magnusson's mind."

"Could simple magic penetrate Magnusson's strong wards?" Abbey put in her two cents. "Something that the mage wouldn't have to fear because it's so…basic?"

"What do you mean by basic?" Andie wanted to know.

"Well, I heard that Fionna's mother has elemental magic, but in its most basic form, right? She can change the state of matter, but she can only change what's already there. I'm new to this, so I might not have understood right…"

"No, that's right," Mrs. MacDonald said. "It's true, and Magnusson scoffed at that when he met Rosa. There was nobody else in our coven who volunteered to have his baby, so he was stuck with her, but he thought she was beneath him."

"So changing something that's already there could work if we can count on Magnusson's hubris," Abbey suggested.

"I know!" Penny exclaimed. "How about we find a way to change Fionna's hair—to a more intense red? Like alarm-beacon red. That would be easy for Birdie to find, provided Fionna is outside or in a building with windows."

Andie looked skeptical. "How are we supposed to do that from afar, though?"

"Great idea." Mrs. MacDonald's eyes sparkled. "I know a way to do that. Andie, do you know where Fionna keeps her hairbrush?"

The brunette witch nodded.

"All right, can you get it for me? This will take a while," the coven leader said. "I suggest we prepare the ceremony to invoke the winds, like we did the last time, Jem—"

"We don't need to."

"What?" Mrs. MacDonald looked at Jem in confusion.

The weather witch turned pink. "Like I said, I practiced. I can do it by myself."

"With just your words?" The old lady looked impressed.

Jem nodded. "I'll have to get my staff, though."

"You do that, and I'll take care of this." Mrs. MacDonald grabbed the hairbrush Andie had fetched and consulted with Penny.

The herb witch dashed home to grab ingredients for the ritual.

Half an hour later, they all met in the garden behind the Simmondses' house. They had turned on all the outdoor lights and brought out more lamps with extension cords.

Fionna's strands of hair in the brush glowed like fire in the dark.

Jem raised her hands and spoke a few words in a language that Abbey presumed to be Gaelic.

A light breeze lifted everyone's hair.

Soon, the breeze turned into stormy currents, whipping Abbey's dark locks into her eyes.

She could still see enough to witness how Jem's staff—which looked like a wooden walking stick with symbols carved into it—lifted into the air.

The weather witch grabbed it and swung up onto it. It took a few attempts for Birdie to sit astride it too.

"Hold on," Jem shouted, then called out another spell.

Within seconds, the two witches sailed up into the suddenly very dark and cloudy sky.

"Let's get back inside and wait there." Penny gestured.

Everyone followed her in. They all stared out the kitchen window, watching the trees bend in the wind and loose leaves whip by.

Nobody spoke, and it seemed to Abbey like an eternity until Jem and Birdie landed in the garden again.

In reality, their search had probably not lasted more than twenty minutes.

The two witches swayed when they stepped off the staff. They waved at the faces behind the window, indicating that they'd come inside.

Andie opened the patio door, and Jem and Birdie dashed inside.

Jem was out of breath when she shouted, "We found Fionna. She's on Inveruglas Isle."

CHAPTER THIRTY-FOUR

FIONNA

In her haste to get away, Fionna tripped over one of the stones still strewn about from the fight between Magnusson and his son.

She tried to catch her balance, but to no avail. She managed to stretch out her arms just in time to catch herself, but a sharp pain in her wrist made her wince.

Fionna told herself that it was better than falling flat on her face and knocking herself unconscious. Ignoring the pain, she jumped back up and ran—a little more carefully this time—toward the opening in the wall.

On the other side, she staggered down a grassy slope. Dense vegetation blocked Fionna's view, but she soon arrived at the shore.

Magnusson hadn't lied to her; it seemed that they really were on an island.

The full moon was bright enough for Fionna to recognize Loch Lomond. She was familiar with the shoreline, and she was pretty certain they weren't that far from Tarbet.

She thought she was facing in the direction of Inversnaid.

Fionna stood in a narrow sandy bay, but to her right and left, the shore was overgrown with vegetation.

If she was right about her location, she'd have to get to the other side of the island to get to the other shore of Loch Lomond, which was much closer.

Maybe there would be a boat there. She wasn't entirely sure how Magnusson had brought them to the island—she felt he'd used a magic trick, and he had talked as if they couldn't get off the island with normal transportation. But Magnus might have arrived by watercraft.

Fionna didn't have any other choice but to walk back around the castle or fortress ruins. She was scared. There was no telling how long the mages would be contained in the dungeon. Nonetheless, she kept close to the stone walls so she wouldn't lose her bearings.

Her right wrist still throbbed, so she used her left hand to steady herself. The stones felt rough and cold. Fionna was more and more convinced the ruin was an old castle. Even though it was dilapidated, she could still make out the Z-shape of a typical Scottish castle. There was a rectangular tower with two smaller towers located at diagonally opposite corners.

Fionna guessed she was stuck on Inveruglas Isle, a small island in Inveruglas Bay. The castle had once been home to the chiefs of Clan MacFarlane before its destruction in the seventeenth century.

Even though Fionna had been here before, she'd never known the dungeon existed. She pictured the heavy wooden door leading to the stairs, thinking she would have noticed it before and explored any kind of open underground space. Maybe it hadn't been here before, and Magnusson had added it with magical or non-magical means to afford better access to the hidden dungeon.

Finally, Fionna arrived on the other side of the island.

She tried not to worry about how much time had passed since she'd locked Magnus into the cell with his father.

Fionna wasn't sure if she preferred Magnus focusing on breaking out of it—or on battling his father.

By all accounts, Magnusson was a despicable person. But he was Fionna's father, and she had just found him. She wasn't quite ready for him to die yet. Besides, she wouldn't wish her worst enemy to die at the hands of his son. What a cruel fate.

Fionna's thoughts shifted back to finding a means to escape the island when she didn't spot a boat at the small pier or anywhere near the bay.

The shore looked not two hundred yards away, but distances could be deceiving when it came to swimming in open waters.

Fionna wasn't a great swimmer, and the Loch was cold and dangerous—even more so at night.

Maybe there was a boat hidden in the vegetation surrounding the bay, Fionna hoped.

Suddenly, it got very windy—and dark. Fionna wrapped her arms around herself and looked up into the night sky. Thick clouds had moved in front of the moon.

The wind loosened the knot she had tied her hair into, and strands of it flew into her face. It seemed strangely colorful.

Fionna grabbed a lock. It was glowing neon red!

Panic rose up in her. Was this Magnus's doing? He might not be able to escape the cell, but his magic could have reached her here, outside, despite the wards. Was she trying to harm her in some way? The glow-in-the-dark color could be a sign of poisoning. She didn't feel anything, though. Or had Magnusson put something in her tea after all, which was only now taking effect?

Maybe it was simply designed to freak her out. She let

go of the red strand and focused on searching the bushes and trees for a hidden mode of transportation.

The storm at least meant that swimming across the loch was absolutely out of the question.

Fionna stopped in her tracks, swaying a little in the strong wind.

Fast weather changes weren't unusual in Scotland, but something about this storm seemed out of the ordinary to her. Anxious, she looked at the sky again.

There, something appeared on the horizon.

It was bigger than a bird, but it was flying in a similar way, sort of like it was riding the storm.

Fionna stood like a rabbit caught in headlights when she realized the object was coming straight toward her.

Was this Magnus's doing, too? Was he hunting her with a missile or something from inside the dungeon?

Her knees went weak with relief when the moon shone through the clouds again and she made out a woman on top of the flying object. She had a lot of long hair. No—there were two women. Another smaller person sat behind the tall one. It had to be Jemima, the weather witch, and a passenger.

That explained the sudden storm.

Were Jem and her passenger looking for her? Fionna jumped up and down and waved her arms. Jem waved quickly and made a gesture that Fionna interpreted as "We'll be back."

Then the flying witches disappeared, and the storm died down as fast as it had arrived.

Fionna was plagued by indecision. It seemed wrong to just stay and wait where she was. She felt like a sitting duck.

On the other hand, she expected to be rescued by her friends. They wouldn't leave her hanging, would they?

She considered going back into the dungeon to grab her mother, discarded the idea, and changed her mind back and forth another dozen times. In the end, she was too scared to face Magnus.

Thankfully, Fionna didn't have to wait too long. Inveruglas Isle was about three miles from Tarbet. Fionna spotted something on the water, and she fixed her eyes on it. The last of the clouds moved away from the moon, and Fionna recognized the boat.

Birdie's father ran a water taxi company, and his boats were pretty distinctive. The witches must have borrowed one.

Soon she made out the small figure at the helm. It was, indeed, Birdie. Jem was next to her, and she saw Abbey, and Penny, and Andie…

Fionna ran toward the pier and waved at them.

Tara was with them, too…and Mrs. MacDonald! Andie helped the old woman off the boat.

"We have to free my mother," Fionna shouted at them as they all came toward her. "She's locked in a cell. When I left her there, she was still unconscious. The problem is that I tricked Magnus and sent him behind the bars of the cell that had been designed for me. Magnusson is in it, too. It's supposed to be escape-proof and warded, but I've seen them perform magic in it, however weak it might have been. I don't know what the two of them combined can do. I'm scared their magic might penetrate the bars after all."

"Hang on!" Abbey cried as she followed Fionna to the castle ruins. Some of the others ran after them, too. "Magnus? We thought Magnusson kidnapped you and your mom."

"Yes, he did. But then Magnus came here to kill me."

Abbey grabbed her arm. "Wait a minute! What?"

"He's jealous of me," Fionna said impatiently. "It's a

264

long story, and I'll tell you all later, but in a nutshell, Magnus is my half-brother. He doesn't think I'm deserving of my father's attention because he wants it all to himself. He's worked all his life to impress his father, to prove to him that he's a worthy successor, and here I come and ruin it all for him."

They arrived at the door to the dungeon, and Fionna pushed it open.

There was nothing but silence and darkness greeting them; nobody asked any more questions.

"Fionna shouldn't go down first after everything she's been through," Andie whispered.

"I'll do it," Penny volunteered.

"No. I'll go first," Fionna heard Mrs. MacDonald's croaky voice. "If the Magnussons attack, I can best defend myself."

The witches let Mrs. MacDonald through.

"Um, guys," Tara said. "Don't be mad, but I'm going back to wait with Jem and Birdie on the boat. A lot of stuff happened here, in this castle. It's kind of a lot. And I don't even want to know what I'd have to see in a dungeon."

"That's fine, Tara. It doesn't make sense for all of us to go down, anyway," Fionna said. "Andie, you wait up here and hold the door open."

Fionna, Abbey, and Penny followed Mrs. MacDonald down the stairs. The darkness lightened a little, as the fires in the wall sconces were still burning. The flames flickered from the air coming through the door at the top of the stairs, creating spooky shadows.

In the ghostly light, Mrs. MacDonald didn't seem at all like an old woman descending the stairs. On the contrary, she appeared pretty agile.

Fionna took her eyes off the coven leader when she spotted her mother in the cell.

No sound emanated from the cell with the Magnussons further down the corridor.

Fionna wanted to ask her mother if she was all right, but she couldn't speak.

Mrs. MacDonald was busy trying to open the padlock of Rosa's cell.

Fionna's feet moved as if by themselves, as she crept to peek into the other cell.

Her heart was pounding, and there were goosebumps all over her body.

She didn't want to face the Magnussons, but with the support of her coven at her back, she felt she had to check on them.

After all, they were going to have to decide what to do with them.

They couldn't very well just leave them here to rot in the dungeon, could they?

Fionna held her breath and took the last step, peering around the first bar.

Magnus lay motionless on the floor.

Fionna couldn't spot the old man at first, but when she crept a little further, she saw him crouching in a dark corner.

She thought Magnusson was trembling.

She didn't know if she should say something.

Mrs. MacDonald stepped up next to her. Abbey and Penny followed, both clearly apprehensive about Magnus.

"It might be a trick," Abbey hissed.

"Yes, I don't buy it, either," Penny agreed.

Magnusson noticed the women standing in front of the cell. He flinched, then looked up.

His face was in the shadows, so Fionna couldn't read his expression.

"I had to defend myself. He attacked me, and no

matter what I said, he just wouldn't listen. He turned into an animal...a rabid dog." Magnusson's voice was strangely emotionless. "I didn't mean to kill him, of course. My blowback spell caused him to fall awkwardly. His head cracked against the wall. The sound...it was awful."

"We believe you didn't intend to kill your own bairn, Magnus." Mrs. MacDonald's voice sounded uncharacteristically soft.

"Maryanna? Is that you?" Magnusson leaned forward, then slowly straightened.

"Maryanna?" Abbey repeated, and she and Penny exchanged a look.

The glow of the closest oil lamp now illuminated Magnusson's face. In her father's eyes, Fionna saw sadness and regret. She couldn't help but feel pity for the old man.

Her father.

Only now did the full weight of that revelation hit Fionna like a ton of bricks.

Her knees buckled. Penny, who noticed first, grabbed her before she slid to the floor.

"Are you all right?" Her friend looked concerned. "Is it Magnusson? Did he do something to you?"

"No." Fionna shook her head emphatically. "No, it wasn't like that. He actually brought me here to teach me magic, to show me what I can do. He's..." She swallowed. "He's my father."

"We know." Penny told Fionna about the scene Tara had conjured up in the Simmondses' basement.

"So it's true," Fionna said hoarsely. "Like I said, he didn't bring me here to do me harm. It was his way of making things up to me, I guess."

"Then you'd be the only child of his who could say that." Mrs. MacDonald sounded sad. "Because he has done harm to each and every one of his children. And now it has come to this." She looked at Magnus's body. "Magnus. What more has to happen for you to give up your obsession with powerful progeny? Does the Magnusson line really have to continue with the most powerful mage-witch ever? How many children do you want to bring into this world who aren't physically or mentally equipped to be here? How many of your children have to die for this? Is no price ever too high for you?" Mrs. MacDonald's voice shook. "I know you have a childhood trauma to overcome, and I'm partly to blame for it. But this has to end."

Magnusson looked at his son's body, and then at Mrs. MacDonald.

"You didn't kill my mother, Maryanna. You—"

"No, but my mother did. She was as obsessed as you are, and she almost infected me with it. It's like a curse that gets passed on from generation to generation. We have to put a stop to it."

Fionna didn't know what they were talking about, but Abbey looked like she was experiencing a light-bulb moment.

Penny also seemed to be in on whatever Abbey was thinking. "Her mother?" she whispered to the private detective. "But that can't be. That would make…"

"…Mrs. MacDonald over a hundred years old," Abbey finished the sentence.

The coven leader didn't pay any attention to what the two were whispering about because she was too preoccupied with Magnusson.

"You're right, Maryanna," Magnusson said. Tears were welling up in his eyes, making the blue even more sparkling. "The end has come. Because I think I have found what I was looking for all this time." His gaze went to Fionna.

She shivered. Everything inside her screamed at her to run away.

Instead, she said, "I don't fully understand what you're talking about. But I don't buy that you've... changed now. You don't even know me. You've spent a couple of hours with me. I don't see how we can trust you."

"I know, my child." Magnusson nodded. "I have to earn your trust first."

"You can start by telling me how to free Rosa from the cell," Mrs. MacDonald said.

Magnusson told her the spell. "Fionna will be able to do it," he said. "With a wand."

Fionna was nervous about performing this sort of magic in front of the others, but it was for her mother, after all. She had to get over herself.

She pulled the improvised wand out of her coat pocket and got the lock to open on the second try.

Magnusson called out from his cell, "Rosa is just sedated. I wasn't going to do anything to her."

Abbey and Penny picked Rosa up. She came to but still seemed very groggy. At least she was able to help a little as the two women took her between them and half pulled her out of the cell and up the stairs.

Fionna wanted nothing more than to follow them and get out of this hellhole. But what would they do with Magnusson and his son?

Mrs. MacDonald took the decision away from her.

"You go with the others, Fionna. Get off the island. I'll talk a little more with Magnusson. Then I'll take appropriate steps to get him off the island. And his son, too."

Fionna hesitated. That sounded potentially dangerous, but if anyone could look after themselves, it was their coven leader. "What about you?"

"Leave me a phone. I'll call, and someone can pick me up."

Fionna went up the stairs and told the others. She

asked Abbey for her phone and brought it down to Mrs. MacDonald.

She didn't need a lot of persuading to get out of there. She was more than ready to leave Inveruglas Isle.

There was another holdup, though. As Birdie was about to unmoor the boat, Abbey remembered she had to give Mrs. MacDonald the pin for her phone, otherwise it would be useless to her.

She ran back to the dungeon to give it to her.

When she came back, she looked deathly pale.

"Are you all right?" Penny asked.

"Yes. It's been a long night. I need something to eat and then sleep," Abbey said.

"Ugh, me too," Fionna said.

Only now did she realize how tired she was. As the boat made its way across the smooth water of Loch Lomond, the island grew smaller, and the dungeon with Magnusson in it seemed to decrease in size in Fionna's mind. It became almost unreal, like a bad dream.

"Did that really happen?" she murmured. "Did I really find out Magnusson, the dubious mage, is my father?"

Even though she hadn't really asked anyone, Tara answered. "Oh god, yes. And we all wish we could erase from our memory how you were conceived."

Fionna rubbed her eyes. "I'm sorry, what?"

Penny told the story about the Devil's Children ritual again. Fionna could only shake her head.

She finally knew who her father was. Her biggest fear had been confirmed, but it hadn't turned out quite as bad as it could have.

Some might call Magnusson the devil, but Fionna had always imagined a much darker force. Her grandmother, Matilda, had convinced her that Satan himself had sired her.

Surely her real father couldn't be that bad.

It didn't really matter, because knowing the truth actually was worth everything.

She had been afraid that the truth would explain why she had always felt like an outsider, like a freak of nature.

And it was true, in a way, but it was good to know anyway.

It wasn't all bad.

Fionna was different from all the other witches. She had a father who was a mage, and she had been conceived under some pretty freaky circumstances.

She had to deal with the fact that she might have powers nobody knew anything about.

The times of self-sabotage were well and truly over.

She couldn't tell herself that she was a failure, anyway.

Everyone would know how special she was, and with that came expectations.

She had some experience with not meeting expectations. Falling short in the eyes of the person who was supposed to love and support her, no matter what, had almost broken her.

Even though she felt almost delirious with lack of sleep and had experienced the most surreal twenty-four hours of her life, Fionna vowed not to fall back into old patterns.

She pulled her coat tighter around her and let the night wind blow through her hair, now back to its normal color.

There was one thing that had been missing all her life.

It was something that she would have to rely on going forward, dealing with all that was to come.

In the past, it was the terrible secret she'd held so close that it had made her lonely.

The evil she had always feared finally had a name.

She could say it; it was out there.

It was much better than the nameless terror that had haunted her.

As they approached the Tarbet pier and Inveruglas Isle disappeared into the dark night, Fionna looked around her.

These women had really come through for her.

She might differ from her witch sisters, but they were a coven.

They would support her.

She was no longer alone.

She had friends.

EPILOGUE

SIX MONTHS LATER

A bbey unlocked the door to Christopher Harris Investigations, then let it slam shut behind her.

Her first port of call was the coffee machine.

It had been a long night, and she had a conference call scheduled this morning with her boss. Chris was manning the Glasgow office he had opened to be closer to his girlfriend, Penny.

Abbey's working hours seemed to be shifting increasingly from day to night. It turned out that investigation of cases that fell into the realm of the paranormal was more likely to take place in the dark of night than in broad daylight.

Not really a surprise, and Abbey didn't mind. She loved her new job.

She hadn't been so sure about it at first.

Sure, she'd been immensely grateful when Penny's partner, Chris, had extended the offer. He needed someone to hold down the fort in his London office while he was away.

On the other hand, she wasn't sure how much of that offer was the witches doing her a favor, and she always liked to be successful on her own merit. She didn't want to be just a glorified personal assistant like she'd been at Sly Investigations.

Chris had clarified that he was still going to take responsibility for his cases, even though he was away.

After a month or so of doing the routine tasks she wasn't terribly keen on, when she was starting to get bored and thinking about striking out on her own instead of keeping this secure, steady-paying job, Chris came to her with a proposition.

He wanted to create a special branch of his detective agency dedicated to cases involving the paranormal. "There're witches and mages and who knows what else out there. People usually get laughed at when they have problems that involve something supernatural, but now they would have somewhere to go to. Nine times out of ten, the cases would probably resolve themselves with a pretty rational explanation, but the rest...I think there's a niche there. We'll have to see how much of a demand there really is. The job could be pretty interesting."

He didn't have to sell Abbey on it. She was all in.

No more cases with cheating spouses or boring all-night stakeouts observing low-level crooks. Her new job was exciting, unpredictable, and more than a little dangerous.

The demand had turned out to be pretty huge. Abbey could soon pick her cases, and she even made a name for herself in a very short time.

Today's conference call with Chris was because they needed to discuss hiring extra people for the London office. They needed someone for the position Abbey was originally hired for and another assistant for Abbey, who rarely worked during the day.

Abbey set her coffee cup down on the desk and looked through the mail.

She recognized the black ink handwriting on an envelope addressed to her personally.

A shiver ran down her spine.

Abbey didn't have to open the letter to know what was inside.

Mrs. MacDonald had already sent her three of them.

They always contained a simple request.

"Abbey, please come to Tarbet. We need to talk."

She'd actually replied to the first letter, her hand so shaky that she wondered if the recipient could even read her handwriting. She'd written, "Don't worry. Your secret is safe with me. I won't tell anyone."

But it seemed as if Mrs. MacDonald wasn't happy with that.

In truth, Abbey didn't quite know herself why she wasn't more eager to discuss the matter with the head of the coven.

She was curious, inquisitive, and open to the paranormal. It was her job.

It wasn't like her to avoid things.

For some reason, she thought she wouldn't be able to take what Mrs. MacDonald would reveal to her.

Thinking about it made her pulse race and her throat close up. She set the letter on the desk, sat down on the desk chair, put her head between her knees, and took slow, steady breaths.

In the last six months, she had seen a lot of things she would have never thought possible before. She'd had to adjust her sense of reality. Her entire world view had shifted.

But what she'd seen that day on Inveruglas Isle when she'd returned to the dungeon to let Mrs. MacDonald know the pin to her phone…Every person had their limits, and the secret the coven leader had kept somehow pushed Abbey to her limit.

Cold horror gripped her as she remembered how she'd opened the heavy wooden door and stepped onto the uneven, slippery stone stairs. She could smell the musty dampness of the dungeon and see the flickering of the oil lamps.

And then, forever burned in her memory, was the sight of Mrs. MacDonald, the old coven leader.

Except she wasn't old. And she didn't look like Mrs. MacDonald.

She looked exactly like the young woman who had caught her snooping in the Thistle Inn on the night of the spring equinox.

Because it was the same woman.

Maryanna.

Magnusson had called her that, and somehow Abbey knew it was the same woman Tara had seen in the woods. The young woman begging Magnus the Great for a child —over ninety years ago.

It was the same woman Abbey had found in all the photographs in Mrs. MacDonald's house. The one who looked same in all eras. The logical explanation, that they weren't the same woman at all, but ancestors who all looked similar, was wrong.

There was only one Maryanna.

It was Mrs. MacDonald.

"It's a spell," had been the coven leader's simple explanation when she'd seen the look on Abbey's face. "It makes it look like I'm an old crone. But in fact, I'm—"

Abbey hadn't been able to listen to the rest. She'd turned around and rushed up the stairs.

Ever since that day, Abbey had pondered what creeped her out so much about Mrs. MacDonald's secret.

She'd been okay with witches conjuring up scenes from the past, freezing people into statues, flying through the air, and much more. She'd had to accept that mages could really beam themselves from place to place. She had witnessed fairies eating desserts, for goodness' sake!

What did she find so terrible, so horrifying, about a woman who didn't age?

Maybe it was because she grew up with the idea that eternal youth and beauty were things to be coveted. Her mother had tried to instill that belief in Abbey, and she'd fought her whole life against it. She knew what some women, no, some people, would give for it. What price they would be happy to pay.

Abbey had come to accept some truly *para*normal things in the last few months, but this, to her, really seemed contrary to the laws of the physical world. Was there something fundamentally *un*natural about Mrs. MacDonald?

Abbey knew her curiosity would eventually get the better of her, and she would go to Tarbet and talk to Mrs. MacDonald.

But perhaps she needed a few more paranormal cases under her belt first, to work herself up to Mrs. MacDonald's supernatural secret. There were rumors about vampires roaming the London underground, and someone wanted to hire Abbey to find one. They were immortal and even scarier than a young witch who had been turning herself into an old crone with a spell for nearly a decade…

Absentmindedly, Abbey tore open a small package. All thoughts of Mrs. MacDonald's secret left her when she saw the contents.

A big grin spread across her face.

Chris had told her about a surprise, and now she'd accidentally ruined it for him.

Excited, Abbey took out a stack of business cards from the package.

She'd been searching for her place in this business, and now she truly felt like she'd arrived.

It was official.

On one side of the black cards it said "Abbey Fine, PI."
And on the reverse, embossed in silver:
"Paranormal Investigations."

FIONNA NERVOUSLY PUSHED a strand of hair out of her face
and smoothed out the little black dress she'd bought especially for the occasion.

She felt a hand on her shoulder.

When she turned around, she looked into Drew's
chocolate-brown eyes. She immediately felt calmer, but the
butterflies in her stomach were still going crazy.

Fionna knew this had nothing to do with the reopening
of The Kirk. Or that she now was the proprietor of a
restaurant and bookstore.

Well, one of the proprietors of a restaurant. She and
Drew were equal partners, since Fionna had invested the
money she'd made with her antiquarian book business into
the necessary renovations.

Rosa had called her nuts, but Fionna put little stock in
what her mother said these days. It was much easier to
ignore her since she had moved out of the house and found
herself a small apartment of her own.

One of Fionna's stipulations for the partnership had
been a new business model. Drew had been only too happy
to oblige when he'd heard what she had in mind.

The Kirk would specialize in traditional Highland
cooking. They utilized the recipes Fionna dug up in old
books. These sorts of cookbooks, antiquarian and new,
were now also available to buy in the little bookshop they'd
installed in the restaurant's transept, where the old organ
had originally taken up a lot of space.

There was only one downside to the whole exciting
new venture.

Now that Fionna and Drew were business partners, surely any romantic relationship was out of the question. At least that's what Fionna told herself for the hundredth time as she looked into Drew's dreamy eyes and almost melted on the spot.

Well, maybe not right now, a voice whispered in her head. But a girl can dream.

Fionna suppressed a smile. Dreaming about being with Drew—and maybe some light flirting—felt like just the right pace for her.

She wasn't in a rush to jump into a relationship now that so many other things in her life were changing.

Added to that was the fact that she already had someone new in her life. Mrs. MacDonald had gifted her an adorable cat as a housewarming present. It was a ginger half-Maine coon with tufted ears and giant paws. Fionna had always considered herself to be a loner, but the lazy cat she had named Monster was just the right companion for her.

Someone cleared their throat. Fionna didn't even know how long she had been standing there, looking into Drew's eyes. Embarrassed, she took a step to the side.

The person who had discreetly made their presence known was the first guest of the evening.

Fionna's eyes widened in surprise when she recognized the man. "Mr. Dudley! What…um, what an honor."

"I heard about the reopening. I think I let a few things slide the last time I was here, which isn't like me at all."

Mr. Dudley's brow creased, and Fionna noticed her hands were getting moist with perspiration.

"I'm glad to see you made some changes, anyway. I don't know why I feel so drawn to this place. The food was very good, I guess. I'm looking forward to whatever you're serving today!"

Fionna was so relieved that the health and safety

inspector didn't seem to remember anything unusual from that fateful evening when the Fool recipe went wrong, she told him his meal would be on the house tonight.

Fionna waved over at the new waitress.

Sally had been committed to a psychiatric clinic. Even though Fionna should be glad that Sally couldn't carry out her threats and expose the witches, she felt sorry for the woman. After what had happened on Inveruglas Isle, she was convinced that Magnus had let Sally keep her memory of that night on purpose, and probably had added an unhealthy dose of paranoia.

But it appeared that the mage had done nothing to the other customers' or Mr. Dudley's memories. That was a relief.

Dessie and Declan came in next. "We came early, hoping we won't have to wait very long for the food to arrive," Dessie said, instead of a greeting.

Declan rolled his eyes. "It's the first time we've been out since Davy was born, and Dessie's a little nervous. I keep telling her that our babysitter is very reliable and that we're only a phone call and a few minutes away, but—"

"I'm fine. I'm totally fine." Dessie grabbed a glass of champagne from the tray the waitress brought over. A few sips seemed to calm her down. She was smiling and paying attention as Fionna told her about the exciting specials they had planned for that evening.

When Declan led her to the table, she seemed almost relaxed.

Fionna smiled when she saw her friends coming through the door next. The young witches hugged Fionna and congratulated her.

The group had come together more and more during the past few months, even though they all had such different personalities. Fionna really had to wonder why she'd always felt like such an outsider. Each and every one of them was unique. And that was a good thing.

Fionna passed around the champagne but nearly dropped her glass when the next guest stepped into the restaurant.

It was her father.

On a whim, she'd sent him an invitation, but she hadn't really expected him to show up. Now that he was here, Fionna worried about how her mother and Mrs. MacDonald would react.

She really didn't need an argument or any kind of drama on their grand reopening night.

Mrs. MacDonald might be fine—after all, she had somehow made a deal with Magnusson, allowing him off the island, making sure he wouldn't bother her or the witches of her coven anymore, and somehow sweeping kidnapping and manslaughter under the rug. They must have also come to an agreement about what to do with Magnus's body.

But then there was Rosa. Fionna had no idea what her mother remembered from that day and night. They had never talked about the experience.

Eventually they would have to because Fionna had some questions she intended to ask.

She wasn't sure, though, how her mother would react if she heard Fionna was in contact with Magnusson and receiving magic lessons from him.

Fionna's stipulation had been that he stop his experiments with the Devil's Children ritual immediately and take full fiscal and emotional responsibility for all his children in care homes.

Her relationships with both her parents were precarious, and it was possible the balancing act would be upended if her mother and father came face to face tonight.

She really hadn't thought through Magnusson's invitation to the event.

On the other hand, she felt an acute sense of pride now as he greeted her with delight and congratulated her on her business venture.

Perhaps it couldn't be helped. Children sought their parents' approval. Fionna was all the happier to see genuine admiration in her father's eyes because she knew that neither side—her father nor the coven—was entirely happy with her career choice.

Now that it was confirmed that she had the potential to become a very powerful mage-witch, everyone was waiting with bated breath to see what important path she would choose, so she had to justify her non-magical career even more.

Fionna thought she was doing the right thing by focusing on something that had nothing to do with either of her parents. She didn't want to jump into anything. With the kind of powers that slumbered inside her, she couldn't be too careful. The actions of her half-brother had only proven that.

Plus, it felt good to be able to choose. Andie had given her the envelope with the results of the genetic testing only last week, and she still hadn't opened it. Andie knew the results and had told her that apparently there *was* something like a witch gene. Fionna didn't know how she felt about that yet. It was a bit too predetermined. Just because she had magic in her blood didn't mean her life had to turn out a certain way. She wanted to have a say in her future.

Magnusson had taken a seat at a table at the back of the restaurant when Rosa, Mrs. MacDonald, and a few of the older-generation witches came in.

They might not understand her non-magical career choice, but at least they showed their support, Fionna thought.

As the other ladies picked up their glasses of champagne, Mrs. MacDonald took Fionna aside.

She pulled a small parcel out of her purse. It had a rectangular shape, and if Fionna wasn't much mistaken, it was a book wrapped in brown paper.

"We decided you should have this. It's the cookbook. The other four copies are safe with me, but…well, Matilda was your grandmother. And after everything you've been through and discovered because of it, it seems only right for you to have it."

"Thank you. I'll make sure it doesn't fall into the wrong hands."

True to her word, she brought the parcel to the kitchen to place it in a safe place. Once there, though, she couldn't resist tearing off the paper to reassure herself it was Matilda's cookbook she was holding in her hands.

Fionna didn't even notice Drew looking over her shoulder.

"What do you have there? *Magical Highland Cooking?* Sounds perfect for us. Can I see?"

Fionna moved it out of his reach just in time. "Umm, I don't know if it's any good yet. I'll take a look and let you know."

Drew looked a little disappointed, but when Fionna asked if he didn't have a lot of cooking to do, he jumped back to the stove, focusing on the job at hand.

Fionna brought the book into the storeroom.

"We'll run a magic-free restaurant from now on," she silently vowed to herself.

Fionna opened the safe and stroked the old leather binding of the book before rewrapping it in paper and pushing it behind some paperwork in the far corner.

The cookbook no longer gave her a feeling of unease.

It had lost its threat of unveiling terrible things about her.

It could no longer do that—it was just a book with magical recipes.

Yes, she may have some dubious mage genes. Perhaps there were some dark forces inside her that had had a part in her conception.

She was aware of the possibility and trusted herself to notice them, should they steer her wrong. If in doubt, she still had friends who would do that for her.

What made her so sure of that was, despite the fact that dark truths about her had finally been revealed, no matter who her parents were, what blood ran in her veins, and how she'd come into the world...at heart she was still the same Fionna she had always been. And that just felt right.

Book nerd. Foodie. Witch. Freak.

AFTERWORD

Thank you for reading **COOKING UP A WITCH**. I hope you enjoyed reading it as much as I loved writing it. If you did, I would greatly appreciate a review on Amazon or your favorite store or book review site. Reviews are crucial for authors as well as for readers who are looking for their next book—even just a line or two are so helpful. Thanks!

I love to chat with my readers, so if you'd like to contact me, visit felicitygreenauthor.com.

Do you want to know what's next for the **SCOTTISH WITCHES?** Read book 4 in the series: **A WITCH THROUGH TIME**.

If you would like to know more about the other books in the **SCOTTISH WITCHES MYSTERY** series, get information on latest releases, and receive a free book, please sign up for my newsletter on felicitygreenauthor.com.

Happy reading!
Felicity Green

9 783911 238021